# DUTCH HEX

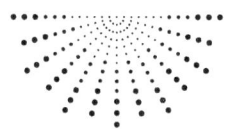

# DUTCH HEX
## A TAYLOR QUINN QUILT SHOP MYSTERY

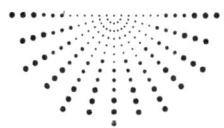

## TESS ROTHERY

Copyright © 2020 by Tess Rothery

All rights reserved.

No part of this book may be reproduced in any form or by any electronic or mechanical means, including information storage and retrieval systems, without written permission from the author, except for the use of brief quotations in a book review.

❋ Created with Vellum

## CHAPTER ONE

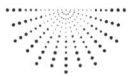

Taylor Quinn
Flour Sax Quilt Shop
Vendor / Mentor
Friend of Cascadia Quilts

The ribbons flowing from her name tag said a lot, but none of the interesting stuff. Sure, she was Taylor Quinn, owner of Flour Sax Quilt Shop. And she was at the Cascadia Quilt Expo at Comfort College of Art and Craft in Comfort, Oregon. As a vendor, she had a table in the marketplace to sell stuff from her store. As a mentor, she had shifts in the work room where she could answer questions and generally help out. And as "Friend of Cascadia" she had donated some bucks to the program. As a member in good standing of the Comfort Quilt Shop Owners Guild she had even put a lot of time and effort into convincing the Cascadia people to hold their event at the college. The Expo, with hundreds of quilters staying on campus for days on end, was going to be great for the economy of her little hometown.

What those little ribbon-stickers didn't say was that she was feeling free and happy for the first time since her mother's death over two years ago. She hadn't pushed the dresser in front of her bedroom door for safety in weeks, and she had been steadily dating just one man for almost five months—Hudson, that handsome handyman with the patience of a saint. She smiled at just the thought of his name.

But the most exciting news was that the Flour Sax Quilt Shop YouTube show was making folks rich.

Not her videos, of course.

Her mom's were the ones bringing in the big bucks.

And not on the YouTube channel, actually. But still, in some small way, Taylor was a part of something big.

The videos that were making money now were outtakes from the Flour Sax Quilt Show, as Taylor's mom Laura had christened it. The regular show had been a steady source of side income for the business both while Laura had been alive and now that Taylor was hosting it. But the outtakes were something else entirely.

Taylor's friend and employee, Roxy Lang's teenage son Jonah, had mentioned in passing one afternoon that outtakes might be fun on a kind of new app called TikTok. He'd asked permission to see what he could make of them.

Roxy was a single mom.

Roxy worked her tail off and Taylor couldn't pay her nearly enough.

So, Taylor had given Jonah *carte blanche* to make what he could of the outtakes on this TikTok business. And he had.

Boy, he sure had.

TikTok loved Laura Quinn.

And Jonah was getting rich from it.

Taylor did not begrudge him his success. After all, Jonah had made minimum wage editing the show for the last several years. His work had saved her store.

Anyway, if his TikTok hadn't taken off, she'd have offered to help with his college.

But this was better.

This way he was doing it himself.

Besides, now that she was officially over-thirty, Taylor knew the harsh reality of life. Like all things Internet, TikTok was a fad. Its popularity would fade eventually. Very few things online had the staying power of Amazon, or YouTube, or Facebook.

You had to strike while the iron was hot with these apps, and the only one who had the time or know-how to make the most of TikTok was Jonah.

He deserved every penny he earned using it.

Taylor took a deep breath, trying to soak the atmosphere of the College of Art and Craft deep into her soul. The smell of lemon oil and wax used to keep the wood of the main gallery gleaming was intoxicating to her. Underneath that, she could sense hints of the linseed oil the painters used, and somewhere in the mix were memories of pine being carved and clay being formed.

It was a good place, Comfort College of Art and Craft. A place that nurtured talent and hope and dreams. She would always love her alma mater. Taking two weeks off from the store to work at the Expo was a gift to her soul.

The Cascadia Quilt Expo was the first large scale quilt conference to come to Comfort. It was a financial boon for the small town, and not a bad deal for the college either. Comfort was a cozy little town right in the middle of wine country, just over an hour from the beach, nestled in the shadow of the Coast Range Mountains, and not too far from some major college towns. It was ripe to become a great tourist destination. It had been ripe for over thirty years now, and someday one of these efforts was going to put them on the map. Why not this one?

Comfort College of Art and Craft had offered up its campus during fall gallery break—a tradition at the art school that gave instructors two weeks in October to travel for art shows or work on their own projects and gave students time to do the same thing.

Cascadia Quilt Expo promised an audacious two weeks of activity. The first week was a traditional conference with classes, speakers, a marketplace, and lots of socialization. It would end with a large quilt show open to the public. The second week was small, intense masterclasses. The college students had gone home or doubled up to make room in the dorms for out of town quilters, though plenty of guests were driving from local homes or coming just for certain day's events.

"Pass me that cord." Roxy waved her hand up at Taylor. She was on the ground fiddling with the set-up for their booth in the marketplace, but the cord had come unplugged. Flour Sax Quilt Shop was playing Laura's old videos on a loop, just as they did in the shop. Though Taylor and Roxy were constantly filming new content, Laura had that special something that Taylor lacked. Her videos were still more popular and getting more views even more than two years after her death.

Roxy got the video working and Laura's light and cheery voice came through, extolling the virtues of making-do. There was no need to go out and buy the latest gadget, she told her audience. You have plenty of stuff at home to quilt with, including those "skinny clothes" in the back of your closet that you knew you'd never wear again, even if you did get back to that size.

Despite a life filled with tragedy, Laura had been a happy woman, and she glowed with that joy on screen. Taylor never went a day without feeling deep gratitude for these videos. Her dad had died when she was just eleven, and they didn't have much film of him around. Nothing like her mom's YouTube show.

Laura's voice brought a smile to Taylor's face every time she heard it. Even when it hurt.

Taylor had learned in the counseling sessions she'd started

that spring that this was normal, and good, and okay. Most of her feelings were.

With the video sorted out, Roxy got back to greeting quilters and shilling pattern books and vintage print fabrics while Taylor stitched on a project. She worked on a wall hanging that she had secured in a makeshift frame of paint stir-sticks and clothes pins, her fingertips protected by nothing more than well-seasoned calluses. One of Laura's more popular outtakes was the one where she tried to show how to make just that quilt frame, but no matter what she did, it fell apart. It was popular on TikTok because she dropped the F-Bomb. It was the first and only time Taylor had ever heard her mom use that word. Taylor figured she might as well tap into some of the TikTok enthusiasm and show folks how the crazy idea really worked.

Not only did they have the video playing, but Clay, Taylor's ex-boyfriend and current employee, had created a series of pattern books based on the projects in the videos. Self-published, sure, but he claimed that's where the genius was. They kept a higher cut of the royalties doing it themselves.

Today was the first day of the Expo. Taylor doubted their pattern books would hit a best sellers list but she was willing to give it a shot.

A group of young quilters wandered over to the table. Taylor thought they looked about her sister's age, late teens, early twenties. One short young woman with a shaved head flipped through a fabric color wheel. Her three friends, one with purple hair, one with a nose ring like a bull, and one exceptionally tall, watched the video.

The tallest girl caught Taylor's eye. "Do you sell DVDs?"

"No." Taylor's brow folded in legitimate confusion. DVDs? Who bought those? Why would these kids want that?

"Oh, wow." The tall girl shrugged at the shaved-head girl.

"Ug." The nose ring crinkled her nose. "Do you know if Flour Sax has any plans to put out a DVD?"

"No." Taylor felt herself retreating from these girls. "But wait, why?"

"Throw-back—" the tall girl began to explain but was interrupted when the purple-haired girl grabbed her by the elbow.

"Look!" The purple-haired girl held out her phone with a shaky hand. "Jonah says his mom is here somewhere! Do you think he'll show up?"

The tall one blushed. "No...."

The shorter girl with the shaved head wandered off and the others followed her.

After Roxy's son's fangirls had passed through without buying anything, Roxy leaned in. "You should have heard the women in line for coffee."

Taylor had at least a dozen questions for Roxy, starting with: What on earth did those girls want DVDs for? But she'd settle for gossip. "Do tell."

"There was a group of ladies in front of me in line who were livid. They hate the keynote speaker, but it is more than just hate, it's like a deep resentment. The group in front of me were mad because she isn't even a quilter."

"You have to admit it's crazy the keynoter isn't an actual quilter." Taylor harbored a little resentment over this herself. The guild had received over fifty amazing pitches for speakers but the owner of Dutch Hex, Shara Schonley, had convinced the Cascadia folks to hire an author of Amish fiction instead. Dutch Hex was a competitor designed to steal customers from the similarly named Flour Sax, and an Amish fiction author was perfect for driving sales to Shara's Pennsylvania-Dutch-themed shop.

"I agree, though she did write an Amish quilt book. There was another group of ladies really mad about that. They called it cultural appropriation. I mean, this lady is from LA. Born and raised. If she's ever seen Lancaster County, it was on a tourist bus."

"But isn't her name something German?" Taylor fiddled with

a stack of papers and found the Expo program. "Albina Tschetter."

"Are we sure that's a real name? It feels like just a bunch of sounds," Roxy said with a little laugh.

"Albina is a real name."

"Maybe yes, maybe no, but it's not *her* name, and Tschetter isn't an Amish name."

"Who would pick Tschetter as a pen name? It's hard to spell and it sounds cheesy." Taylor snickered at her little pun. There was a delicious sense of justice in the idea that Shara had been duped by a fake Amish author. Taylor said the name again more slowly. "Albina Tschetter. Nope. Doesn't sound Amish to me." There was a small but vibrant Mennonite community in their region of Oregon, not Amish, but they shared many of the same surnames. Yoder? Heibert? Miller? Sure. But Tschetter? No way.

"I played around with the letters while I was waiting in line but can't figure it out. It's not backwards for something else, not an anagram. It's just some dumb sounds she pulled out of the air."

"Could be her real name. It makes more sense than picking something like that as a pen name." Taylor set down her papers and picked her quilt back up. It was true you could quilt with all sorts of things found around the home, but this little quilt frame was almost worse than nothing.

"Nope." Roxy showed Taylor her phone. She had it open to the Facebook profile of a young blonde woman in resort-wear at a beach. She was tan, glistening, and wearing a heavy gold chain. Across the banner of the page it said: "McKenzie Forte writing as Albina Tschetter." Albina's headshot in the program was demure. Her blonde hair was pulled back from her face but cascaded over her shoulders. A sweater set and pearls. Same tan. Same youth. Same woman. "You can't convince me her real name is Mackenzie Forte, either. I wonder how many identities she has."

Another gaggle of artsy young people came to the table. A

girl with hair the color of Maraschino cherries, and bright white plastic glasses leaned in close and whispered, "You wouldn't be selling any original Flour Sax projects, would you?"

"Sorry." Taylor shrugged.

"What about DVDs? She was a genius, you know." The young woman eyed the stack of pattern books. "A self-taught genius. Kind of a pioneer in modern primitive." She picked up a copy of each book. "I want them all. Here's my card. If you find out that the family is selling any of the projects she did in her show, please call. Money is, like, no object."

Taylor stared at the young woman in disbelief. Her mother was a highly trained artist. Just because she made simple projects online to teach beginners didn't mean she was a primitive. She crinkled her nose. Not long ago a famous 'primitive' had been murdered in Comfort. But that woman hadn't been any more primitive than Laura Quinn.

And what was primitive supposed to mean anyway? Quilts had always been, and should always remain, an art of the people. People without means or access to expensive material and training had always been capable of exquisite work.

This had become Taylor's mantra. Her education at Comfort College of Art and Craft had left her with a knowledge of how great art was made, but without the natural ability to make it. She could make good quilts. But not great. That kind of thing didn't come from school. It came from talent. And there was nothing 'primitive' about talent.

She sighed.

She had to get over her feelings of artistic-inferiority. She hadn't had that at all as an art student. Her work back then had been fraught with meaning and overwrought. Like all good art students. It was only once she began to spend all her time with women who really quilted that she saw what she had always lacked.

The young woman was staring at her.

Taylor was staring into the distance, lost in her thoughts.

Roxy stepped in, accepting the business card. "Thanks so much. We'll let you know if anything comes up."

The cherry-red-head wandered off and the gaggle of young women with her followed.

"Valerie Ritz. Related to the hotel, maybe. No wonder money is no object." Roxy slipped the card into her phone case. "Jonah told us we needed to sell off the projects from the show."

"Do you know how angry Mom would be to hear herself called a primitive?" Taylor murmured.

"Forgive the child. She said money is no object," Roxy laughed happily.

"Mom went to Comfort College." Taylor wanted to say more, to boost her mother's achievements and brilliance, but the truth was, Laura had married at eighteen and had Taylor by twenty. She hadn't finished her degree, but she was far from primitive.

"Don't worry about that. The kids adore her. Laura would love them."

Taylor forced a smile and, in a moment, found herself laughing. Her mom had always loved teenagers and she would absolutely have loved those goofy kids with their extremely artsy outfits. She loved business, too, and wouldn't have turned down an offer to buy her work.

Taylor's phone pinged—an alert that Jonah had posted a new video, she suspected. He was uploading videos faster during the Expo as advertising. She ignored it for a moment.

"I'm serious about this keynoter business. In addition to the people mad she's not a quilter and the ones mad she's not Amish, I ran into a third group of ladies who were mad as heck." Roxy settled into her folding chair with her own quilt project.

"All right. Spill." Taylor leaned back, project in hand, needle loaded.

"A group of Amish authors."

Taylor paused, needle midair. "How many Amish authors are there in the world?"

"There are about five extremely popular best sellers you can buy at Walmart or wherever, but there are hundreds of people using Amazon. I would guess these women fell into that category."

"What was their problem?"

Roxy grinned that smile that seemed to start at her toes and extend far beyond her petite frame. "They're out of their heads angry because Albina's books aren't even Amish."

"Someone in this world is out of their head angry about the content of someone else's fiction title?" Taylor loved books as much as the next girl from a small town with not much to do, but that seemed absurd.

"Yes, indeed. These four women were going on and on about Amazon categories and cheating. The writers were fit to be tied because the keynoter got her Amish life wrong. One woman was convinced they were Hutterite stories. Another was convinced 'Albina' just made up whatever she wanted, and the other two were convinced that it was a secret cult that 'Albina' herself had grown up in. Either way they were mad because she was manipulating her sales...but..." Roxy paused and took a long drink of her coffee. "See, you and I are using Amazon to sell Laura's books, so we know how it works. Albina, on the other hand, has a publisher. She doesn't pick her keywords. She doesn't have anything to do with the sales categories. The authors should be mad at the editors, or publicists, or whoever."

"Or, even better, they should mind their own business." Taylor rolled her eyes and started stitching. Clay knew Amazon, and categories, and all that. Like Jonah and TikTok, she had let Clay have his way with the pattern books. Not the royalties of course. That would be absurd. She laughed softly. The books had brought in a solid twelve dollars since they had gone live.

The TikTok thing had brought Jonah within a hairsbreadth of one-million-dollars.

To steal the words of an extremely old Knight Templar, she had chosen poorly.

And she still didn't understand how one monetized TikTok.

## DUTCH HEX

It had something to do with tips and sponsorships. For every few videos of Laura, Jonah posted one of himself. He was cute, with curly brown hair, big brown eyes, and a grin that lit up a room like his mom's did.

Taylor had watched a few. At first she thought he was just a big fan of the Oregon Ducks, but eventually she recognized it as college spon-con—sponsored content—and then realized it wasn't just for the college, but for Nike, the college's biggest corporate sponsor. She still didn't get why the college was using him and his videos of Laura's outtakes to recruit students. He had explained it once: Nike wanted diverse representation. Jonah was, in his own words: pretty, soft, and popular, a target Nike hadn't focused on much. It sounded unlikely to Taylor, but the sheer amount of Nike and U of O swag didn't lie. They were banking something on Jonah's big audience.

"Earth to Taylor," Roxy grabbed Taylor's attention again with her ringing laugh. "You say these ladies should mind their own business, but you were pretty mad about Shara's new quilt frames."

Taylor glanced in the direction of her rival's Dutch Hex booth. "She's selling paint sticks and clothes pins, Roxy. She one-hundred percent stole that from us, just like everything else."

"You're just mad at yourself because you told me we shouldn't do it." Roxy stared at her own project. She had rejected the silly frames and was using the standard PVC tubes. Much handier.

"I'm mad because making use of what you have is a depression era thing, like making clothes out of sacks from feed and flour bags. The Amish are known for their fine craftsmanship. An Amish quilt frame should be something sturdy, handcrafted, and made to last. You know I'm right."

"Point taken." Roxy gave Taylor a worried look, one Taylor hadn't seen from her friend in a long while.

"Never mind. I'm probably just kicking myself for saying no." Taylor tried to lighten the mood. She was happy for Jonah and Roxy's new-found wealth. She was glad the event had been booked solid for both the main week of events and the specialty training.

She had no complaints, no matter what Shara did or didn't sell at her store or booth.

The Cascadia Quilt Expo organizers—Sue Friese was the big guns of this event—had worked to fill the marketplace. In addition to tools, gadgets, fabric, services, and other things related to quilting, the Scientologists had an auditing booth, the Comfort antiques mall had a few booths where they sold their rusty gold, both Herbalife and Mary Kay made their presence felt, the 4-H was recruiting volunteers, and something with a big sign that only said "Ladies Club" was handing out free cups of coffee. The crowd at that booth was impressive.

Across from the Flour Sax table, in the farthest corner of the marketplace, was a beekeeper. Her table had pizzazz, that was for sure, with her beekeeping helmets on mannequin heads and large ceramic beehives for display. She was selling raw organic beeswax for waxing the quilting thread—a simple and effective tool for hand quilters. Taylor needed to grab some before she went home. Not only did the quilting go more smoothly, it made your hands smell delicious while you worked.

A person could only make so much money selling disks of wax though, so the beekeeper also sold beeswax candles, jars of honey, tubes of lip balm, and little tubs that were probably some kind of skin cream. The way Taylor's hands dried out working with fabric she could see a special balm being useful. In fact, after first thinking of the beekeeper as some kind of hanger on like the Scientologists, she had recognized the genius. Here Taylor was, selling fabric and patterns, which only quilters would ever want, while the beekeeper had come up with a side hustle that could be marketed a million ways from Tuesday and sold everywhere and anywhere. Smart girl.

Not that Taylor would have wanted to be a beekeeper. Running Flour Sax was a far cry from the corporate job she had dreamed of, or even the management job at Joann's she'd actually had, but it was good to be home running the business her grandmother had founded many years ago. It was very good.

The crowd in the marketplace had thinned out again, but another group of young quilters gathered at the Flour Sax booth. A perfectly normal looking young person with Cascadia Quilt Expo T-Shirt spoke out of the blue. "No, you're totally right. Shara stole the idea for the quilt frame from the videos. I heard her talking about it. She got paint stirrers custom printed with that quilt block—the Dutch hex from her logo. She's making a mint." The girl turned to Roxy. "Any original projects for sale?"

"No, sorry." Roxy gave her an overly apologetic smile.

"Bummer." The agreeable girl and her friends wandered off.

The large gallery of Comfort College of Art and Craft emptied out, and they closed up their booth. It was time for dinner followed by the first keynote of the event.

As TAYLOR MUNCHED her way through a salad of baby kale and slivered zucchini with a pretty basic honey-mustard dressing, she wondered what 'Albina Tschetter' was getting out of the week. She hadn't manned her book table, so she wasn't after the rush of fame. She wasn't a quilter, so she didn't have patterns or technique videos to sell. Each seat in the crowded dining room had been provided with a complimentary copy of *Quilted in the County*, the first in her "In the County" series of Amish Family Drama, so she clearly wasn't after book sales. The book was a slim paperback. The image on the matte cover was of a quilt drying on a line in front of a white farmhouse. The image was faded, in tones of blue and sepia. Very calming. Under the title it said, "a novel" in small, modest letters. It had been given the full literary fiction treatment.

Taylor wasn't an expert in Amish culture, but she had been around the quilt scene her whole life, and she had never heard anyone refer to Lancaster, Pennsylvania as "the county." By the time dessert came, Taylor was more than curious.

Salad had been followed by plates of curried lamb and sweet potatoes served with a broccoli cake. The wait staff cleared those and replaced them with tall, old-fashioned Sundae dishes filled with raspberry trifle. A yellow cream between the white and pink layers made it especially pretty and tasted like guava, but the pine nuts sprinkled on top made Taylor think the kitchen staff watched Chopped in their spare time. Nonetheless, she planned on eating the whole thing.

The evening's MC, a man in a sharp suit and a patchwork tie, welcomed Albina Tschetter to the podium.

Despite her modest navy-blue pants suit with cream blouse and hair back in a bun, it was clear Albina was from LA. She was a great speaker—funny, disarming, and smooth. She admitted frankly that she wasn't crafty and wasn't Amish, and then went into great detail on how she had prepared for her series by befriending a sweet grandmother in Los Angeles who had been moved across the country by her apostate children.

The grandmother had been fighting cancer.

She had died.

The audience dabbed at their suddenly wet eyes.

Albina claimed, in heart-melting tones, that she would cherish the quilt they had made together and honor her memory in literature, which lasted forever.

And that was why the Cascadia Quilt Expo had hired her.

For all the things Albina did not do, she was pretty outstanding at public speaking.

Taylor cleared her throat, but it wasn't because she was crying.

For the first time in too long, the sad, sad story of someone's death hadn't completely broken her. The counseling was working.

But, over the course of the speech, a small tickle had grown in the back of her throat, and then her nose had begun to drip.

She had a last spoon of trifle, savoring it. Berries, whipped cream, custard, and that tropical guava curd. The curd probably had coconut in it.

Taylor always had a hard time convincing people she had a coconut allergy, so despite writing it on her meal service form, she had received a dessert she shouldn't have.

She pushed the cup away. As Albina had just reminded them all, life was precious. She wouldn't waste a minute of it fussing over the inconvenience of a mild allergic reaction.

Whatever Roxy's gossipy quilt ladies had to say about the keynote speaker, Taylor was sold on Albina and planned on sitting in on her smaller class the next day. According to the program, Albina would be teaching on quilt as literature. Taylor was into that. Stories told with fabric were stories of the people.

## CHAPTER TWO

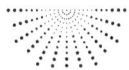

Taylor's little house was quiet without Grandpa Ernie. Through the last couple of years, Taylor had often resented the way her dad's mom Grandma Quinny had interfered in her life, but the offer to take her Grandpa Ernie (her mom's father) to the beach during the Expo was one she could not turn down. Having the house to herself in the morning and evening after a long, long day's work was a luxury she valued more than she liked to admit.

After a quiet night and morning, Taylor was refreshed and ready to network, learn, and sell stuff.

She walked the few blocks back to the college in the dreary fall rain without a worry on her mind.

"Good morning!" Roxy offered Taylor a thirty-ounce cup of something from the town's new coffee shop, Comfy Cuppa. As much as they had liked the bakery items at Café Ole, it was already gone. Quilt shops did well in Comfort, but cafés were hard to sustain.

The fall day was chilly and dark. Distant clouds threatened to roll over the event. And as Taylor sipped the new coffee from the new shop, she shivered.

Taylor was staying in her own home instead of on campus in

the dorms. But Roxy was taking advantage of the escape from parenting. After all, her son was a senior in high school. He'd be fine home alone while she stayed in the dorms. Probably.

They met for the day at the front of the school. In their absence, Clay and Willa were running the Flour Sax. Willa, the ever faithful, had come out of retirement again—the last, last-time, she swore.

Taylor had welcomed Roxy's gift with open hands. The paper cup warmed her stiff fingers and her heart. The aroma was like a gift from heaven.

"I think we'll sell out of the pattern books today. By the end of day yesterday we'd cleared out two thirds of them." Roxy's smile warmed the cold, dark morning.

"That's amazing. What do we do the rest of the week, then?"

"Don't worry, I put in a rush order for more books. They should be here by tomorrow morning."

"Great." Taylor wrinkled her nose and wondered if the money they made selling the books would cover the cost of overnighting the new batch. Books were heavy and overnighting wasn't cheap.

"Don't worry. This *is* great. Plus, I got us a spot on the how-to panel this morning. They didn't have any creative problem solvers. Do you want to take it?"

"You can have it." Taylor inhaled the dreamy aroma of the fresh brewed magic potion. She might regret not taking the spot at the panel, but the longer she filmed her mom's show, the more she became convinced the wrong person was behind the camera. Roxy would kill it on YouTube, if they switched places, and she'd kill it on the panel.

"Someday you'll sit on one of these panels and you will adore it." Roxy was always enthusiastic in the morning. If she hadn't been, the show would have failed long ago.

"I'm sure you're right. In the meantime, I'll network."

"You're teasing, but that is your talent. We wouldn't have any of this without you."

Taylor shook her head. "You overstate the case, but thanks."

Roxy was right that Taylor had used her connections to help the Expo planners fill the hall with booths, but she was hardly responsible for the whole event.

"Jonah and I came to a compromise." Roxy rolled a cart loaded with Rubbermaid bins full of product behind her as they went to set up for the day's work.

"Always good to hear. Anything important?" When they were back at their spot in the marketplace, they stowed their bins under a charming farmhouse kitchen table that had been provided. They covered it with an embroidered tablecloth Taylor's Grandma Delma had made as a young bride. It hid their bins of books, fabric, notions, and electronics.

"He's Snapchatting for us."

"Why?" Snapchat seemed old news. Did anyone even use it anymore? Taylor shook her head to get the dust and cobwebs out, then sipped her coffee.

"Snapchat videos disappear." Roxy beamed with pride. "Like the Facebook Live and Insta-stories, but its own thing."

"I know what Snapchat is. But he can't just give up his new influencer career. That would be insane."

"He's not, don't worry," Roxy said. "He said Nike is cool with him doing fewer quilt clips and more of just himself." Her smile took on an impish quality. "If you've heard some of the younger folks around here, I can see why Nike is 'cool with it'. The girls love my Jonah."

"That's great." Taylor had seen Jonah blossom recently. He'd gone from her invisible editor whom she had only seen from a distance once or twice, to a regular at the shop, stopping in to see his mom, and now to this…an internet star. "Tell me more about his Snapchat plans."

"He's going to use it to promo the event. He can drum up more young folks. Ticket sales. Book sales. Fabric sales. It's good stuff."

"And he'll send them to our YouTube show, right?" Taylor

had a sneaking suspicion she was losing viewers to Jonah's more interesting content.

"Definitely. He'll post the outtakes on Snapchat, somehow. He said he had a way. He's good at all the tech."

"He is." Taylor did some quick googling. "Hmmm."

"Yes?" Roxy settled the crazy but adorable little pin cushion hat on her curls.

"You can run ads on Snapchat."

"That's neat," Roxy said agreeably.

"But not on TikTok."

"With Nike money, he hardly needs ads, right?" Roxy asked, this time with a hint of concern in her wide eyes.

"Of course, he doesn't need them." Taylor opened Snapchat and found Jonah's account. She hadn't been on Snapchat in years. As far as she could tell, there was no way to see how many followers he had. "Tell him his favorite boss says thank you."

Roxy straightened a stack of print on-demand paperbacks. "He's really going to do it, isn't he?"

"What's that now?" Taylor had moved on to TikTok and was distracted by shots of her mom sticking her tongue out in frustration to the tune of 'I want Candy.'

"Make his first million before he graduates."

Taylor exhaled sharply.

A million dollars.

For a senior in high school.

It seemed insane, but Roxy was right. Jonah was going to do it. "He sure is."

Roxy reddened, embarrassed by her own pleasure at her son's success. "So, today…I do the panel, and you work the table? Are you sure?"

"Absolutely, and then we meet for lunch," Taylor smiled as she said it. She refused to regret her decision. Nike wouldn't have paid her tons of money for sharing outtake clips, even if she'd bothered to learn how to use TikTok. And if Jonah managed to push his income into insane levels by getting all those TikTok followers to be his friends on Snapchat, all the better. The world was for the young.

She and Belle didn't need the money. Anyway, Belle was a scholar. Doing serious things like…

Taylor wasn't sure. All she knew was that Belle was working with her birth-mom's step-daughter Ashleigh at a living history museum in Seattle right now. But Belle had been accepted to grad school and would start after Christmas.

"And we'll work the table together in the afternoon?" Roxy asked.

"There's a workshop I'd like to go to after lunch, is that okay?" Taylor fiddled with her coffee, slipping the coffee stirrer up and down in the lid.

"Of course! Get out there and work your networking magic. I wanted to sit in on the thread painting lecture at four anyway."

"Perfect."

Taylor kept the cash box in her sewing bag and slipped off to the dining hall with Roxy to see if breakfast was still being served. Taylor wanted a poppy seed scone to go with her coffee. Roxy wanted to hear more gossip about Albina.

There was plenty to listen to. In the line in front of them, two women whispered their real opinions about the star speaker.

"She's just too young," a thin-voiced grandmother said. "What do I want to hear from some kid for?"

"It's not her age that's the problem," the second lady disagreed. "I think she's an actress."

Taylor tilted her head to listen better. Albina had absolutely seemed like an actress.

"Obviously." The grandma sounded disgusted.

"I think the publisher hired her to pretend to be the author."

There was a long pause.

The second lady spoke again. "I don't think she wrote those books at all. Did you read the one they gave us?"

"No, not yet."

"I read it last night. I think a computer wrote it and they hired this actress to play the author."

"That's just science fiction." The older woman dismissed her friend with the fluttery wave of a small hand.

Taylor mulled over the gossip as they walked back with their scones. "Albina Tschetter. *Quilted in the County.* Both of those sound just ever so slightly off, don't you think? And yet her speech was delivered to perfection. What if that lady was right? What if someone used a computer to write a book and hired an actress to play the author?"

"You know what would spice up this quilt shindig?" Roxy sipped her coffee, a twinkle in her eye. "If you investigate this and entertain me with your crazy ideas."

Taylor laughed. "It would make a nice change from investigating murder. And the story rings true from a psychological point of view." Her phone pinged before she could elaborate. It was an update from Jonah's TikTok. "Your son is always on his phone."

"So are you. Your point?"

"I'm not supposed to be in school right now."

Roxy scrunched her lips, that hint of worry playing in her eyes again. Attendance hadn't been an issue in the summer, when he'd started the account. But school had been in session for a while now and he sure managed to post content when it seemed like he ought to have been doing his senior year classwork.

Taylor clicked the alert. Jonah had sent an invite to follow his new Snapchat. She tapped the screen a few times and did the deed.

Roxy went off to find her panel.

Taylor expected to see the grinning mug of Jonah Lang on Snapchat. Instead, she found her mom's bright smile and sunny hair. She stood at the worktable where she had filmed all of her videos. "Taylor! Can you see me?"

Taylor stared.

Snapchat was supposed to be live, and though she knew it was just a film of her mom, she was startled by it. Her mind told her that this Snapchat was live, even when she knew better.

How had Jonah managed it? Set up a screenshare with his laptop maybe? She wanted her mom to say more but that was all there was to it. If she could have seen the whole clip, she would have known what video it had come from. She could have placed it in space and time and made sense of it. She knew her mother wasn't alive, but those quick seconds of the Snapchat had left her feeling off kilter.

The feeling lasted all morning.

AFTER LUNCH TAYLOR settled into a cozy little classroom, usually the calligraphy space, where Albina Tschetter would be teaching about quilts as literature. The walls were covered in samples of teacher and student work. Elaborate ink that wouldn't have been out of place in a medieval library to modern pieces stark in their simplicity, but equally moving.

The classroom was packed to the brim with people and buzzed with the fluttering of programs folded into fans. Outside rain pelted the land, driving deep into the clay soil. The school had overshot the heating needs with this crowd, and the small space was steaming.

From the window on the far wall, Taylor watched as sheets of rain turned the world a pewter gray—the sky, the land, the silhouette of Evergreen trees on the distant hills. But a world shrouded in punishing rain was nothing new in Comfort, Oregon, and she wasn't distracted by it for long.

Taylor shifted in her seat. This would be a good moment to network, and the conversation in front of her had caught her attention. Two women with gray hair, and a big bear of a man were locked in a heated debate.

One of the women had been talking a blue streak, fast and

loud, her voice younger than her hair, when a familiar name caught Taylor's ear. "Nonetheless, Jonah Lang ran the text through an app that proved definitively that McKenzie Forte did not write that book."

The shorter of the gray-haired women adjusted her glasses. "I don't know who Jonah Lang is, but authors use different voices for different books. McKenzie Forte *didn't* write *Quilted in the County*. 'Albina Tschetter,' her Amish pen name, did."

The bear of a man looked up from his phone. "Kaitlyn was almost right. Jonah compared the book to a collection of McKenzie's writing and showed she didn't write it, but then he ran it through a different app and that one showed it had to have been generated by a computer program."

Kaitlyn, the taller woman with gray hair, turned to look at the door. She was young enough to be one of Jonah's fans. Her silver hair was just a trendy dye job. "If a computer writes a best-seller, it means the death of literature."

"*Quilted in the County* is hardly a bestseller." The older lady dismissed the claim with a snort.

"Ranked number one in Amazon," the bear-like man said.

"For?" the elder lady challenged.

"Family Drama, Amish slash Mennonite."

"People are so free with the term, bestseller, these days." The elder woman held her phone out like a menu, adjusted her glasses, and tapped the screen. "No Tschetter title has made it to the New York Times list."

Taylor had her phone out as well, texting Jonah about how he was the talk of the Cascadia Quilt Expo.

He didn't respond, but he did post another Snap. This time Taylor's mom's happy smile was embellished with a dog nose and some freckles. "Who'd have thought it, right?" She let out a laugh and disappeared.

This was a trick that Taylor didn't appreciate.

Jonah had figured out some way to make her mom seem alive

and chatting, using clips from the various videos. Outtakes only he had access to. Things Taylor hadn't seen before. Pairing them with filters made the illusion even more real. She held her finger out to unfollow but couldn't do it. She couldn't shut her mom out.

She put her phone down, not wanting to nurse an unnecessary melancholy. Her grief counselor told her she was doing really well, that the pain and sadness she experienced was well within normal ranges. But the counselor encouraged her not to dwell in the sadness if she could help it. There would be times she couldn't. During those, she had to survive. But today she had other things to think about.

The bear of a man had brought up Jonah again. "I don't see why you all are hanging on Jonah Lang's every word. He's just an opportunist."

"Amen," Taylor hadn't meant to say it out loud.

She didn't resent Jonah.

Or hadn't before these snaps of her mom started appearing.

The big bear of a man turned with a smile. "I noticed you at the Flour Sax table. Any relation to Jonah?"

"Just a friend. I'm Taylor Quinn, Laura Quinn's daughter."

"Oh!" the silver-haired young woman turned with wide eyes. "Are you selling any of her projects?"

"I'm sorry, no."

She sighed dreamily. "Someday you need to have a gallery show."

The elderly woman was still looking at her phone. "Whatever Albina Tschetter has actually written, she doesn't seem to want to talk about it. Her session is half over and she didn't bother to show up." The older woman and the man left, he with one more smile in Taylor's direction.

Taylor decided to wait a little longer. She Googled Tschetter while she waited.

Albina had four books in her Amish series. One focusing on quilts, one on cheese, one on childbirth, and one on horses. The random nature of her subjects seemed to support the computer-generated theory.

Taylor ordered all of them for her Kindle app.

Albina never showed.

AFTER THE FAILED class and Roxy's later thread painting class, they met at their booth. Roxy had another coffee waiting for her.

She accepted it with pleasure, though something about the regular gifts of coffee made Taylor wonder. Was Roxy really that worried about her? Or was she feeling guilty for something? Maybe she was feeling guilty for the money pouring Jonah's way…and worried about how Taylor would handle it all.

"Have you been getting Jonah's snaps?" Taylor held out her phone, but the videos in question had long since disappeared.

"No, I haven't downloaded it yet."

"It's really…real. Like, it feels like she's live."

Roxy frowned sympathetically. "That must be really hard. I can tell him to stop." She pulled out her own phone and tapped at it, probably downloading the app.

"Don't pester him about it yet. The YouTube videos were hard at first too…maybe I'll get used to it." Taylor stared at the crowd in the marketplace. It was just as hot in the marketplace as the classroom had been, and quilters wandered around in squeaky wet shoes, dripping with excitement for the event.

The Flour Sax booth was quiet for the moment, so Taylor opened one of Albina's books to have a read. But it only took a few minutes for a happy, wet crowd of fans and quilters to descend on the booth. She'd have to read later, but it was worth it. They sold the last how-to books to the first customer with cash. After only two days.

# CHAPTER THREE

The last event of day two, directly before the night's keynote, was a Q and A with the author. Taylor decided to hit it up before heading home. She wasn't interested in the keynote or the dinner, not with the promise of a quiet night waiting for her, but she wanted to learn more about this mysterious author.

Like the earlier class, this crowd found themselves waiting for Tschetter. Taylor attempted to eavesdrop, hoping to hear some more crazy conspiracy theories but no one nearby was saying anything new.

The big bear of a man from earlier spotted her and smiled. He ambled over. "Can I join you?"

"Of course."

The short, bearded man was built like a football player, all shoulders and broad chest, but he had the huggable vibe of a giant teddy bear. His hair had just a hint of gray in it. "Let's see if our diva makes it this time."

"I hope so. I have a lot of q's for her to a." Taylor fiddled with her phone, both hoping for and dreading Jonah's Snapchat alert.

"Has your friend's son uncovered any more trouble for our favorite Amish author?"

"I hope not, he was supposed to be in school today." Taylor didn't want to rat Jonah out to a stranger, but at the same time, how could he possibly keep up his TikTok, Snapchat, school, *and* digging into Albina Tschetter's background?

"He's something special." The man's beard bristled as his round face broke into a smile. "I thought his quilting stuff was good, but his online detective work is outstanding."

Taylor scrunched her nose but laughed. "I hope the attendance office at his school isn't a fan. He might have heck to pay. But maybe I'd better catch up on it this evening."

"You won't be sorry." The bear of a man hesitated for a moment, then, "I'm Bruno Stutze. Sorry I didn't introduce myself yesterday."

Taylor glanced at his name tag. His ribbons included "faculty." She shook his offered hand. "It's nice to meet you. How is it being one of the only men at a two-week-long quilting expo?"

"Not bad, to be honest. If the other guys knew what I know, they would give up the gun shows and hit the quilt circuit. There are never any single women at gun shows." His eyes twinkled. "I used to come to these events with my wife." He looked down at his hands for a moment. "After she passed, I got a little desperate and tried to contact her through this online medium. Grief makes you do crazy things." His cheeks above his beard pinked up.

"I get it. Nothing in life has made me feel quite as crazy as losing my mother." Taylor's hand went to her phone, as though she expected her mom to Snapchat.

"The medium told me that I wasn't letting my wife go. She said I wasn't going to find her online. If I wanted to be with my wife, I had to go where she would go." He gave an embarrassed laugh. "I signed up for a quilting conference as soon as I hung up the phone. There weren't any nearby, so the one call ended up costing me over two-thousand dollars once you added in hotel, meals, and airfare, but it opened up worlds to me. Turns out, I'm pretty good with a long-arm quilting machine." He grinned with pride. "A year after that call, I was able to quit my day job and quilt full time."

Taylor tried to look like she wasn't staring. An online medium? Grief could make you do some strange things, but she'd never even thought of that.

"It's been a few years now. I tell the story in my memory quilt workshops. The quilters love it, but I can't tell it without getting a little choked up."

Taylor pulled herself together. "It's charming."

"Glad you think so. I wear my heart on my sleeve."

Taylor's phone pinged. "You might like this. Jonah's been sending me Snapchat clips of my mom's classes, but only the outtakes. Stuff I've never seen before." She held out the phone so they could both see it. First, Laura Quinn looked from side to side as though she was looking at both of them.

Before he could respond, Bruno's phone rang. "Excuse me." He shrugged apologetically and stepped away.

Laura leaned forward on her table, eyes straight at the camera. "Go grab Roxy for me!" It was like a direct request, and Taylor had a difficult time not doing it. It felt so real. Rather, it was real, but who knew how long ago that clip had been made. And Jonah was probably the one behind the camera who Laura had been talking to, not Taylor.

But it felt real.

"Sorry, Mom." Taylor whispered and closed the screen. Maybe it was the rain. Maybe it was the stress of a new thing going on, but this was too hard.

The video popped back up. "Please?"

Taylor stared at her mom's face, pleading, but in a teasing way. What was Jonah's point in sharing this? Was *he* asking Taylor to get Roxy? If so, wouldn't a text be simpler?

"I'm sorry," she said to her phone, because it felt right. "The speaker is about to show up."

Taylor had a gut feeling her grief counselor would consider

talking to Snapchats of her mom as regression, but she had longed to talk to her for two years now, and this felt so real.

One more snap came. "She's not coming?"

Yes, Laura Quinn said it like a question, as though maybe Jonah had said his mom Roxy wasn't coming. But that's not what it felt like. Not at all.

Taylor turned the phone off and shoved it deep into her purse. She'd have Roxy talk to her son. This wasn't going to work.

Bruno came back. "Funniest thing. The number was my daughter, but there was no one there. We don't call them butt calls, she and I. We say it's Mom calling us. My wife, I mean. When one of us butt calls the other, we say it's Dana trying to get in touch. Our dark sense of humor. My daughter says Mom is 'ghosting' us." He was rambling, surprisingly awkward for a man who travelled to conferences for a living. It was probably because Taylor was staring into the distance not listening.

A ghost call interrupted him from seeing the video of her dead mom. How appropriate.

The buzzing, thumping noise of someone tapping on a microphone pulled her attention back to the here and now. "I am very sorry to say there has been an…" Sue Friese, the director of the conference gripped a paper cup of coffee in both hands, "an…an emergency and this session is cancelled." She stood stock still, staring at the room, her mouth slightly opened.

The MC from the night before joined her, put his arm on her waist, and led her out of the room again.

"Never hire an actress to do an author's job," Bruno grumbled. "I travel to a minimum of seven conferences a year and the farther the distance the keynoter has from the craft, the less satisfying they are to work with. Want to go get a coffee?"

"Yes." Taylor had meant to make a polite excuse, but her mind wasn't working correctly. She followed him to the coffee cart.

She ordered a decaf. She felt like she'd had enough caffeine for a full week.

He ordered an iced coffee. They took a seat at one of the little bistro tables that had turned the school lobby into a temporary café. Within seconds they were joined by three other women.

"Bruno! I can't wait for your class." The gushing speaker was around thirty. She wore small, rimless glasses and had very red lips.

"I've been dying to get into the class," a quieter, older woman said. "I inherited a stash of fabric from my grandmother and want to use it to make a memory quilt."

The third woman practically jumped on the end of the quiet woman's words. "Bruno, we met in Albuquerque, remember? You used my newspaper print quilt as an example of a fine-art memory quilt."

"I'd never forget." Bruno had a knack for sounding sincere that Taylor didn't trust. "That was a beautiful piece of work. Ladies, I'd like to introduce you to Taylor Quinn. She's the daughter of the legendary Laura Quinn."

"Nice to meet you." Taylor smiled at them.

"Laura Quinn ," the pushy newspaper print quilter said. "I love her work."

The other two nodded.

"Then I recommend you get to the Flour Sax table at the marketplace. Also," Bruno added, "you need to convince Taylor to get in on the teaching. No one like Laura's daughter and heir to keep the Flour Sax traditions alive." The name of her mom's show rolled off his tongue as though he was an honest fan.

"Yeah, you definitely need to," the first woman said.

The quiet woman backed away a little. "I'd better be going...."

"Say hi next time I see you, okay?" Bruno reached across the table to grip her hand in farewell.

Her face glowed, but she didn't respond.

The lady with the red lips hesitated, then turned toward the quiet lady. It looked as though they had followed Bruno together. "See you in your class."

"Sounds good." He waved as she walked away.

The newsprint-quilter planted herself in a seat. "Fit to Print is at the Museum of Craft and History in Wichita." She leaned back and sipped her coffee.

"Well done. You're making a real name for yourself in the fine arts world." Bruno's smile was wide and sincere.

She nodded, a small smile on her lips. "I am. I've been approached by others, and there's a tour happening soon."

Bruno turned to Taylor. "Her grandmother was an early journalist. She made a memory quilt of the clippings. It hadn't been done before."

"Trudy Franklin." Trudy didn't offer her hand. "If you aren't a part of the fiber scene in fine arts you might not be aware of my work."

Taylor's phone pinged again. She didn't remember turning it back on. But maybe it hadn't really pinged. Maybe she had imagined it. This woman was stressing her out, but Bruno noticed it too.

"Do you need to check that?" He asked in a low voice.

"No." Taylor folded her hands on the table. So, she hadn't turned it off like she thought she had. She still wasn't going to see what Jonah had sent this time.

"You must know Jonah Lang," Bruno said to Trudy. "He's created quite a stir by using clips of Laura Quinn's work on TikTok. You'll appreciate this. The kids are in love and consider her a primitive genius, but as you and I know, she attended this very school for a while, and was considered one of the greats, at least regionally, even before her show took off. I asked Jonah about why he didn't straighten his audience out and he said something about working with what works. Didn't make sense to me."

Trudy swallowed. "Oh, sure. I know about Laura Quinn. And Jonah." She looked out beyond Bruno, like she was embarrassed.

"Mom was a complex woman," Taylor murmured. Yes, she was here to promote her mom's work, but she was desperate to get away.

And Bruno was a complex man. How did he know all of that about her mom?

"I wish I had known her." Bruno had something like affection in his eyes. "She didn't get online till long after my wife was gone, but Dana would have loved her." The little round cheeks just above his beard turned pink again. "I had hoped I'd get to meet her someday, at a conference maybe, or just a trip out here. Your mom..." He whistled softly.

Taylor's phone was pinging like crazy, which distracted her from Bruno's fanning. And crushing? This man had developed a crush on her mom from the videos?

"Are you sure you don't need to handle that?" Trudy said a little tensely.

"Yeah, excuse me. I just need to turn off my notifications, I think." Taylor excused herself and headed for the bathroom. She locked herself in the stall and opened Snapchat.

"I did tell you." Laura looked out from the screen a twinkle in her eye.

Taylor scrunched her face and replayed the other snaps in her mind. The only thing her "Mom" had told her was that "She wouldn't come" or something along those lines. Had Jonah been trying to tell her that Albina wasn't coming?

Taylor shut Snapchat and texted him. *"What do you know that I need to know?"*

He didn't respond.

Taylor stared at her phone, then slowly and carefully, paying complete attention, shut it off. Between online psychics, ghost calls, and that man holding a torch for her deceased mother, she thought she was losing it. She was sure one more snap from Jonah would send her over the edge.

She went back to the lobby-cum-cafe but Trudy and Bruno were gone.

The evening was wet and misty, not painfully wet and stormy like earlier.

The college campus was a collection of small buildings connected with breezeways and sidewalks. She wandered the sidewalks breathing deeply, in and out, slow and steady, trying to relax her nerves. Other quilters were out as well, enjoying the brief respite before dinner. Taylor walked till she was far enough from everyone that she felt alone.

She needed to call her counselor, but the phone had pinged another alert, and she couldn't bring herself to look. Either she had fooled herself into thinking she had shut it off, meaning her subconscious wanted these snaps and longed to disconnect from reality, or she was imagining the alerts from the app for the same reason. She stood there, willing herself to look at her phone and see which delusion she was operating under, but couldn't do it.

She stared out at the field full of cows where the campus met a neighboring farm. A common enough sight in Comfort. Fields and forests, trees and cows. This was good. This was home. She stared. Reality in its earthiest, right there.

Nope.

The cows were doing nothing for her.

She needed Roxy and a sure shot of reality. She changed directions and headed back toward the marketplace, but the phone buzzed, the distinctive buzz of a text rather than chime of an app update.

She pulled it out, sure now that she had unconsciously on-purpose not turned her phone off. A new and unpleasant grief reaction, long after the loss of her parent. Just when she had finally gotten her life and emotions back under control.

*"To all of the educators and representatives at the Cascadia Quilt Expo. We have an important emergency meeting in the conference room."*

The phone rang. The number was the same. She answered it and a prerecorded message repeated the content of the text. She went back to the main building and found a seat in the conference room.

Sue Friese, the director of the Cascadia Quilt Expo, stood at a microphone in the front of the room with the man who had been MCing. Her face was ashen.

Taylor's phone pinged.

She turned the volume off.

It pinged again.

She had a serious problem, but it looked like Sue Friese and the Expo had a bigger one.

After about four minutes of waiting the door was closed and Sue began. "It is my deep sorrow to announce the sad passing of our delightful guest and keynote speaker Albina Tschetter." She paused and dabbed her eyes with a handkerchief. "Albina was my dear friend. A woman I had known for several years through the world of quilting and Amish fiction, of which I am a devoted fan." She took a deep breath and looked away. Then she stepped back.

Taylor's phone pinged again.

The gentleman in the suit took Sue's place at the podium. "Some of you might know me. I'm Morgan, Sue's husband. We've been running The Cascadia Quilt Expo for two decades now and have been looking forward to our first event at Comfort College of Art and Craft. This tragedy is a first for us. I cannot tell you how torn we are. On the one hand, it only seems right to shutter our doors and put on our mourning, but as you know, talented men and women from around the country have come to stay with us, to learn from us, and to have their lives enriched. Sue and I have thought and prayed about this and feel that the show must go on, in honor of Albina. The keynote after dinner will be cancelled tonight. And tomorrow, instead of the scheduled talk from Albina, we'll have a memorial. We are truly blessed and honored in our replacement speaker. Bruno?" From the first row Bruno Stutze stood.

"As you all know, Bruno is a nationally recognized quilter

and a teacher with deep expertise in the art of memorial quilting. He will speak in Albina's place about her, her memory, and how we can use our art to keep our dearly departed near to us."

Sue had collected herself and took her spot back at the podium. "The rest of Albina's engagements will be cancelled, but her agent will be here to man her booth. I am sure it will be a comfort to people to be able to purchase a book to take home. Thank you all for your understanding, and please don't forget, we have many wonderful events, including our quilt show, to look forward to." She paused. "Thank you."

With that she and her husband left. The crowd slowly stood and began to leave as well.

Taylor stared ahead of her trying to make sense of everything she'd experienced during the last two days. The living Snapchats of her deceased mother. The books that were fraudulent—created by computer instead of life. Like the Snapchats, that way.

Had Jonah really sent that snap of her mother saying, "She's not coming?" or had Taylor's mind created that from the bits and pieces, the clues around her? It could be that.

Two years ago, Taylor had worked hard to discover who had killed her mother. It was meant to help ease her sister's grief, but it had only increased her own trauma.

And since then she'd found herself mixed up in two other murders. Maybe somewhere, deep inside her, she'd known something was wrong when Albina didn't show up for her class—something deeply wrong—and it was too much for her.

Perhaps Taylor had snapped, figuratively. She wrinkled her nose at the pun. But that's what it had to be. Trauma. PTSD. Grief. One of those things had triggered a kind of mild break from reality, and so long as she wasn't doing anything dangerous, like operating heavy equipment, it would be fine.

She just needed to find Roxy. Whatever had motivated Jonah to send that Snap, he'd been right.

And yet she remained seated, waiting for her phone to ping again.

Bruno found her. "You should probably answer that. I bet it's Jonah wanting updates about Albina's death."

"Hmm? Oh. Yes." Taylor stroked the back of her phone, not wanting to look at it. "But how could he know so soon?"

Bruno indicated a knot of young quilters at the side of the room. "They call themselves Jonah's Juvies. They've been keeping him updated in comments on TikTok."

"Jonah's Juvies? Like delinquents?" Taylor cringed.

"Or like young quilters?" Bruno laughed. "Kids never make sense to me. But if that kid ever starts traveling to quilt conferences, my days as most popular man in quilting are over." He picked up his computer bag. "Sorry our coffee was interrupted. Rain check?"

"Sure. Sounds good."

"Invite your partner." His ever-ready smile deepened. "I met her at your booth, but I'd love to get to know the woman who raised Jonah Lang." Those brown, bear-like eyes of his twinkled.

Roxy, hmmm? Roxy could do far worse than connect with this kind and thoughtful man.

Something like a weight lifted from her shoulders. She hadn't even realized that she'd been guarding herself. Not that Bruno wasn't lovely in his own way, but she had just settled into a real-life relationship with Hudson, and Bruno had seemed so attentive. Too attentive. "How's dinner after the memorial tonight?" Taylor asked. "We can make it a double date and bring my…." she paused, blushing, "boyfriend."

"That sounds terrific. I happened to pick up your card from your booth…is that the number I can reach you at?" He held out the Flour Sax business card, a little hesitantly.

Taylor took it from him and added Roxy's cell number to the back. "My phone's been acting funny. That's Roxy's number. I'll tell her I gave it to you."

He grinned.

They parted ways, Taylor to find Roxy, him to greet the hordes of women waiting to thank him for stepping in, for caring, and basically for being a good-looking man at an event full of women.

She headed to their booth hoping to find her friend and, maybe, a sense of peace and normalcy. The booth was unattended, and the marketplace was empty. Taylor settled into one of the folding chairs and stared at that phone of hers.

Right now, it was a perfectly normal phone. Not pinging, ringing, snapping, or buzzing. Just sitting there, being off.

She tipped back on the legs of her chair and closed her eyes. Mindful meditation was always good for stress.

Her counselor had told her to start simple. To think about her toe. It felt ridiculous, like calling a grown man boyfriend, but she was willing to try anything once.

So, she considered her big toe in a very thoughtful, meditative way. It was the biggest of her toes. It was not painted. Wait. Mindful. The toenail was not painted. The toe, how did the toe feel? It felt a little sore. She'd been on her feet a long time. No. Be mindful. How did it 'feel.' The pain was like an ache which was like a warmth focused on that one spot. Too much warmth, heat, in one spot was pain. That's all pain was. The pain was nothing. The toe was nothing.

The phone rang.

Panic ripped through her chest. Her eyes flew open.

It rang again. It was just a normal phone doing a normal phone thing.

She answered it breathlessly, "Taylor Quinn."

"Hey. This is Bruno. I know we just made plans, but it turns out I need to stay after the memorial to speak with some official people. Not sure what it's about, but it doesn't seem fun. Can I offer you a rain check, please?"

"Sure." Taylor was sorry for Roxy but didn't mind getting some alone time with her *boyfriend* tonight.

"I am sorry. I mean it." Bruno did sound sorry. Sorrier than seemed reasonable.

"Life happens. Can't be helped." Taylor was anxious for the call to end, as though it was keeping her from seeing her mom.

"Thanks."

They both hung on the line, quiet for just enough time to feel awkwardness seeping through the receiver.

"Um, now you have my number, so call, or text, or something if you hear from Jonah. I'd love his take on all of this. Sue seemed pretty literal when she talked about Albina," Bruno said.

"Sure. Maybe McKenzie Forte was actually a stage name and Albina was the real one."

"That's exactly what I was wondering. We can discuss it over breakfast. Roxy too."

"Sounds good." Taylor hung up. Roxy and Bruno…what a lovely thought. Maybe something good could be born from this tragedy.

## CHAPTER FOUR

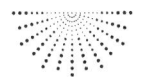

*R*oxy hadn't shown up at the booth yet, so Taylor sent her a quick text, packed up, and headed home. A quiet evening at home sounded better than dinner at the Expo.

The college campus was just blocks from Taylor's house and she took the walk back slowly, pulling their merch in a garden wagon behind her. The wagon wheels splashed through little puddles, muddying the ankles of her artfully torn jeans.

Bruno had made her curious. What was Jonah up to with his armchair detective work? Once home, she commandeered the kitchen table and stared at her phone wondering where to begin.

She had dozens of notifications from Snapchat, so she opened it, wary. Was she up for this? Could she handle more of these clips that felt so much like her mom was truly making them live?

The camera zoomed in for a close-up of Taylor's mom. She wore pink sapphire earrings—the last gift Taylor's dad had ever given her, and as she spoke, she reached up and touched them. "Just one last thing, okay?"

Taylor bit her bottom lip. One last thing.

She didn't want one last thing. She wanted Jonah Lang to have thousands of hours of film that he could roll out over the course of Taylor's whole life, all new. All fresh. But she also wanted to see it all right now.

But she didn't want it ever to end.

"No," she whispered to the screen of her phone. "Please don't be the last thing."

"You've got to trust me, okay?" Laura Quinn seemed to be staring directly at Taylor, right through the screen, her large, blue eyes sincere and so young looking. "Promise me you'll trust me? I know this feels crazy, but it's going to work, and when it does…" She shook her head, her smile growing. She touched the earring again. "When it does, neither of us will ever have to worry about money again."

Taylor dabbed her eye.

The snap ended. Taylor opened the next one in the queue. Jonah, that handsome kid stared at her this time. "Okay Juvies, I told you that this chick at the quilt Expo with my mom wasn't a real author, but I'm telling you, she's really dead. If you're at the Expo, be careful. I think it might have been murder." The video closed. The ten seconds over.

Murder, again.

She hoped Jonah wouldn't get too much advertising money out of this, or he might look like a suspect.

She got up, restless from the videos. Mindful meditation hadn't helped. Coming home hadn't helped, though she recognized it was her own fault for checking her phone. Maybe she just needed to walk it off.

She locked up her house and headed away from the school. But Comfort was a rather small town, and less than a half an hour later she found herself back at the Expo, wondering what news there was about Albina Tschetter.

Taylor made it as far as the doors to the dining hall when she was way-laid by the young woman with dyed-gray hair. The gray girl cleared her throat softly. "My name's Kaitlyn. We met waiting for Albina's class on quilts as literature. I was wondering…. can I join you?" She looked around the dining hall nervously. "I'm just feeling really alone…"

Taylor waved at some seats. "Make yourself comfortable." The girl didn't look much older than her sister. And she looked as scared and lost as she sounded. "Are you here from out of town?"

"Depoe Bay. I think I might go home though." She lifted her eyebrows like she wanted Taylor to answer that as a question.

Taylor's heart was melting towards the girl. If this had been her sister, she'd want someone to take her under their wing and look after her. "What led you to decide to come for such a long, expensive conference?"

"I recently finished my MFA in fiber arts."

Taylor nodded. "Go on."

"And I need to make professional connections in the field." She ran her hand through the front of her hair. "But the only people I meet are the girls obsessed with Jonah. I like him as much as they do, but I'm here to launch a career, not giggle about some guy on the Internet."

"I can appreciate your frustration." There was something comforting about talking to a girl who wasn't into Jonah. "What kind of quilting do you do?"

Kaitlyn took a deep breath. "I create quilted materials with handmade fabrics that, put together, speak for the unwritten history of the land." The words spilled out like she was afraid she might forget something.

"Not a bad summary. Slow down and relax, and after you get that part out, talk about why. What feeling do you want to create in people when they view your work?" Taylor tried to remember what her professors had taught her about artist statements, but it was foggy and mixed up with ad copy in her mind.

"I want people to feel connected, rooted in the past that they haven't been taught." Kaitlyn's face was pale and her hands shaking.

Taylor let them sit in quiet for a moment, hoping it would

help her calm down. "That's a good motivation. What's your process like?"

"I spin and dye my threads, then weave my fabric. I use my own fabric to create quilted wall hangings." She moved her hands like a shadow show of her art.

Taylor was impressed. She had liked spinning and dyeing and weaving in school, but not enough to try and make a living at it. "That's an incredible amount of work."

"It's why I don't have much yet. Not enough for a one woman show."

Taylor smiled, hoping to show humor and affection. Anything to make the girl feel more comfortable. "Then don't be a one woman show."

"Right. Exactly. That's why it was so important to come here. I can anticipate being able to create one piece a year until I have more of a fabric library to work with. I can't feed myself on one piece a year—yet. I need to find people, like-minded artists who I can collaborate with. Artists I could grow together with." Her large, dark eyes were filling.

Taylor didn't mind if this girl cried. Crying was good for the soul, but Kaitlyn gritted her teeth like she didn't want to cry.

"Coming here makes perfect sense to me." It wasn't that Taylor thought Kaitlyn's vision was a good one. The work was too slow and unfashionable to be smart business, but at least she was at the right place to meet people. She wouldn't have encouraged her sister to do anything like that, but this girl wasn't Belle.

"And yet being here makes me feel like I need a gimmick, like I need to set aside my goals for quick cash. There are so many ways to do it quicker, easier, for more money. I could design fabrics to sell at Spoonflower where they have print on-demand fabric. I could make how-to videos or books for any part of my process. With nothing more than an Internet connection I, too, could be famous." Kaitlyn sounded both exhausted and disgusted.

Taylor glanced around the room filled with mostly women

who had dedicated years of their time, obscene amounts of money, and their whole hearts to their hobby, craft, and passion. She thought Kaitlyn was being a bit cold toward them. While Taylor cared about this girl's worried heart, she also remembered the not so long-ago years in her twenties when she had thought that everything around her was insincere. She knew better now. Kaitlyn would too, someday. "What do you wish your career could look like for the next twelve months?"

Kaitlyn squared her shoulders. "I want to spend ten hours a day or more in the studio creating. I have a piece in mind about the scablands—it's a geological region in Washington—the scablands are prehistory at its deepest, most misunderstood. I want to create. Just…create. But I have to eat."

"Then deliver pizza at night. If you're hungry enough, you'll make it happen." Taylor clenched her phone. Her words hadn't come out kindly, and she had a feeling she'd be punished for it by a well-timed snap from Jonah/her mother/her delusion. It would be a coincidence, of course, but she could feel it coming.

Kaitlyn gritted her teeth, but appeared to ponder what Taylor had said, without shutting down.

Taylor's phone pinged.

She bit her lip but turned the phone over.

Snapchat.

She opened it.

Her mom, on the screen, hair up in a ponytail, shiny pink earrings glittering. And a dog-faced Snapchat filter. "Do I look fat in this?" She laughed, that warm, musical sound that Taylor missed so desperately.

How had Jonah gotten a filter on a video clip? It wasn't right, but Taylor couldn't pull her eyes away.

"Video ads ten pounds. But listen, we're getting burgers after this anyway. You're doing the hard work and you deserve it." This video had to be a practice video. One from the first days of filming, when Laura and Roxy were just goofing around getting used to things. It was so natural and silly.

The ten second snippet ended. Taylor was unsure what Jonah's motivation was, but now she wanted a burger, and anyway, she *was* doing the hard work. "Do you have Snapchat?"

"Sure. I'm following Jonah. He's going a little crazy about this murder."

"What do you mean, 'following'? I'm new to this."

"He posts stuff for followers. I follow it." Kaitlyn didn't elaborate. "He's posted a ton tonight about poor Albina. I kind of feel like it's not his business, you know? I guess I can't blame a guy for wanting to make a living, but it does feel like it's in bad taste."

"What's he been saying about her?"

"I haven't watched the videos, but on Snapchat he shared her IMDB credits, shared some of her modeling shots from a million years ago. He outed her as McKenzie Forte. It seemed like a lot for a couple of hours." She dragged her phone out of a little purse and glanced at it.

"I agree. What does he gain from that?"

"Murder is a big deal." Kaitlyn narrowed her eyes.

"Officially murder?" Taylor tapped the back of her phone, wondering if she should get away and watch more. She hadn't seen the McKenzie Forte revelation snaps, only the Laura Quinn stuff. Maybe she was following something more personal. Something Jonah was making just for her. If it was out of gratitude for the fame he'd gotten, he was off target.

"Jonah is saying it is, and he's using his...pardon me, these are his words...elderly mother and her friend in a small town with a murderer on the loose as a hook." Kaitlyn shrunk back a little as though she were afraid of how Taylor might react.

"He is unreal." Taylor rolled her eyes.

Kaitlyn smirked. "I agree."

"If he was my kid, I'd ground him for saying that." Taylor lifted an eyebrow and chuckled, hoping she came across as not that bothered.

"It's rude, right? Roxy can't want to be called elderly."

Kaitlyn relaxed

"She's not. She's just barely forty."

Kaitlyn looked confused.

Taylor bit her tongue.

The phone pinged again.

"I do think he's scared for you. If Albina was murdered, then there might be a murderer wandering around." Kaitlyn's face flushed—a young person's excited response to the dramatic. She might claim she wasn't here as one of Jonah's Juvies, but she sure was informed on what he was up to.

Taylor's phone pinged again.

"Check it and see what he's saying now," Kaitlyn urged.

Taylor turned it over. It was her mom again. The account that was probably private to her. She still had the ponytail in, so it was probably from the same session. They must have filmed for hours that day. "It's a secret," her mother said. "No one can know till we get it just right." She picked up the pin cushion hat, Roxy's favorite, and stuck it on her head. "No? You don't think? But I love it." She patted it.

The ten seconds ended.

The hat had been her mom's idea?

If Jonah was trying to communicate about the murder, what did he mean when he said it was a secret? Taylor needed to talk to Jonah, face to face. And the sooner the better.

Kaitlyn stared at Taylor, her face hopeful.

Taylor sighed. "This week might not get any easier. Let me give you my cell number." She passed her card. "If you need something, just text. As you said…there might be a murderer on the loose."

Kaitlyn lowered her eyebrows in suspicion.

"If you were my sister, I'd want to know someone was concerned."

"Okay. Thanks." Kaitlyn slipped the card into her pocket. "Bruno said he'd help too. It means a lot to me to know that people care."

## CHAPTER FIVE

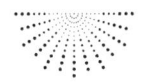

Comfort College lobby was bustling the next morning. Quilters who ought to have been in the dining hall for breakfast were lined up three deep and down the hall at the coffee cart. The attraction seemed to be the four sheriff's deputies holding court in the middle of the well-appointed arts and crafts era building. Isaiah, Taylor's old friend and head of the college office, Sue Friese, the director of the Expo, and Shara Schonely, owner of Dutch Hex, were in conference with the officials. Likely they were answering and asking questions in equal measure.

Taylor was drawn to that scene, but decided to hold back, the sheriff's warning to keep her nose out of crime still fresh in her mind after the recent murder that led to an explosion at the town's only old folks' home.

Bruno was off to the side, by himself, in one of the golden oak chairs outside a classroom door. Taylor sat next to him.

"You get the call too?" He was drumming his thick fingers on his knee.

"No. What's going on?"

"Don't know yet. The sheriff wanted to have a word with me."

"Looks like they aren't in a hurry." Taylor and all the quilters in line for breakfast and coffee watched the huddle of law enforcement and Expo staff. "Are you ready for the memorial talk?"

"I was, but Albina's literary agent came—he was just up in Portland. He wanted to take over." Bruno stared into the distance. His thick brows were together, drawn in worry. He glanced at the group in the lobby, then at his phone.

"They can't make you wait here forever, right?" Taylor offered it as empty comfort while she and the rest of the quilters watched the show.

Bruno shrugged. "Who knows."

Taylor switched subjects again. "I'm glad you're taking over as keynoter. With your focus on memorial quilts, it just makes sense."

The crowd began to break up. Two deputies headed off into the heart of the school and two came closer.

"It's a little weird, to be honest, but I couldn't turn down the opportunity." He tipped his head back and stared at the ceiling. "The deputy who called made it sound like the chance to jump into keynoting was something I might want to kill for."

"Absurd." Taylor smiled at him, hoping it was a confidence boosting kind of smile.

He shrugged. "After I got 'invited' down to talk, I was afraid everyone might be thinking the way they are."

"A person would have to be a lunatic to kill for a chance to work more. Besides, from what I've seen, you aren't suffering from lack of fame."

"Can I put you down for a character witness?" His big soulful eyes looked sincere.

The classroom door opened, and a quilter Taylor recognized from a show on her public television station stepped out with tear-stained cheeks. Maria, one of the deputies Taylor had met in the past, held the door open. "Bruno Stutze?"

Bruno stood. "That's me."

"Come in."

Taylor smiled at him one more time, but he didn't look back, just took a few shaky steps into the classroom.

Taylor stood, but wasn't sure if she should leave. Bruno might like someone to talk to when he came out.

Who was she kidding? She wanted to know what the deputy had to say.

Her phone pinged.

She pulled it out of her purse. "Hey, Mom." She knew it was just Jonah, and that he couldn't hear her, but the words fell out anyway.

Her mom smiled, a phone to her ear. "Good evening Taylor. Are you there?"

Taylor closed her eyes.

"You'll never believe what I'm doing right now."

Taylor remembered this phone message. She'd come home from a long day at work. Her phone had rung. She'd seen it was her mom's number and let it go to voice mail. She didn't hear the message till the next morning.

But she could hear it now. And see it, too, if she'd open her eyes. She didn't open her eyes.

"Well, I don't want to say it in a phone message, so I guess you'll just have to call me. But trust me, it's big."

Taylor sat down, again, resting her phone on her knee.

"Psst, Taylor."

Taylor looked down at her phone.

"Over here."

She looked up.

Roxy took the seat next to her. "I've been looking all over for you. Have you heard the latest?"

"Probably not."

"Jonah just texted—miracle, I know—it turns out Albina Tschetter was murdered."

"I've heard the rumor. But how does he come to that conclusion?"

"He said he has inside sources but won't reveal them. He thinks he's so smart." She shoved her phone back into her hand-quilted-patchwork-purse. "He thinks with the help of his fan girls he can solve the murder, but I think we can beat him to it, don't you?"

"It does keep the numbers up." Taylor tried to keep her voice light, but she had a feeling he was keeping his audience engaged in the murder for sake of the advertising money. She'd helped in murder investigations before, and it was never for money.

Roxy folded her fingers together and stretched them out. "I think we should at least try. Once word spreads about the murder, it's not like anyone is going to stick around to buy our books."

"Got any ideas where to start?"

The classroom door opened. "Thanks for your time. Don't make any plans to leave town." Maria held the door for Bruno.

Bruno shook her hand but remained in the hallway.

Roxy jumped up. "Excuse me, ma'am."

"Yes?" Maria gave her a quick once over.

So did Bruno.

"This is Taylor Quinn. You probably know her. Everyone does. She's solved three murders."

Maria's eyes glazed over, but Bruno's didn't. Bruno turned and stared.

Reg, Taylor's old beau, joined Maria in the doorway just in time to hear Roxy's declaration.

"Taylor…" The last time Reg and Taylor had spoken she'd promised to steer clear of murders.

"This isn't my idea." Taylor stood up quickly. Her phone fell to the ground pinging a new alert as it did.

"A healthy young woman died for no reason." Roxy threw her shoulders back and smiled proudly at Taylor. "And Reg, you of all people know that Taylor could help. She's got a gift."

"The sheriff doesn't work with volunteers, sorry." Reg's jaw flexed.

Roxy held out a business card. "In case you lost her number. You and I both know you'll want to call her eventually."

Reg pocketed the card. "Taylor, why don't you come in?" He stepped aside.

Taylor gave Roxy a stern look of disapproval. But Roxy didn't notice. She only had eyes for Reg.

Bruno, on the other hand, only had eyes for Roxy.

"Have a seat." Reg pulled out a chair for Taylor. Roxy followed her in and seated herself.

Maria sat at a desk in the corner, her eye on the door.

"Roxy, are you nuts? Do you know how mad the sheriff was last time Taylor got involved in one of his investigations?" Reg stared her down for a moment, then turned back to Taylor. "We've been talking with people who were closest to the deceased, as well as a few other folks here." Reg had a homey, country kind of accent despite having lived on the west side of the Cascade mountains since he was born. "It's not normal for a woman in her twenties to pass away like this. You can imagine we want to find out what happened as quickly as possible."

"We really didn't mean to bother you. I just stopped to talk to Bruno." Taylor's face was hot with embarrassment. She had promised she'd not get involved in another investigation.

"I'm glad to hear it." Reg frowned at Roxy. "But since you're here, maybe you can tell me what you think of this Bruno Stultze."

"I don't know him." Roxy held up her hands in surrender.

"I didn't ask you." Reg sighed, a little exasperated. And yet, he hadn't sent them away. It probably didn't hurt his feelings to have someone he knew to talk to right now. The Quilt Expo had over two hundred guests in addition to the staff. Getting to the bottom of a mysterious death was going to be an insane amount of work.

"I just met him, but he seems very nice. He loves his work." Taylor nodded and smiled as she spoke, probably looking foolish, but wanting to look encouraging.

"What did he have to say about Albina Tschetter?"

Taylor hesitated.

Reg noticed.

"When I met him, he and several other quilters were wondering if she was who she claimed to be. But really, everyone's been asking that."

"What did Bruno conclude?"

"He seemed interested in the idea that she might be an actress hired to pretend to be an author." Taylor tried to say it lightly, as though it was no big deal.

"Was he bothered by this?" Reg's fake casual tone only made the question sound weightier.

"I would say he found it entertaining." Taylor fiddled with the edge of her nametag. "We just met, but he says quilt conventions are a big part of his career. It might get boring sometimes. This controversy added some interest." Taylor was trying to hint that Bruno wouldn't have wanted Albina dead, since she offered entertainment. Her phone pinged. Jonah's impeccable timing.

"You don't think he'd try and create some excitement, do you?" Reg leaned forward, eyes narrowed.

"I would say he was enjoying the gossip." Taylor bit her lip. Tell him about Jonah or no? Her phone pinged five times in a row. "I'm sorry about that." She patted the purse the phone was safely inside of.

"We're still waiting on the results of the autopsy, but you might hear something that wouldn't be said around our uniforms. A little gossip from the living could go a long way." He stared over Taylor's head. "Officially, I don't want you getting messed up in this."

"Of course not." Taylor began to stand.

"But people tell you things. If you happen to hear something, you'll call, right?" He looked stern, like Taylor had better call.

"I won't go looking for trouble."

"Let's pretend that's true. But when trouble finds you, you'll call me, right?"

"Yes, of course. Obviously." Taylor was frozen. Had she just been unofficially deputized?

※

TAYLOR'S HOUSE was too quiet that night. She got in her car and headed toward the beach where all of her grandparents were in one house, watching TV or playing cards or whatever it was grandparents did when the kids weren't around. She wanted to be with people, but not be at the Expo.

Loggers, the little bar at the edge of town, was closer though and had a packed parking lot. The bright lights and cheerful noise vibrating from the familiar old building drew Taylor in. She changed her plans picking immediate gratification.

Taylor found her way to an empty seat near a very busy table. She ordered a peach shrub—drinking vinegar with peach syrup, a dash of lemon essential oil, and a few muddled mint leaves. It was incredibly refreshing and not a bit alcoholic. She felt unbalanced enough without alcohol today.

She sat alone in a room full of hubbub wondering if she should call Hudson. She heard a lady to her left say murder, so she waited and listened for more.

"She was hot." The loudest voice was a man Taylor had seen around town. She thought he might be Max or Matt. He was slender and wearing the Loggers Bar standard Wranglers and tight t-shirt. He had a small tattoo of a gun on his wrist. "Seriously hot. I have no idea how she found her way to this old lady show, but it was a bad idea." He laughed and tipped back his beer.

"Dude." A woman with large hoop earrings had a hint of disapproval in her voice. Taylor didn't recognize her. "The chick is dead."

"That's what I said. It was a bad idea for her to come here. You think getting killed was a good idea?"

"It's not like the old ladies murdered her," the earrings argued. "She probably OD'd on coke or ennui."

"On who?" Max or Matt guffawed again.

A younger guy who Taylor sometimes bought coffee from at the cafe that had been Cuppa Joes, then Café Ole, and was now Cozy Cuppa, cleared his throat. "You didn't hear what I heard at work yesterday."

"Spill it," the earrings said.

Taylor frowned. The town was playing a game of telephone. What did she care what the barista from Cozy Cuppa said he heard yesterday? The police could never use information like that.

"A couple of smokin' ladies were in line to get some real coffee."

"Not from the same group then," Matt or Max said.

The barista—baristo? ignored the interruption. "They were talking about stripping, so I listened in."

"Yessss." He got nods of approval from all of the men and a snort of disgust from earrings.

"It was a major letdown because apparently stripping is just cutting fabric, but they did say that they were pretty sure that the dead chick was a real stripper."

The earrings groaned and pushed her way out of the crowd.

Taylor copied her and moved to the other side of the room. Some of the Jonah's Juvies crowd were huddled around a table in the far back. Jonah was still in high school. Did these Juvies of his have fake ID's or was he attracting an older crowd?

"Hey." Taylor recognized the girl with the red hair and white glasses who had said money was no object. Valerie Ritz.

"Taylor! Join us." She stood up slightly and motioned toward an empty chair.

"Thanks. How are you all doing?"

"It's been wild," Valerie said. "Jonah seems to have gone to bed, but I don't think he did anything but post all day. I've never seen him so fast with his editing."

From the corner of the table a mild-mannered girl with bangs in her eyes spoke up, "It was strange. It made me uncomfortable." She paused, all eyes on her. "How did he have time to film and edit?" She looked down at her hands, took her time considering them, then looked up, eyes dramatically wide. "I don't think he made those videos today."

The table met her hint with silence.

A familiar looking girl with the shaved head spoke up. "You're trying to make us think he planned the murder and prepared the videos in advance. You obviously don't know Jonah."

Taylor lifted an eyebrow. While she agreed whole-heartedly with the shaved-head's common sense, she wondered who she was and why she thought she knew Roxy's son so well.

"You work for him," Valerie said. "What do you think?"

Taylor kept her voice serious. "I've been working *with* him for a while now. The idea that he might kill is ridiculous. In addition, he is very quick with his video edits. I've seen him film, edit, and post in an afternoon."

"But he's been doing this all afternoon. Video after video," the girl with the bangs in her eyes whispered slowly.

"How does the quality compare?" Valerie asked. "I think she's talking about full edits of the Flour Sax classes, not just the TikTok stuff."

Taylor was surprised Jonah hadn't had that mystic psychic connection and sent her more snaps. She hadn't opened the ones he sent during her chat with Reg. Maybe he wouldn't send more till she did. But somehow it seemed like he'd know he was being talked about.

"How did Albina Tschetter die?" the dramatic whisperer asked.

"Albina? You mean McKenzie Forte," a girl seated next to Taylor scoffed. "I bet she got a pair of Ginghers through the heart."

Taylor flinched. The last time she'd been caught up in a

murder, stabbing had been the method. "I don't think it was anything obvious. I've heard they're waiting on an autopsy to see if it was natural causes."

The atmosphere lifted.

"She probably OD'd on coke and ambition," a bookish girl in a button down said.

Valerie snorted.

An extremely thin girl with pale skin and dark hair spoke for the first time. Her voice was raspy. She stared at Taylor. "You should ask her."

Taylor fidgeted. How could she ask a dead girl?

Her phone pinged.

Valerie waved down a waiter. "Can we get some pretzels and fondue? Pretty please?"

"Coming right up."

The thin girl didn't take her eyes off of Taylor.

"Did anyone get the chance to talk to Albina?" Taylor asked the group.

They all shook their heads.

"Look at my finger." A girl Taylor would have never recognized in a crowd held up her right hand. "It's all torn up. I bought those stupid Band-Aids instead of using a thimble," she pouted.

Two other girls offered their fingertips for comparison.

Taylor moved away from the table, finished her shrub, and set the glass on the counter.

Nate, the bartender, paused. "Any word on the dead lady?"

"Word's gotten all over town, has it?" Taylor leaned a little closer.

He laughed. "Another murder in Comfort? Of course it did."

"What have you heard?"

"I heard she was AI. You know, a cyborg."

"Ah," Taylor said. "So, word has gotten out." She tapped the side of her nose with a chuckle. After she paid her tab, she drove home. She'd been mistaken. Being with people was not better than being alone.

Once at home she double checked the locks.

From a stripper pretending to be an author, to a cyborg book writer. She didn't think this was the kind of gossip Reg was after.

Much later that night, she laid her head down on the pillow and contemplated whether she had maybe ought to drag her dresser in front of her door. She took a deep breath, held it, then let it out slowly, trying to do the circular breathing her counselor recommended for the panic. She felt a strong urge to do something practical, and in her life that meant buy something. It was almost overwhelming, so she turned to her phone. It was harder to shop from the phone than the laptop.

And besides, those alerts from earlier were probably messages from her mom. Well, from Jonah but also her mom.

Most of the snaps were about Albina, but the last one wasn't.

There her mom was again, this time close to the camera, her eyes and her pink sapphires sparkling, the silly hat in her hands. "That's all for today, darling. Goodnight." Maybe Taylor's mom was speaking to her imaginary audience, the one she dreamed of as she plotted her YouTube empire. Or maybe she was talking to Roxy.

Or maybe, just maybe, this was for Taylor.

❦

THE NEXT MORNING the mood at the Expo had changed dramatically. Less loud gossip, more whispering. Fewer people in the marketplace, more people in the lobby of the school, huddled in small groups, looking over their shoulders. Taylor peeked into the classrooms and saw fewer people engaged in learning. There was also a line at the front office desk, people with their rolling suitcases and scared looks on their faces, probably wanting refunds before they went home.

If Taylor had been a killer, that's what she'd be doing. The autopsy results hadn't been in the news. In fact, the death itself wasn't on the radio or in the local newspaper. Albina must have died of something subtler than a pair of fancy scissors to the throat. Something quiet that would take a long time to find, like poison. A woman's weapon.

But in the modern world obsessed with crime television, a man might use poison to purposefully throw the scent off himself.

Taylor watched the quilters line up to leave the Expo. Only two men were slinking away with the crowd, one was a scrawny thing with thinning hair and shirt buttoned all the way up, the other a soft dinner roll of a man with a pleasant face that dimpled even when he wasn't smiling. Maybe, ignoring gender entirely, poison would be a quilters weapon of choice.

Her phone pinged.

Taylor took a seat in one of the golden oak chairs that lined the lobby and opened Snapchat.

"I feel like she was just here yesterday." Taylor's mom stared off camera, toward what was the front door of the store. "I miss that damn kid so much." She turned toward the camera and nodded to something Taylor couldn't hear.

"Sorry." Taylor apologized to the video, sure as anything her mom was talking about her.

"You know what? It's poison to our relationship."

Taylor swallowed.

Jonah was being a jerk. If he hadn't been in school at the moment, she'd have had it out with him for sure.

If he wanted her to know that he also thought Albina had been poisoned, all he had to do was text. He didn't have to send videos that made her feel sick with guilt.

"Don't you have the directions?" Laura asked from the phone screen.

Taylor snapped to attention again. Directions? She did have directions, from the police. How had her mom…

No.

How had Jonah known?

Or did he think he was giving her directions?

She hated the compulsion to open this thing every time it pinged.

But...her distance from home life *had* poisoned her relationship with her mom. She couldn't ignore her. Not now. Not ever again. Especially because the pain of seeing her was a sort of punishment, a penance for having been a self-centered twenty-something.

Penance aside, Taylor did have her directions. Or permission anyway, from Reg. The deputy had heavily implied she should be his ears in the crowd. Listen and report. Even if all he had said was report, she knew what he'd meant. Somewhere on campus someone was saying something useful, and here she was, watching disappointed and grim-faced crafters beg the office for a refund instead of hunting down clues.

## CHAPTER SIX

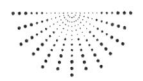

Roxy hadn't shown up yet, so Taylor headed over to the dorms to find her. On the way she found Bruno leaving the dining hall. He offered her a sheepish smile and joined her on her walk through the campus.

"Glorious morning. You'd not know it was fall in the rainy part of the world," he offered as an icebreaker.

"No…you wouldn't." The day was remarkably clear and dry. Taylor thought she owed him some kind of small talk but had hoped to have Roxy to herself for a while first, to discuss Jonah.

He cleared his throat. "Sorry I ran out on you last night."

"It's nothing, don't worry."

"You looked like you were about to get in some trouble that was none of my business."

"Honest, it's okay. Reg and I … go way back." The first crime Taylor and Reg had solved together had been when she was a freshman in college and Reg was a newly minted deputy.

Bruno nodded in a knowing way.

Taylor paused. Could he tell? Did he know just by the way she had said that, that Reg and she had dated for a while? Surely not. Men weren't known for their relationship insight like that.

"I'm from a small town too," Bruno said. "In Kansas. Everyone there goes way back."

They got to Roxy's room, but Taylor didn't knock. She still wanted to think of a way to get rid of her new friend.

"It looks like you and Roxy are a big hit here. Are you going to do any traveling this year?" Bruno asked.

"We run the shop here in town. No time to travel."

"You should reconsider. A little travel can be good for business."

He had hit her favorite word, and she was torn. Confront Roxy with complaints about her son, or talk to this guy who had new and even interesting ideas about how to improve business? "Are you traveling much this year?" she asked, still undecided.

"I'm doing a smaller event in Portland at a church next, just a weekend thing. My daughter is meeting me out there for some daddy's-girl time. Then I'm headed down to New Mexico. There's a fine arts fiber fest that I never miss. You should consider that one."

Taylor shook her head. "We're not really a fine arts brand."

"Bummer." Bruno raked his hand through his salt and pepper hair. "I don't think I mentioned it earlier, but I've been a fan of the show since it started. Discovered it after I quit my job to quilt full time. Your mom's a treat. I don't mean to be rude about Jonah, but it seems unfair for her skills to be minimized in those TikTok videos." He stopped. "I'm sorry. I shouldn't."

Taylor chuckled. "I can't say I disagree with any of that. I don't love the TikTok blooper real he's running, but the thing he's doing on Snapchat right now is even worse. But then, Mom made the show because she knew she and Roxy needed the money, and man, Jonah is bringing in the bucks, so maybe she wouldn't mind." Taylor's phone pinged. She stared at the man who so freely confessed that he had used an online medium to contact his deceased wife. He'd probably understand the real reason these snaps from Jonah were getting under her skin.

Bruno looked at his watch, then looked around, realizing

they had been standing in a hall, not going anywhere, for longer than is natural. "I'd better head out. Say hi to Roxy for me, if you see her."

The door opened as he spoke and Roxy stood there, shining and bright like she had a good day ahead of her.

Bruno beamed.

She looked from Taylor to Bruno and back again. "Good morning."

"Let's get coffee." Taylor didn't try to explain Bruno's joining them or why she wasn't checking her phone, which pinged three more times as they headed toward the coffee bar.

Before they could order, they were joined by Kaitlyn, the young girl who had dyed her hair silver. She was breathless and red-faced, having just run into the school at top speed. "I tried to send you a Snap, but you didn't check it. I'm dying here." Her face was flushed with excitement. "He did it!"

"Whoa, Nelly." Bruno's voice was a low rumble. "Who did what?"

"Jonah Lang hit his first million dollars! He just posted a video about it." She grabbed Taylor's arm to hold herself up.

An embarrassing wave of envy rolled over Taylor.

Roxy grinned.

She glowed.

She quivered with excitement and pride.

Taylor held her breath.

This was it. This was what her mom had been working for. And Roxy, and Jonah, and even herself. They had all been working for this.

She wanted to be happy for him, for them. But she really, really, really wanted him to stop.

She stared at her friend. The chasm between Roxy's reality and Taylor's seemed impassable right now.

Young people gathered around their little group, drawn by Kaitlyn's excitement. Voices congratulated Roxy. Expo programs fluttered asking for autographs. Taylor's turn came at the coffee stand and she ordered, mindlessly.

Bruno slipped into the crowd, back to his quilting work.

Taylor's mind spun. This was absolutely the wrong time to ask Jonah to slow down, to change his game. To stop doing what was working so well. But maybe those snaps, just the snaps, that wouldn't be too much to ask, would it?

She was surprised a video of her mom hadn't popped up with something weirdly related to her misgivings.

But then her phone buzzed. A slightly different sound from the Snapchat alerts.

This was a text, and from her baby sister Belle. "*I could kill Jonah.*"

Taylor responded. "*Same.*"

"*I begged him not to do it this way.*"

"*with all the weird apps?*"

"*yeah.*"

"*this sucks*"

"*yeah.*"

Since her early college admittance and graduation, Belle had been flirting with an academic career, something, anything to do with history. She seemed to float around between museums and internships, always talking about finding her focus, that one thing she could do her thesis on in grad school. She had recently decided to do a retrospective on their Grandma Delma Baker who had founded Flour Sax Quilt Shop.

Belle never said it outright, but Taylor suspected her sister held some resentment that Laura, their mother, was famous for what had really been Grandma Delma's life passion. Belle had talked about wanting to write a real book for a university press. Something that highlighted Grandma Delma's struggles against the patriarchy, against small town culture, against the pressure of the early eighties when a woman was supposed to have it all and do it all.

It sounded a bit overwrought to Taylor. As far as she had

ever heard, the transition from Grandpa's tailoring shop to Grandma's quilt shop had been smooth, and everyone had loved it. But it was Taylor's policy to support Belle no matter what she decided to do. So, she supported her in this as well, and had to agree that Jonah getting rich off their mom's show felt wrong.

Taylor sent her one more text: "*get writing.*" Then pocketed her phone.

They both knew Belle's book would be academic, true, respectful, and nowhere near as popular as Jonah's little internet clips were. But the book would be nothing at all, if Belle never wrote it.

Shortly after the text exchange, the morning's first session ended and the classrooms spilled their quilters, hobbyists, artists, lifelong passionate crafters, and new, earnest learners. Fewer than before the death of the keynote speaker but still determined.

Taylor let herself be swept along with the crowd and deposited into a classroom.

The instructor had a variety of fabrics pinned to a cork board on an easel. She began her lecture with the history of the samples. Where they had come from, what purpose they had served, and why they had eventually been replaced in popularity.

As Taylor let herself absorb the information, her phone pinged.

The woman in the next seat glanced over in response to the noise.

Taylor checked it. This time it was just a short, sweet clip of her mom, the famous quilting YouTuber in the silly pincushion hat. "Let the children sort it out themselves." Her mom was looking at a stack of notes on the table rather than the camera. She must have just been chatting with Roxy, giving her advice, mom to mom. She wondered if Jonah and Belle were fighting, and if it had been about the show. She couldn't take the wondering anymore and sent him a text via the app. "Why, Jonah? What are you trying to tell me?"

The rest of the lecture went over her head, though no more videos came, and Jonah didn't reply.

She ought to let the kids sort it out, not get into the rivalry that was developing between her sister and Roxy's son. She couldn't afford to make it a thing between Roxy and herself. She would never be able to replace Roxy at the shop, or in her life.

The workshop ended and the quilters and Taylor made their way to the dining hall where they had both their meals and their keynote events. Taylor was stuck in the middle of the crowd, mostly individuals alone like her, but a group of women to her left were in deep discussion, voices hushed. She edged closer to them and listened.

Shara Schonely, the owner of Dutch Hex who had been persuasive in hiring the Amish author, was in the middle of the crowd. She wore a long navy-blue dress with a white trimmed collar. It wasn't exactly Amish, being tailored to perfection, but it had those vibes. "My husband won't stop texting. He's demanding I come home, but I won't leave before the quilt show. I refuse."

"What is he so scared of?" The second lady was tall and built like a runner. Her matter of fact voice cut through the shuffling noise of the crowd.

"Murder." Shara's voice was dramatically rough. That annoying vocal fray so popular a couple of years ago with influencers.

Taylor sighed. Leave it to Shara to make this about her.

"Don't be ridiculous," the runner said. "Albina probably had a heart condition. You'd be surprised how many people are walking around right now with dodgy tickers."

Shara's hand fluttered to her chest. "If it was just a heart thing, the police wouldn't still be here, would they? Half of the workshops were cancelled because the instructors are all in interviews with the police. A heart thing would be easy to prove with an autopsy."

"But so would murder," the runner said.

"Not if it was poison." Shara's whisper carried easily to where Taylor lingered behind the group.

"Please." The runner's voice practically rolled its eyes. She pushed her way past the group. The four women huddled closer. They had made it to the dining hall now and found a table together. Taylor joined them. Roxy would never be able to find her in the crowd, but that was okay. She had plenty of Jonah's Juvies to sit with and celebrate.

"So, you think it was murder?" Taylor asked Shara.

Shara stared, realizing who had joined them. "I suspect so, and I think I can prove it." Her voice lost a little of its confidence.

Taylor leaned forward. "You do?"

"Yes, I'm a huge mystery novel fan, and I think I can find the clues I need to find before the police do."

"Ah." The idea that Shara was somehow a better detective than Reg, and Maria, and all the others from the sheriff's office annoyed Taylor. She recognized the irony, but she had never thought she was better than the officials. Just…helpful to them.

Shara tilted her head up so she could give the impression of looking down on the ladies at the table. "I have a very, very keen sense of intuition, and I can feel things." She leaned forward this time and lowered her voice. "I feel things very strongly, and I feel something is wrong with the investigation."

"Do tell me more." Taylor's voice sounded sarcastic. She could hear it herself.

The woman sitting next to Taylor, whose name badge said Nan, gave her a sharp glance.

"To start with, when Albina Tschetter was a no-show for her first workshop, I knew she was in terrible danger. I told my roommate, didn't I, Nan? I said I didn't like it one bit and that we'd need to keep an eye on her."

"I remember you saying you didn't like it and being a little annoyed that she was a no-show." Nan wore one of the navy-blue cotton Cascadia Quilt Expo shirts that was for sale in the marketplace. She seemed familiar, like she might be related to Shara.

"Not annoyed, concerned, but that's okay, you were preoccupied. You see, her work bag had gone missing." Shara lifted one eyebrow. "You still haven't found it, have you?"

"I did find it, Shar. It was in the closet, under a spare blanket." Nan sounded exasperated.

"Ahh…" Shara nodded, her eyes narrowed. "I suspect that is important, but I don't need to tell you why, I'm sure."

"Please, pretend I'm stupid and tell me." Taylor tilted her head in innocence.

Shara shook her head. "No, I'd better not, but I will tell you this: the Expo has been on pins and needles since the first morning. Nobody has been at ease with Albina Tschetter. You cannot have this many artists together and not have our collective intuition pick up on a problem." Shara turned to Nan and spoke too low for Taylor to hear.

Shara wanting to turn the story, make it seem like she had been suspicious of Albina all along, didn't surprise Taylor. Shara was a woman who liked a false narrative. She seemed to truly believe that Dutch Hex didn't have the same sound and feel as Flour Sax. That her store was almost just as old as Flour Sax, even though she literally opened it what, twenty years later? Before this was over, Taylor was sure Shara would be telling people she had warned the Cascadia committee that having an author as a speaker was a bad idea.

The dinner—a nine layer béchamel and Portobello lasagna edifice served with chicory wrapped brie and quinoa bundles—was served. It took concentration to eat it without making a mess, and for a while, conversation died. When they cleared the table for desserts, Taylor excused herself. She had seen the desserts being served to a table down the row—a bread pudding with crème fraîche. Probably delicious, but she wasn't wasting dessert calories on bread pudding. Shara had teased her with delusions of being a detective and left Taylor hungry for real clues. She needed to find someone who actually knew something.

There was an open seat at a table toward the front of the dining room, so Taylor took it. It had probably been Albina's regular seat. Bruno was to her left, Sue Friese, the conference director, and her husband were to his left. "Do you mind if I join you?" Taylor asked Bruno specifically.

Bruno was dolled up for the evening in a crisp plaid shirt and new creamy sweater with leather elbow patches. "I would love it. Did you eat? Can we get you dessert?"

"No, no. I'm fine. I was just at a table with strangers, and… even though we've just met, you feel more comfortable than a stranger."

"I'm glad to hear you say so." His smile was definitely avuncular. Taylor appreciated it. He could save all his romantic longings for Roxy. The last thing she needed was another man to worry about.

"Is there any way I can be of help?" Taylor directed this question to Sue Friese.

Sue looked at Taylor with no recognition, which made perfect sense since they hadn't spoken except via phone and email. "It is very nice of you to offer." She waved her hand, dismissing the idea.

"We've had nothing on our mind but the sad loss," Sue's husband Morgan said. "I've been begging Sue to tell us a little something about her last trip to Czech Republic, but she won't. Sue travels to source materials for her work. She found the most beautiful vintage bohemian embroidery to include in her family tree quilt."

Sue sighed. "Morgan, dear, it just doesn't feel right. I wish I could make you understand." She laid her fingers gently to her forehead. "The only thing of comfort right now is that Bruno

Stutze is prepared to give us a wonderful night's encouragement."

Bruno pushed his bread pudding away. "I'm glad I can help. Morgan, do you mind helping me set up my computer? I want to make sure I have it right." He led the husband away.

Sue let out a deep breath, clearly relieved. "I love him, I do, but he has no sense of the weight of this." She pushed her fork in and out of her dessert. "A young person I considered a dear friend has lost her life. She's dead. Gone."

They weren't alone at the table. To Taylor's right was the PBS craft show star, and next to her a couple of the other big-name teachers, but until this moment they had been politely ignoring the conflict between spouses.

Audra Market, the television star, spoke up. "Sue, I feel so strongly for you. I can't imagine what you're going through. I had only just met Albina, but she was the loveliest girl. Such a bright light. I know you feel obliged to stay, but couldn't you go home for a day at least and rest?"

"Even if I felt I could," Sue said, "the police have requested I not leave town. Can you imagine?"

"Don't you live in Portland?" Taylor asked. Portland wasn't right around the corner, but the idea of making Sue stick around Comfort when her home was within driving distance seemed extreme.

"Our home is in California. Some of our board members live in Portland, so we keep a business PO box there." Sue stared at the empty stage. Bruno would be on soon, and Taylor's chance to learn something would be gone.

"I'm sorry. It must be incredibly painful for you, and stressful as well." Audra the television star interjected her sympathy.

"But have we heard yet what the cause of death was?" This was from one of the teachers Taylor didn't know but recognized as the athletic woman she had overheard in the hall. The one who looked like a runner. Her name tag said "Ellen Sprow."

"No. Morgan found her, and I saw her. She looked, oh, she

didn't look well at all. There were no injuries, but her face…I'll never forget it. A look of shock, of pain…and so red. I just wish her parents were still alive, then I could talk to them about family health issues. Anything, anything at all, to get a sense of reality back." She turned to Taylor and then to each of the women at the table. "It feels unreal."

"Sue, dear, you need to call your doctor. Let them give you something for your nerves." Audra's voice was firm and supportive.

It was weird, outdated advice from someone Taylor's own age. She would have expected Audra to tell Sue to go to yoga, or meditate, or something like that.

"No, I couldn't. I have so much to do before the quilt show tomorrow. Please," she stood, shaking, "will you all excuse me? I think I just need to lie down."

"Oh darling, please go rest. Let me walk you to your room."

Sue tilted her head toward Audra, a small motion of agreement.

They left, and Taylor was alone with Ellen Sprow, who looked as though she was a runner, and the lady she didn't recognize.

Ellen Sprow exhaled loudly. "I know it is tragic. I feel for them all, but Sue is just so dramatic."

Taylor had to agree. Something about Sue's performance at the table had felt like…a performance. She half expected Jonah to send a timely or pithy snap to that effect, but her phone was silent.

"Don't all jump in to disagree with me." Ellen gave a wry smile. "Sue ought to go see her doctor, or go home, or go for a run. Not sit here having fainting spells or whatever she's doing, but, I suppose it takes a person who likes attention to put on a show like this."

"You should be careful about what you say," the lady who was a complete stranger spoke. Her name badge was turned backwards, but she had a flurry of ribbons hanging from it. She was someone important. "You'll make people think she killed her friend for attention."

"If people think that, then people are idiots." Ellen Sprow sipped her water. "A person who loves attention and drama doesn't have to go out of their way to get it. They just make the best use of situations as they present themselves. I'm sure Sue is truly heartbroken, and I'm sure she'll make the most of it for a long time."

The house lights lowered, and a stage light came on. Bruno took his place at the small oak podium. Behind him was the projected image of a pretty, red-headed woman, skinny and petite, standing in front of a very simple quilt hanging on a wall. "This is my wife Dana, three years before she died," he began.

Taylor's phone pinged.

She glanced down but didn't dare play the short video sitting here at the front table, right by the speaker.

## CHAPTER SEVEN

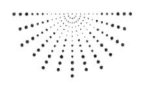

Taylor was seated at the front table of a darkened dining hall listening to a new friend talk about how quilting had brought him a sense of peace when he lost the love of his life. The only light came from the spotlight on him, his fuzzy beard, and his fatherly smile.

Quilting had brought Taylor a lot of things in life. Frustration at first as she sat at her Grandma Delma's side learning how to make perfect stitches. Then hope and dreams as she worked on her fiber arts degree in this same college. There had been a time, early on, when she thought she'd be some kind of artist. The kind who shaved one side of their head, and wore tunics, and did things that had never been done before, just to shake up the system. But most of all quilting had given her a touchstone to her mom, and a way to reconnect with her family in the face of tragedy. A job, and a goal, and a purpose that kept her from completely losing it as her family fell apart around her.

Quilting had been good to her. And she loved it and couldn't live without it.

From the Dove-in-the-Window quilt on her bed, made by Grandma Delma, to the stack of quilts in the closet made from scraps, so many scraps, of costumes from school plays and summer dresses, and sheets that had gone threadbare in the middle. Her life would have been so much colder without quilting.

"It was this quilt," Bruno was saying, "that became the life of me."

Taylor smiled. His timing was almost as good as Jonah's.

The quilt on the slide show was simple, like the one his wife had been standing in front of in the first slide, but the quilting, clearly machine done, was impeccable. He had used a black thread over the creams and whites of his nine-patch, and it struck a chord with the audience. Intricate lace drawn with thread on fabric. He was an artist, and that was why he had been able to make a career in this crazy industry.

"This quilt only won second place, but I began to get calls, orders, jobs. I was doing finish quilting for money and if you have been in a workshop with me, you know how the rest of that turned out. What you don't know is that as I stand at my machine directing the arm, I can hear Dana. I talk to her. She talks to me. She speaks to me from the pattern, more often than not. Giving me her approval. Does that make me sound crazy? It's just the tip of the iceberg, but there was one thing I was able to say to her through quilting that I hadn't thought I would be able to do, ever." He paused, his head turned sideways to view his quilt. "I was able to say, 'farewell.'

"It wasn't at the funeral or at the cemetery that I made my peace with her loss, but at the long-armed quilting machine. I knew, even though I still talk to her when I quilt, that she was gone, but she was happy. That she was at peace, and I could be as well." He clicked to a new screen, this time a photo of him and his daughter displaying a quilt of immense beauty, all tiny hexagons in brilliant jewel tones cascading from top corner to bottom corner in a prism of color, the opposing corners the same piecework, but in shades of charcoal and grey. "This is my daughter's latest quilt. I lost a wife, but she lost her mother very young, and in quilting together, I think I was able to keep her memory alive." He paused his eyes glued to the beautiful, young woman in the photo with him. "But that is a story I will share with you tomorrow. Thank you all so much." He made a clumsy bow.

The audience erupted in applause, every single one of them in love, Taylor suspected.

There had never been anything in history like a man talking about how much he loved a woman to make all the other women in the room fall in love with him.

It was hardly fair to the handful of other male quilters at the event.

Taylor slipped away before he came back to the table. She stood outside the door of the dining hall breathing the warm, familiar air of her alma mater.

She was overly emotional, filled with sadness over the loss of her own mother.

She patted her phone, hoping Jonah would send a timely snap, but the phone was silent.

She couldn't take the silence, so she called Hudson East, the man she had grown to love dearly.

She left a voicemail, very sorry she had asked him so nicely to give her some space during the Expo, because she'd be so busy.

She headed to Roxy's dorm room, glad her friend was staying on campus, nice and close. The students who left for the week had cleared their rooms out entirely, nothing personal left behind. Taylor remembered stowing some of her friends' things in her dorm during fall break when she was a student here. It would have been simple for her to go home, to the little house she still lived in up the street, and take her friends things with her, but she hadn't. She chose to stay in the half empty school working on her projects. Every year but her senior year.

Roxy stretched on the extra-long twin bed, reading glasses perched on the end of her nose, e-reader glowing lightly. "Jonah called."

"Oh? Is he in the middle of an all-night celebration?" Jonah was a two-minute drive away. It was silly that they weren't with him right now, celebrating his success.

"No." Roxy stared, her eyes red from crying. "YouTube shut down the account."

Taylor sat on the other twin bed with a thump. "What?"

Roxy had locked down as tight as a panic room, obviously exhausted, unable to collapse into her feelings. A feeling Taylor had shared more than once in her life.

"I don't know. He said he has to call during business hours. He might need to call a lawyer. He hit his million-dollar mark, but those payments would be coming in the future, and YouTube has frozen all of that. No more videos, no more payments."

"Help me understand. I thought he was making money on TikTok and maybe Snapchat." Taylor rubbed her temples. She didn't like that she needed to really understand this stuff to make a living selling quilt fabric.

"He makes some on TikTok, with coins, I think. But the income for him from TikTok is mostly the Nike money. It looks impressive to have a sponsor, but they didn't pay him all that much. Mostly free product and a little cash. TikTok feeds his YouTube and our YouTube. Snapchat does as well. But YouTube is where the real money is."

"Did the YouTube people say why?" Even with her own misgivings, Taylor wanted to wrap her arms around her friend. This was a severe blow. To have a sure future in the morning, and nothing at all by night had to be terrifying.

"Someone complained about how he was talking about Albina. Someone said he was offensive. My Jonah. Oh, I don't understand, I really don't. He's the nicest boy, and he's using his platform to help, but someone said he was abusing death to make money or something like that."

"I don't see how they could shut down an account for that." Taylor took her shoes off and tucked her feet under her. She told herself it couldn't have been Belle, that Belle would never have done this, but Belle had been so upset. Or at least her texts had felt upset.

But no, it couldn't be her. She was upset about how he was handling their mom's videos. She didn't care that he was talking about Albina's death.

"Did you watch his videos? Were they actually offensive?" Taylor asked.

A look of guilt passed over Roxy's face. "I didn't, and now they're gone."

Taylor's phone pinged. Of, course it did. She grabbed it, but the screen was black. She hit the power button but got no response. It was dead. She found a charger and plugged it in.

The pinging had been Roxy's phone, and she was already checking it. She held it out to Taylor. "Watch this."

It was Jonah, Snapchatting. "Hope is not lost. We can still help Albina Tschetter. Visit my website to see the content." He held up a sign with a web address on it.

"Get out your computer. It looks like we have some videos to watch."

Roxy followed Taylor's directions. Taylor moved to the floor next to Roxy's bed so they could watch Jonah's "Desk Chair Detective" videos.

The site was pretty simple, but effective. A logo, and posts that were nothing but videos. Taylor didn't know how easy it had been to create, but to her, it was evidence that this kid really was a genius.

Roxy's finger hovered over the keyboard. "He has a terrible ego lately. He's not been himself at all since he got that sponsorship deal. But I can't blame him. He always lived in the shadows before, not one of the cool kids, not one of the athletes. This was his shot. His time to shine."

For the last two years Taylor had known Jonah as the quiet young man who sent her edited videos to approve. He hadn't had a role in any of her sister's teenage dramas. He had seemed…easy.

Roxy turned on the first video. It was Jonah's analysis of Albina's books compared to her social media posts. The second was about how he put her books through some kind of app that could tell you if it was written by a natural human or a robot. What a world they lived in that there was enough computer-generated content for this to be a tool someone needed to create. The app, and Jonah, concluded the book made no sense and had to have been written by a machine. That wasn't news. Taylor wanted the incriminating stuff that had gotten him shut down.

Roxy scrolled past several videos where Jonah was wearing the same shirt and stopped at the first one with him in different clothes.

He wore a white button down open at the neck, half frame tortoise shell glasses, and a green visor like card shark in an old movie. He rolled up his sleeves and started talking. "McKenzie Forte was a beautiful, rising star in the entertainment world. Her heart was pure, and all she wanted to do was act. When she was hired to play Albina Tschetter, she had no idea that it was a con. No idea that it was going to kill her." He paused dramatically. "It is up to us, me and you guys, my Juvies, to discover what happened to her. I know we can do it."

Roxy paused the video. "The quality is terrible, he's overacting, and…it is in poor taste." Her big eyes were sad. "But I don't see how it's against terms of service. He didn't make a threat. He isn't being lewd or obscene. There has to be more to it than this."

"Let's finish the video. There are several more after it too."

Jonah continued. "To start with, we need to know who hired her. I hope that someone in her hometown down in Southern California will contact me. Find her parents, her friends, ask them. Who was behind this acting job? That's the first task. There will be more." He reached towards the camera and turned off the video.

The next one was similar in style, but with a call to find out who had created the books in the first place, begging anyone who worked for the publisher to dig into it.

The third video of him dressed like an old-timey accountant was different. "I've had several calls. Lots of great information coming my way. I think we're getting somewhere on the who, maybe even the how. I can't believe how amazing Jonah's Juvies are. I wouldn't want to be on the wrong side of you all." He laughed. "We have another job to do, are you up for it? At the Cascadia Quilt Expo, right now, where McKenzie Forte lost her life, are two dear women. Two dear ladies, alone and unprotected, my mom Roxy and her friend Taylor. This is a call out to my girls, Jonah's Juvies: Please take care of my family. I can't be there. I can't get there. You all know why." He paused and glanced behind him dramatically. "I'm relying on you right now."

Taylor hit pause. "First of all, he is here. So, what on earth does he mean he can't get here? And secondly….are you kidding me? He's acting like we're a million years old."

Roxy groaned. "I would be tempted to turn him in for policy violations on that alone. But he has to be in school, so he can't come to the Expo, can he? He's not lying." She seemed to want Taylor's approval, but as a young woman, merely a few months older than thirty, Taylor was not going to approve.

"He's definitely trying to create drama to get page views. He seems to have things plotted out, a strong narrative. He's telling a story and telling it well. These aren't short enough for TikTok though. It feels so…planned."

"I'm going to call him." Roxy shut her computer and chewed her lip.

"I'm going to head home and get some sleep. Let's confer again in the morning." Taylor stretched, then stood. She was afraid if she stayed, she'd want a turn to talk to Jonah, and she wasn't sure she could say what she wanted to say nicely.

Roxy nodded, but didn't add anything.

Taylor texted Hudson on the way home. He met her there, and they talked, long and late.

"I don't blame you for your not-envy-but-actually-envy."

Hudson had his strong arms wrapped around Taylor, snuggled under her Dove-in-the-Window quilt. "But can I say I think it's silly you haven't just headed over there to talk to him yet? It's not like he's hard to find."

"I kept wanting to talk to Roxy first. I didn't want to be the one that made his magic money disappear."

"He hasn't responded to your text yet?"

"Nope."

"Make time to go see him tomorrow." Hudson stopped talking to nuzzle her neck.

"I know you're right." Taylor didn't commit. She had a feeling Jonah wouldn't answer the door, just like he hadn't responded to the text. "I don't wish him ill. I just don't want to keep getting those videos of Mom. At least, not like this."

"Just ask him to stop. Even if he's in the middle of something bigger. You're the adult. It's okay to do this."

She stared at his deep, dark, understanding eyes and kissed him.

## CHAPTER EIGHT

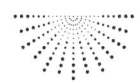

Hudson had to leave early the next morning. He had, after all, been warned to keep busy for two weeks, since Taylor wasn't going to be free. "But I'm picking up a nice bit of extra cash while you're at the Expo, just think of the fun we can have with it." He smiled down at her and then kissed her.

"I do have fun spending money." She blushed, wondering if Hudson knew how true that was.

"I'm thinking we could go away, but we'll figure that out later."

She gave him a lingering hug before he left.

She was feeling better this morning, like talking to Jonah would be easy. She wasn't asking for much after all. And she had a right to ask it. Amara Schilling, her lawyer, had made sure she still owned the rights to the footage, even though she'd given Jonah permission to use it. Not that she wanted to go in heavy handed and with a lawyer. But she felt reasonable and sensible.

A real contrast to both Shara Schonely and Sue Friese. Two women who both seemed to want to get some attention from the sad death of the speaker. Shara was off her head, probably. Her claiming to have some kind of intuition, some kind of sixth sense…claiming reading a lot of mystery novels meant she could solve real crimes. Absurd. But Sue…Sue had known Albina and had seen her dead.

Albina had looked pained, Sue had said. And her face was red.

But was it red like…flushed? Or rashy? Taylor wondered. That could be a way of figuring out what she'd died of. She was tempted to text Reg and ask about the autopsy report, but though he expected info from her, he hadn't volunteered to give her any in return.

The quilt Expo was serving breakfast, which would surely be better than a bowl of cereal in her own kitchen, so still wondering what might have made Albina's face red and then killed her, Taylor went back to the campus. She sent Roxy a quick text, hoping they could meet up.

Taylor went through the line at the breakfast buffet, getting herself one of those fat, cake-like muffins and the largest mug of coffee available.

Roxy was nowhere to be seen, but Bruno was having his breakfast. He waved Taylor down and invited her to his table. "I think last night went well."

"I do too." Taylor sipped the coffee, glad for the sense of normalcy it gave her.

"I'll be presenting the keynote again tonight."

"That will be nice."

He ate a little in silence.

Taylor didn't mind. She wasn't in a hurry to learn more about Bruno.

"I went for drinks with Sue and Morgan last night," Bruno volunteered when his bacon was gone. "Morgan and I tried to draw Sue out, but she was shut down. This has been hard on her."

"What about Albina's family? I guess they'll show up here sooner or later." Taylor picked at her muffin, wondering why Morgan thought taking his wife out for drinks at a time like this was a good idea.

Bruno shook his head. "Albina's agent is here now, but I haven't heard anyone mention family."

Taylor went to Facebook on her phone and looked at McKenzie Forte's page.

It was different. Something had changed. It wasn't right.

She stared at it in silence.

Albina had posted yesterday afternoon.

While being very dead.

The post was charming for a selfie. She had a classy authorial look—cardigan sweater over a lacy camisole with a chunky feature necklace—and stood with her arm around two petite ladies who were holding copies of *Quilted in the County*. The post said, "Having fun as Albina! Expect more updates from the Cascadia Expo soon! #author #Amish #Tschetterforlife."

Had no one told her PR person she was dead?

Taylor passed the phone across the table. "What do you make of that?"

"I think her publisher didn't realize she had posts scheduled. Someone should get a hold of them and have it stopped." Bruno spread jam on a biscuit and shook his head sympathetically.

"I wonder who has her passwords."

"No telling. You could always report it to Facebook and see what happens."

Taylor took the phone back and clicked the "report" button. She didn't think the content was offensive and hoped she made the problem clear in the comments.

Taylor went back to the post and zoomed in on Albina's face. She looked happy. Whether she was an actress paid to pretend to be an author, or an actress using a pen name to start her writing career, she seemed to be enjoying herself.

Even with the start of a red rash around her lips.

Taylor passed the phone back to Bruno. "Look at her mouth. What do you think that's about?"

He put down his fork, drew his brows together, and stared at the picture. "I feel like the answer ought to be something about female suffering under unfair financial obligation enforced by power of male gaze." He looked up. "But you're wearing lipstick, too, so maybe it's just not her color?"

A burst of laughter escaped Taylor. "Wow. Uh, no. I wasn't thinking about her lipstick. She seems to have the start of a rash around her mouth. Do you see what I mean?"

He took another look. "Can't tell."

"So, it might not be there?" Taylor chewed the inside of her cheek. Was she just seeing it because Sue had suggested it?

"It's hard to say." He tried to zoom in closer, but it was as good as it got. "She does look a little red around her mouth. Could be normal though, or she might have just had her lips done."

"They are very nicely shaped."

"A little unnatural though, don't you think?" He gave Taylor a kind smile.

Taylor took the phone back. "I don't remember her having a rash the night of her first keynote."

"Make-up could have covered it."

"Then again, make-up could have caused it too."

"Think her mouth rash killed her?"

Taylor put her phone away. "Probably not." Surely that hint of a rash on her mouth hadn't killed her, but then again, what if it had?

Taylor ate her muffin without thinking much about it, then Bruno walked her back to the marketplace where the booths were set up.

They were stopped by Reg, the deputy, in the doorway to the bustling hall. "Got a minute?"

Taylor froze. "Of course."

Reg ushered them into a quiet corner far from the marketplace. Before addressing them, he spoke into his two-way radio. "I've got her in the lobby." Pause. "Yes sir." He clipped his radio on his belt. "I have to take you down to the station, Taylor. I'm so sorry."

Bruno put his hand on her arm and shook his head. "You can ask her whatever you want here."

"I've got my directions." Reg's face was fully professional, with no hint on it that they were friends, or had dated, or that he felt any kind of way at all.

Taylor's Snapchat alert chime went off. She grabbed it out of her purse, face hot and starting to bead with sweat. Reg was arresting her?

She fumbled for the power button, trying to turn the phone off. This was not the time to get a lecture from her mom's blooper reel. Her nerves got the better of her, and instead of turning it off, she opened the app.

Her mom stood at the worktable, wrestling with a slippery piece of fabric. "STAY PUT!" she hollered at it, then laughed.

Taylor's face heated up, and she got the app closed.

The timing.

The timing.

How could Jonah know?

She looked behind her, and as she did, a slight male figure seemed to slip around the corner.

But then again, maybe it wasn't a slight male figure. It could have been anyone.

She took a deep breath. "Reg, can we compromise?"

He scowled.

"We could go into the office and have a private talk. You know me. You know I'm not going anywhere and that I will tell you anything you want to hear."

For a brief moment, his eyes flickered, as though he too remembered that time at dinner when she had said exactly the opposite of what he wanted to hear.

She wished she had worded that differently.

"I'm under orders to bring you down to the station. Full stop. Roxy is there already. You know I don't want to do this. But I can't show favoritism."

All of the blood she had ever had in her body rushed from her head to her feet and she swayed.

Bruno put his arm on her back in a steadying way. "Is she under arrest?"

"Not at this time."

"Then Taylor won't leave the grounds. It's more than generous of her to be willing to meet in the office, but she won't do that alone."

Taylor was gulping for breath and her phone pinged again.

She knew Reg.

She trusted Reg.

She didn't know Bruno.

Why did everything feel backwards?

"You should answer that," Bruno said quietly.

Regretting what she might see, she raised her hand to look at the phone.

Reg turned to the side and spoke into his radio again.

Taylor stared at her phone. She didn't have a snap from Jonah posing as her mom. She had a text from Roxy. "Call Amara."

"Do you think I need a lawyer?" Taylor asked Bruno quietly. "I didn't do anything. Roxy didn't do anything. Why does the sheriff want Reg to take me to the station? Why is Roxy already there?"

Bruno held his phone out so she could see the screen.

It was open to Oregonlive, the online version of the newspaper, The Oregonian. A bold, black headline. "Teen Influencer makes Millions after Murder of Amish Author."

Motive.

A millions tiny one-dollar motives.

She hadn't thought.

It hadn't occurred to her.

She hadn't applied this logic to herself. To her own proximity to the funds.

If getting a keynote speaking job was enough for the sheriff to look twice at Bruno, making a million dollars was about a million times more reason to look at everyone who benefited from Jonah's success.

Her fingers shook with dread, but she found Amara's number and sent her a simple text. "Help. Please. Murder."

Reg cleared his throat. "Okay, it will do. Come with me to the office and we'll talk."

Taylor followed Reg, and Bruno followed Taylor

Her phone was silent, but this time she wished with all her heart that it would start ringing. She definitely needed a lawyer.

Reg let her into a private office but shut the door on Bruno.

They both took seats and pretended to get comfortable.

"Jonah's made a lot of money since Albina Tschetter passed," Reg said.

"Not exactly. He'd made most of it already, I'm sure. The Nike thing and stuff." She stumbled over her words, like a kid in a first interview. She was scared. More scared than she had been in years.

"I'm sorry." Reg shrugged awkwardly, his face finally showing some kind of compassion. "I have to follow a certain direction for this conversation. According to our sources, Jonah tipped over into the million-dollar territory much faster than he should have after this death. Since you guys are in business with him, we need to have some long talks. The boss would like to keep you in the jail for a while just in case."

Taylor ignored the threat of jail and focused on the apologetic look on Reg's face. He didn't want to do this. "That's not how it works." She kept each word at the same level and spoke slower than normal. She would get control of herself if it was the last thing she did. None of this was her fault, or Reg's fault, or even Jonah's. "To start with, I have no financial connection to Jonah's TikTok thing."

"His TikTok drives traffic to your YouTube show. According to our research you are a lot closer to a million dollars than you were before the death too." Reg held his hands out, apologetically.

"I wouldn't know. Belle, my sister, handles that end of stuff. And she's up in Seattle. I haven't talked to her. I try not to think about the YouTube thing. I'm not good at it and…"

"And?" he probed.

"And it makes me sad. What Jonah is doing especially. All the clips of my mom…they feel too real. I don't like it."

He frowned, as though the new information really did change his opinion.

"You would rather he not get more views."

"Exactly."

Reg shook his head. "Listen, I don't believe you or Jonah or Roxy had anything to do with this, but on paper in looks bad. The sheriff is breathing fire. I need something better than just you telling me you don't want the money."

Taylor was quiet for a long time. She also wouldn't believe someone who claimed to not want riches. In fact, she had a tingle of excitement at the idea that her YouTube channel was getting a little boost while she was at the convention. She wouldn't have killed for it though.

"Taylor, I hate to ask this, but I have to."

"Go ahead." Her voice was quiet and difficult to get out.

"This is a small town."

"Sure. I know." She nodded and swallowed.

"People talk." He shrugged.

"I know that too."

His voice dropped as though he didn't want anyone to hear him outside. "There has been a noticeable increase in murders since you moved back home."

Taylor slumped into her chair.

There *had* been more murders than seemed normal. And yet, maybe it just seemed that way since two of them would have been written off as accidents if she hadn't been around to help. It made her wonder how many murderers had gotten away with it before she'd come back to Comfort.

# CHAPTER NINE

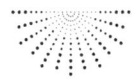

Bruno was waiting for Taylor. They walked together to the edge of the campus. Taylor wanted to go home and talk to Amara. She needed legal advice and she needed it stat.

The police were chasing the tail end of a loose thread—Jonah's money and her proximity to the dead person, but they didn't have reasonable cause. They couldn't arrest her, but they had made their interest in her clear. What she didn't understand was why Roxy had gone willingly with the sheriff and why she hadn't called for help.

At the edge of the campus Taylor's phone pinged. "Do you mind if I check these messages?"

"No problem. I should be heading back anyway." Bruno looked over his shoulder, but hesitated, clearly unsure if he was needed or not.

Taylor turned away and paid attention to her phone. A new snap from Jonah. There was her mom, nodding with a look of approval on her face. "Trust your friends, even the new ones." When that snap ended, another one popped up. This time it really was Jonah. "They've arrested my mother for the murder of McKenzie "Albina Tschetter" Forte, the actress pretending to be an author. This is absurd police brutality, but be assured, my father is on the case, and that is no small thing."

That snap disappeared as well.

Jonah's father.

That was a surprise. Taylor didn't even know who Jonah's father was. But she did know it was after school hours, which meant she ought to be able to catch Jonah and have a long talk with him. How did he know which video clip to send her and when? And would he stop it, please?

Bruno stood with his hands in his pockets, trying to be near, but still giving her privacy.

"Thanks," Taylor said, lacking a better word. "I'm just going to head home."

"OK. Um…if there is anything I can do, you'll call, right?"

Taylor's mom's smiling face encouraging her to trust her new friends popped into her mind. "I will. Especially if Roxy is in trouble."

Bruno began to walk away but stopped. "Are you checking out for the day or will I see you back at the expo?"

"I'll try to come back."

"Send me a text, if you want. We'll grab a coffee. I owe you." He had a distinctly fatherly way about him, and Taylor appreciated it. Parental figures were few in her life.

"Will do."

He ambled back to the event, and she went home wondering exactly how to find a sneaky little high schooler who has hundreds of thousands of dollars to help him hide.

But first, she called Amara and promised to say nothing to the police without her present. Amara wasn't a criminal lawyer by practice, but she knew the law and was better than nothing for now.

Taylor sent Jonah a private message via Snapchat. Then she called and sent a text. She gave him a full minute to respond before she got in her car and drove to the apartment he lived in with his mom.

The little bungalow unit in the fourplex near the gas station was dark and locked. No cars were out front. Jonah might have been hiding inside, but if he was, he was successful at it.

Taylor went to Reuben's Diner, always a popular hangout with teens, but Jonah wasn't there. Not giving up, she headed to the one place she knew teens took shelter. Sissy Dorney's house.

Only Breadyn Dorney, Sissy's middle schooler, was home. She shook her head and shrugged when asked about Jonah.

"You do know him," Taylor insisted. "He's famous on TikTok. The only wildly successful and rich influencer in our county. Maybe in our state. Come on. It's Jonah."

"Cooper's friends are all a lot older than me." She pulled a pink thread of bubble gum from her mouth.

"Cooper and Jonah aren't friends." Taylor crossed her arms. "Breadyn, this is serious. If he's in your house, I just want to talk to him. Please?"

Breadyn looked over her shoulder and then leaned forward. "Jonah hates Cooper. Really hates him. There is no way he'd come here. But…" She grinned. "He loves, loves, loves, loves, your sister."

"But Belle is in Seattle."

Breadyn grinned and shut the door.

Jonah and Belle? It didn't seem likely. Belle was dating…no. She'd broken up with her genius high school sweetheart Levi.

But if Jonah was up in Seattle with Belle, then he wasn't in school.

She got back in her car and called Roxy. She ought to have gone straight to her friend, but the snap from Jonah had distracted her.

"Taylor!" Roxy's voice was near panic. "You've not been arrested, right?"

"I managed to escape. How are you? What's going on?"

"I hated to do it, but I had to call Jonah's dad. He's not local but I put him on the phone with the sheriff and he got it sorted out."

"Is he a lawyer?" Taylor asked.

"Sort of. He's in The Judge Advocate General's Corps. JAG, like the TV show."

"No kidding…and he got it sorted?" Taylor pictured Roxy's ex, the short, rather cute man she had seen only once or twice in her life. It was difficult to picture him as a military officer.

"For now." Roxy's voice was stiff. "I really, really hate having to turn to him."

"Do you need a ride? Where can I meet you? We should talk. Where is Jonah?"

"I don't need a ride, my sister came and got me. I agree we should talk, but she's sort of commandeered me for now." Roxy paused for breath. "I'm at her place in Eugene. As for Jonah, I spoke to the school. Despite his promises of keeping his education his priority, he's not been there for several days. Not since the Expo started."

"Oh, Roxy, I'm sorry."

"Not as sorry as he'll be. His dad has some time available and is on his tail."

Taylor's shoulders dropped, relaxed. It was a relief to know someone well trained was looking after the kid. "So you don't know where he is?"

"Nope. We know exactly where he is." Roxy sounded defensive, almost protective.

"Is it better not to say because of the case?"

She inhaled sharply—an angry tone Taylor had never heard from Roxy before. "He's in Seattle with your sister."

Taylor didn't have an answer for this. The last communication she'd had with Belle made this story seem very unlikely. "I'll call Belle and see what she has to say about this." Taylor had some words for her sister, definitely.

"Good."

"About the Expo…" Taylor cleared her throat. They had obligations, and a whole lot of quilters were wandering around

Comfort College wanting to get their money's worth still. "Don't you have some panels coming up?"

"I'll do everything I promised."

"Okay…"

The unsatisfactory call ended.

Taylor went home, but it was too quiet, dark, and cold. She went back to the Expo and texted Bruno. They met at the little coffee cart in the lobby and commandeered a bistro table.

"Do you know a quilter named Shara?" Bruno asked over their paper cups of brew. "She said she was going to play amateur detective. I'd like to find her and see what she's dug up."

"Sure. She's a local." Taylor decided not to go into her contentious history with Shara. Somehow quilt shop rivalries paled when compared to being arrested for murder. "We can go find her, if you'd like."

Bruno nodded, serious. "I tried to call Roxy, just to check in, but she didn't answer."

"I spoke with her. She has things handled." She didn't mention Roxy's ex being the one handling things. She liked this Bruno character and his crush on her friend. She didn't want to disappoint him.

A group of ladies walked past, their voices carrying in the cozy room with its wood paneling and wood floors. They were discussing Albina's death. Taylor nodded in their direction.

Bruno put a finger to the side of his nose.

They stood together and sidled up to the women. Shara wasn't with them, but they had to start somewhere.

One lady in the group was Valerie Ritz, the young lady with the white plastic glasses and cherry-red hair Taylor had met previously —the one for whom money was no object. Taylor caught her eye.

"Taylor Quinn! I heard you guys got arrested!" Valerie's mouth hung open in shock.

"You heard wrong," Bruno answered.

"The deputies just had some questions," Taylor added. "And frankly, so do I. Does anyone know if there is evidence that Albina was murdered?"

Two of the women from the group of five quietly left. The three who remained circled tighter. One of them was a tiny woman with shiny, dark hair that went to her waist. Her name tag said "Carrie." "I heard the coroner couldn't find anything, and that Albina's doctor said she didn't have any pre-existing medical conditions either." Her voice was surprisingly loud for such a little person.

"Where did you hear that?" Taylor asked.

The short woman looked side to side. "I overheard a policeman talking to a security guard."

"You heard this firsthand from the officer?" Taylor didn't correct her about the officer being a sheriff's deputy and not the police.

"Absolutely. He was a tall man, a little older. His name tag said Reg. He told the security guy exactly what I just said. No cause found, but no medical history to account for it, either."

Taylor flinched at Reg being described as "older."

"I guess they had to send samples to a lab then, yeah?" Valerie asked.

"That's what I'd expect. Blood samples at least." The loud voice of the little woman named Carrie echoed in the mostly empty, mostly wooden room.

"No signs of struggle or signs she might have been poisoned? Don't poisons have some kind of effect? On TV murders they seem to." Taylor directed her question to Carrie.

"I told you all I heard. If there were signs of struggle or anything else, Reg the cop wasn't advertising it. Despite his keeping stuff close to his chest, I think I can solve this one. I've got my ear out for gossip and clues." Carrie handed Taylor a business card. "If you hear anything important, text me and I'll find you, okay?" Her name was Carrie Kyle and her card said she was a photographer specializing in textiles. That seemed incredibly specific.

"Definitely."

"You're *the* Taylor Quinn, right? Owner of Flour Sax Quilt Shop, daughter of Laura? The boss of Jonah who made all that money from the murder?" Carrie leaned in, but her voice didn't get any quieter. "If I were you, I'd lay real low."

Taylor tucked Carrie's card into the back pocket of her jeans. "That's what I plan on doing."

The third woman in the group hadn't said anything. She had just stared, her big brown eyes glued to Bruno. Finally, she broke her silence with a quiet stutter of a voice. "B-B-Bruno Stutze?"

"Yup." He smiled warmly at her, oozing fatherly comfort.

"C-can I have…" she fished around in a workbag probably for a pen and paper, "your autograph?" She looked up again, holding her event program and a pen.

He gave her a big, warm smile. "What's your name?"

"Ellie Smith."

"To Ellie," he spoke out loud what he was writing, "Write your story in thread. Love Bruno." He handed her back her program with a smile.

She was red-faced and incapable of speech.

"I think I gave you a card already," the girl with the white glasses said, "but let me give you another, just in case." She passed a thick linen textured card. Valerie Ritz listed herself as "Creative Consultant".

"Like the hotel?" Taylor asked without thinking, but it would explain why money had been no object on Valerie's hunt for collectible stuff.

Valerie gave a half nod. "Let me know if there's anything I can do for Jonah. I'm a huge fan." Then, surprising Taylor, she also blushed and excused herself.

Taylor tucked Valerie's card in the same pocket. It would be handy to have contact info for these ladies.

The little crowd broke up, so Bruno and Taylor continued

their hunt for Shara. The marketplace was almost empty at the moment, but a large crowd had gathered at a seating area in a far corner and were engaged in a heated debate.

They got near enough to listen.

"I swear on my mother's grave, if I see one more child claim to be a fiber artist, I will spank her tiny bottom." The woman who said this was old enough to be Taylor's grandmother and had a familiar steely glint in her eye.

One of her equally steely peers joined in her disgust. "They act like they've invented imagination. Who do they think they are? And who do they think they are calling themselves 'makers'? Quilter isn't a good enough word for them?"

"Crafter was a good enough word for hundreds of years. Why isn't it good enough for them?"

"Spoiled, that's what they are. Paid for their tickets with their parents' credit cards."

The crowd of women were dedicated to their joint cause, except one lady sitting on the edge of a crowded well-worn leather sofa. She was about Taylor's age and was focused entirely on a piece of embroidery—it looked like a superhero, but it wasn't one Taylor recognized.

"I brought my daughter and granddaughter with me," a woman with a very fluffy scarf slung over her shoulder said. "But will my granddaughter spend five minutes in a row with me? Oh no. She found some group she calls Juvies and thinks it is hilarious to run around with them."

The fiercest woman snorted. "They think they invented cheeky names. We've been calling ourselves strippers for years." She waved a rotary cutter as she spoke.

Laughter bubbled throughout the group.

"And hooker jokes too." The lady with the embroidery looked up. "For rug-makers and people who crochet. We call them hookers."

"And we invented the stitch and bitch groups, but these kids think they are shocking us by calling themselves Jonah's Juvies."

"That Jonah, though, he sure is a good-looking boy," the lady with the scarf said.

"I wouldn't mind if my granddaughter brought him home." A lady with pure white hair added.

"Hey gals." Bruno engaged the crowd. "Have any of you seen Shara? I can't find her anywhere."

"Shara Schonley? I saw her in the work room about half an hour ago," scarf lady said.

"Great, thanks!" He turned away, and the group giggled again.

The college had a large workroom for fiber arts students, and the Expo was making use of it. It was a large, well-lit space set up with tables where you could plug in your sewing machines, and also groupings of chairs where you could gather with friends to work on projects. It had plenty of outlets, so it was a popular place to gather. It smelled like hot machines hard at work and a little like White Musk, a scent that always reminded Taylor of teachers.

Bruno and Taylor stood in the doorway.

"There she is." Taylor spoke low and gave a subtle nod at the gothic-Amish hybrid that was Shara Schonely. They walked casually over to her table.

She didn't look excited to see Taylor.

They joined her anyway. "How goes the investigation?" Taylor asked.

Shara narrowed her eyes. "I stumbled across something very important, but I don't think I should say anything just yet." Her body trembled with excitement. She was dying to spill.

"I completely understand, however…" Taylor smiled, lifted her eyebrows invitingly, and pulled a chair very close. "If you have the sewing machine running, I don't think anyone else will hear it."

Shara put her foot to the peddle and guided her fabric through the machine. "Albina Tschetter was an actual Amish woman. Not the Albina who just passed away. A different one.

But her husband wasn't originally Amish. I think he was a Hutterite and converted. Or she converted, I can't recall. She died last fall. I think," she stopped her machine and locked eyes with Taylor, "McKenzie Forte stole her identity."

"She wouldn't out herself on Facebook the way she did, if it was a stolen ID, do you think?" Taylor knew she shouldn't have disagreed but couldn't stop herself. Her natural response to Shara in general was to disagree, but this time, Shara was wrong. A pen name is entirely different from identity theft.

Shara pursed her lips. "The woman existed, and now this dead girl is profiting from her identity. What would you call it?"

"Sorry. It's just during her first talk she admitted to not being Amish and told us all about how she learned the culture. If she was trying to pass herself off as Amish, she would have, um, pretended, no?"

"That's as may be, but I find it highly suspect."

Bruno had wandered off to sign autographs and talk to his fans.

Taylor had Shara alone, which she liked. "It just seems like if she was trying to steal an identity, like use her credit score, or her social security number, or something, she wouldn't be so open about it."

"The Amish don't participate in Social Security." Shara dropped her voice again as though this was a huge part of the secret.

"Then how could Albina, I mean McKenzie, be benefitting?"

"That's what I need to find out." Shara pressed her lips tight and nodded as though Taylor had finally gotten her point.

"You're on to something there." Taylor gave up. "If I hear anything, I promise I'll let you know."

Shara smirked and bent her attention back to her sewing, clearly dismissing Taylor.

Shara was a good quilter, but she was a bad amateur detective.

Taylor tried to sneak out without Bruno. She wanted to find a quiet spot and call her sister, and Jonah, and Hudson to talk through the whole mess.

She made it all the way to an empty seating area in the hall before he caught up. Taylor sat down and pulled out her phone, a universal sign that a person doesn't want to talk.

"Did you get anything good?" Bruno asked.

Taylor kept her eyes on the phone.

"Are you okay?" He sunk down into the chair next to her. "This has been a very stressful day for you. What can I do?"

"Give me a second." Taylor felt guilty for the strong desire to ditch her new friend. After all, she was the one who had texted him when she was tired of being alone.

He pulled out his own phone and let her have her moment.

While Taylor was trying to decide what to do, Amara Schilling, the family lawyer texted. She was free to meet.

Taylor spent a few minutes setting up their appointment, then apologized to Bruno and left. She didn't feel too bad about abandoning him. He'd have an easy enough time finding someone to keep him company.

A MASSIVE WAVE of relief poured over Taylor when she and Amara took their seats at the old pine table in Taylor's kitchen. "I can't tell you how glad I am to see you!"

Amara opened her laptop and logged into a video conference that was already in session.

Roxy stared at them from the computer. Unlike her normal sunny self, her face was stormy as the wooly fisherman's knit sweater she wore.

"First off, can you tell me everything you said in your interview at the sheriff's office?" Amara sounded cool, collected, and legal.

"They wanted to know how long I'd known Albina, when I'd last spoken to her, and how Jonah paid us. They basically asked those over and over," Roxy said. "I said I didn't know her, had never met her, and that Jonah doesn't pay us anything."

"Is all of that true?" Amara asked.

There was another face on the screen now, not the cute small man Taylor remembered as Roxy's ex. This man had a head like a cinder block, with a very gray high and tight. "You don't have to say anything Roxy, this woman doesn't represent you."

"Of course, it's true," Taylor interrupted.

"You don't have to say anything either," Amara said, still unperturbed. "In fact, it's best if you don't. You don't have first-hand knowledge of how Jonah and his mom are handling his income or of who she does and does not know."

"Like in a divorce," the military lawyer said, "you each need your own representation."

"But we aren't in a legal battle against each other." Taylor's stomach twisted.

Roxy stared straight ahead, her face a mix of anger and confusion. "Do you know who turned Jonah in to YouTube for terms of service violation?"

Taylor shook her head.

Taylor expected Roxy to spit the word out, but her voice was mournful as she said Taylor's sister's name.

"But he's with her now." This wasn't any kind of argument against what Roxy said, but what Roxy said was insane. "And our income from our show depends on him. She wouldn't have done that."

"And yet, she did," Roxy's voice cracked.

"Let's shut this down." Amara seemed to be looking at Roxy's ex.

"Agreed." He gave a curt nod.

Amara closed out the box and shut the computer. "I want to help as much as I can, but we need to find you a defense attorney. Even if you don't get pinched for murder, it looks like you might get sued for slander."

## CHAPTER TEN

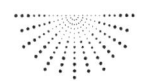

Following a fitful night, Taylor woke early, but stayed in bed much longer, staring out the window into the spindly branches of the dying maple tree.

Tree maintenance.

Life in her condo in the city hadn't involved that.

Life in her condo in the city hadn't involved murder, either.

She wanted to call Roxy and see how she was this morning. See if she'd heard from Jonah, if he had any news about his own legal issues. See if he had an explanation for his suspiciously well-timed snaps. She wanted to call her friend and hear that everything was going to be fine.

But she didn't, because she had a sinking suspicion that it wasn't going to be fine.

Taylor glanced at the clock. It was 7:30 now. She only had a half an hour to get to the Expo to set up her booth.

But with the death of the speaker, did anyone really care if she set up a table in the marketplace to sell notions, and self-published books, and all of that?

Instead, she threw a load of clothes in the wash and began pacing her little house trying to think of other things she could do to stay away from the Expo.

She could catch up on Jonah's desk chair detective website, which might have answers to the questions she was full of. Or she could call Belle, yet again, and find out what was really going on.

She wished she could call her mom. The snaps, well-timed or not, weren't the same. She just wanted her…mom. Her real, used-to-be-alive-mom who would tell her to be careful of men who got familiar too fast, and who would tell her not to waste a good learning opportunity just because of murder.

She wiped her teary eyes on the cuff of her bathrobe.

She would never stop missing her mom.

Her Snapchat alert chimed, and she gave in immediately, actually hoping it was another bittersweet snippet.

Her mother's smiling face greeted her from the fuzzy distance of the computer screen as though Jonah was holding his phone up to the YouTube video as it played. Her mouth was moving but she could barely hear her. Her face seemed to twist from that deep happiness to something desperately sad. "It just doesn't seem real. Any of this."

She faded away.

Taylor fell into her sofa, and hugged her knees to her chest, feeling about fifteen years old instead of just over thirty. A funny thing, being motherless. It didn't matter how old you were, it left you feeling incredibly vulnerable. And no, none of it felt real. Not even a little bit.

She took her time getting showered and dressed, but she couldn't put it off forever. She had to go to the Expo.

She called Belle as she walked to the campus, not bringing her wagon of goods for sale, but she only got voicemail. She left her a message. "I have so many questions, and I suspect you have all the answers. Please call."

Taylor made it in time for the morning keynote, so she went straight there. Bruno was surrounded by ladies. Taylor didn't know how he'd manage to get to the stage.

He didn't notice her which was just fine. She wanted to lay

low, listen, and wait it out. She wouldn't be arrested for a murder she didn't commit. Or for a death that might not actually have been a murder.

Roxy sat at a table alone in the back of the room. Taylor joined her but left a couple of chairs between them. She wanted to ask when she'd got back into town. Wanted to ask who this military man was that she called Jonah's father. She wanted to ask about the sister she'd never known existed. Taylor had a million questions, but she also had a wall of ice between herself and Roxy.

Roxy would always protect her child. Against anything. And though Taylor had similar feelings about her sister, she knew it wasn't the same.

"I spoke to Jonah this morning." Roxy sipped her coffee. "He said Belle didn't turn him in."

Taylor jerked to attention. "I'm glad to hear it." She drummed her fingers on the table. "Who does he think did it?"

"How can he know? He's got millions of followers."

"I see."

"But he swears he believes Belle, even though…"

"Even though what? What reason would she have for damaging his gravy train?" Taylor couldn't keep her frustration in.

"See? That's the reason. Envy," Roxy's voice rose louder and higher.

"Come on," Taylor dropped her voice. "I'm not envious."

"Jonah and I have been working on the Flour Sax show for a few years now." She folded her linen napkin over and over again. "We've been really invested for a long time."

"I see." Taylor sat back in her chair. Roxy seemed to be saying Taylor was an interloper. Someone who didn't belong.

"You might not be envious. That's fine, but you're a grown up." Roxy sighed like she was making a concession. "No matter how far ahead she is in her schooling, Belle is still very young, and she's envious."

"Even if she is, that doesn't mean she'd try and get him in trouble like this. Not with a death to deal with," Taylor countered.

"Jonah says he believes Belle, so I guess that's that." Roxy's words did not match the hurt expression in her eyes.

"I tried calling but can't get through. As soon as I do, I'll talk to her." Taylor began to fold her napkin as well, but it wasn't real linen, just some polyester blend. It wouldn't hold a fold. Synthetic fiber was like that. Once its nature was set, that was it.

They waited in silence while the room began to fill.

Valerie Ritz, the wealthy young woman with the distinctive red hair and white glasses, brought a group of girls her age to their table. "Have you heard the latest?" Valerie took one of the seats between Roxy and Taylor.

"Probably not." Taylor felt defeated. She had thought this Expo would be something wonderful for her and Roxy. A way to make money but also to develop their friendship beyond just filming and working together.

"To start with, McKenzie Forte was not married, despite Sue Friese telling us all that 'Albina's husband' was coming, so they were all-in one-hundred percent on their fake author bio. I haven't seen anyone pretending to be her husband around here, so I suspect the publisher refused to pay out for an actor."

"Go on." Taylor wasn't overly impressed, but she had forgotten they had said Albina was married.

"Supposedly only Sue and her husband actually saw the body." Valerie lifted a thick eyebrow. "I don't think anyone died."

Roxy burst out with a sardonic laugh. "You can think that because you didn't spend the day at the police station yesterday."

"So, it's true!" Valerie's face brightened. "I had also heard that you, Jonah Lang's mother, had been arrested, but how could that have been true if there wasn't a body?"

Carrie Kyle, the loud little one from yesterday who also

fancied herself a detective, took the other seat between Roxy and Taylor. "Everyone knows there was a body because the paramedics came and took her away."

"It could have been staged, just like everything else about her," Valerie countered.

"Not so. I heard at the bar last night that they know what killed her now." Carrie Kyle looked smug, her darkly painted lips pursed in satisfaction.

"Do tell." Taylor couldn't take Carrie Kyle seriously. Her voice was just so loud. Comical, almost.

"Allergies."

"That makes perfect sense," Taylor agreed, just to keep her talking.

"So, it wasn't murder," Roxy murmured. "I can't tell you how good it feels to hear that."

"Oh no, someone murdered her with her allergies. Like in that episode of Death in Paradise with the bug in the matchbox."

"Sure, someone is reenacting a British detective show. Why wouldn't they?" Taylor sipped her coffee, tired already of these sleuths and their ideas.

Carrie Kyle bounced in her seat. "People have to get their ideas from somewhere. It's not like we're a bunch of hardened criminals here, and anyway, everyone knows quilters love mysteries."

"Anyone at the bar tell you what the motive was?" Taylor asked. And then her phone pinged. She looked at the three women and then around the table in general. Two others were on their phone. Could one of them have reported the conversation to Jonah so he'd send a clip to Taylor? Maybe.

In this snap, Taylor's mom leaned on her elbows in front of a pile of fabric that Taylor vaguely recognized. "Trust me," she whispered.

Someone in the background of the video laughed. Roxy? Belle?

"We're going to be stars." Laura Quinn picked up the stack of fabric bits and tossed them so they fluttered to the table like streamers.

"Trust who?" Taylor whispered back to her mother. Trust you? Or trust Jonah who was sending the clips? Or was it about trust more generally? Was she supposed to trust these girls or maybe the system? Or maybe her own intuition?

Or maybe these really were just random.

Or maybe she needed to splice them together, watch them as one long narrative to see what her mom was really saying.

Except they disappeared after watching. Google had told her they could be replayed once, after deletion though. So, she had one chance. One chance to line them all up and see what Jonah was trying to tell her.

If she was brave enough.

If she trusted them.

Valerie Ritz put her hand on Taylor's wrist. "You've had a lot of stress."

Taylor swallowed. She hadn't said any of that out loud, had she?

"It doesn't matter anyway," Carrie continued in her well-projected voice. "I mean, if the killer got the idea from the show or not. The police know what killed her. Now all they have to do is find the fingerprints and it's locked down."

"Nobody leaves fingerprints anymore," some girl across the table said in her best impression of a valley girl who hated everybody.

"I wonder what kind of allergies…?" Taylor asked. Maybe they were the kind of allergies that gave you a rash on your face. "Who did you hear the allergies story from?"

Carrie Kyle leaned towards Taylor as though she were going to whisper. "I heard the security guard tell the bartender in town. The security guy said he was in the room when the paramedics came. The paramedics said it looked like allergies. That's what the security guard said." Despite her body posture, her voice was so loud, heads at the table in front of them turned.

"Interesting." Taylor found herself folding her napkin again, though it was as unsatisfying and artificial as ever. Terrible fabric for quilting. Terrible fabric for mopping up a spill. Only good for creating an appearance of luxury. Paramedics saw a lot of dead people. They could be right. The medical examiner saw a lot of dead people too. Shara Schonley claimed she heard Reg telling the security guard that the autopsy came back inconclusive. "I wonder where I can find the security guard…?"

Bruno took the stage starting his slide show with a clip of his daughter and his wife sitting at a sewing machine together. His eyes twinkled with tears.

"Excuse me. I think I need to go somewhere quiet to think."

Valerie patted her arm. "Very good idea."

Carrie Kyle hollered goodbye, but all the others at the table, including Roxy, had a lovelorn look in their eyes that were glued to the speaker.

Bruno was right. He would have never gotten this kind of attention at a gun show.

## CHAPTER ELEVEN

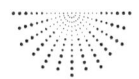

Taylor thought long and hard, and then gave up.
She wasn't a quitter by nature, but her thoughts had gone around and around and gotten nowhere, leaving her feeling like the whole mess was none of her business.

She wasn't the one who had pressed for the Amish author to be the speaker. That had been Shara. Though if it was true that Sue and the author were good friends, then maybe Shara had merely taken credit for Sue's idea. That seemed to fit Shara's overall vibe.

Taylor and Hudson talked late into the night, but he hadn't come over. They both had places to be in the morning.

After hanging up she spotted a text from Ashleigh, Belle's step-sister. Ashleigh asked Taylor to call ASAP. Taylor frowned at the phone. If Belle wouldn't return her calls, she was hardly going to call this Ashleigh, at least not in the middle of the night. She'd sleep on it. If it was urgent, Ashleigh would call.

The next morning was bleak. The dark-gray weather came with a soaking rain that led Taylor to drive the few blocks to the school, something she avoided doing whenever possible. But even the short walk from doors to car soaked her.

She was late, but time didn't seem to matter so much

anymore. Bruno, or someone, would be giving a talk in the dining room at the time.

She could go, and sit, and be inspired. Or she could snoop a little and see if she could learn something while everyone was tied up.

The sheriff's crew were still roaming the school. Taylor went straight to the office they had interviewed her in, but the room was shut tight and locked. She wondered if they had commandeered some private security office with CCTV monitors. The school had to have one of those somewhere.

A young woman in a crisp suit jacket whose Expo ID card said "Cascadia Staff" was standing to the left of the reception desk.

Taylor joined her hoping her wet hair, lackluster clothes, and worried expression would inspire compassion. "Excuse me, I'm looking for security."

The woman yawned. "I'm sure he's around here somewhere." She tapped her phone screen a few times, then spoke into it on speaker. "Karen? This is Aza. Can you get security on your walkie? One of the faculty wants him." She paused. "Mmm. Okay. Sure." She hung up. "He's working right now. Do you have an issue I can help you with?"

Taylor considered. Did she? Or could she just come up with something? "I can't locate my business partner, and with….well…you know, I'm worried." Likely Roxy was in the conference room listening to Bruno, but Taylor hadn't seen her yet this morning, so she was being mostly honest.

Aza didn't acknowledge Taylor, but picked up the phone again, pressed a few more buttons and waited. Then, "Joyce, do you have a minute?" Pause. "Yes, another one. Ah. Sorry." She hung up and opened her mouth like she was going to speak but yawned again instead.

"Can I get you a coffee?" Taylor wanted to buy Aza's affection if possible.

Aza's phone rang. "Yes, she's waiting here in the front office.

Okay, thanks." She hung up. "Security will be here in a minute. Just wait." Aza turned so her back was slightly to Taylor and returned her attention to her phone.

Taylor waited.

The clock on the wall ticked.

Taylor's phone was silent.

A man about Taylor's height in the white button-down and black pants of private security ambled toward her. "What's the problem?"

"My roommate disappeared." Taylor walked toward the locked office conference room.

She put her hand on the doorknob and frowned.

The security guard unlocked the door and opened it. The florescent light overhead sputtered to life automatically.

Taylor took a nervous seat in a folding chair and leaned forward, elbows on her knees. The guard's name tag said "Joe."

"Joe, it's been pretty scary here, I'm not going to lie, and with my business partner missing, I'm worried."

Joe was older than Taylor but it hadn't looked that way at first. He had a full head of hair and his face was almost wrinkle free, but his hands showed age that couldn't be hidden.

"Yeah, I can see why you're worried. Think she might have checked out without telling you? Gone home maybe?"

"I just don't know," Taylor lied.

"Have you tried calling her?" He was asking the obvious questions, the ones Taylor expected.

She wrestled with ideas for how to turn the conversation to Albina's body. Even if it hadn't been Joe at the death scene, the security staff must have talked about it. "With this death hanging over us, I just fear the worst."

"I suggest you try calling her. Did you happen to get into an argument?"

Taylor nodded. She didn't actually want to get the police involved in a fake missing person's thing, so the less serious she made this sound the better. Plus, it was true, which would make it easier to remember. "Do you all have CCTV? Could we check if she left in the night?"

"How about you call her, see if you can get hold of her first, okay?" He hadn't taken a seat yet.

Taylor needed to get him to stay. She considered crying, but it seemed like too much effort. "I'm afraid she ran from the police."

He sat.

She bit her tongue. This was not the right strategy to use if she wanted to keep this a quiet, police free affair.

"What would she be running from?"

"Uh, well, they took her down for questioning because of her son and his videos." Too much truth came out, on accident. But it was too late to reel it back in.

Joe frowned, his whole face folding into a look of disapproval. He reached for his two-way radio.

"Wait—I'll call her first. I'm sorry I didn't think of it. I'm just so overwhelmed by this situation. They told us not to leave. I'm all alone now. I don't know what's happening with my friend. I can't…." Taylor ran on, words spilling fast, a panicky sound brought on by actual panic that he would call someone to arrest Roxy for fleeing.

Joe held out both of his hands. "It's gonna be okay. Calm down. If you had a fight, Roxy might just be avoiding you."

Taylor stared. Of course Joe knew her. Of course he knew Roxy. She couldn't place his face, but she realized as she stared at him that she'd seem him in town. At the market. At the diner. At the gas station. He was a local and knew more about Taylor than she was comfortable with now. "Yes, you're right, I'm sure. She didn't do anything wrong. She doesn't need to run from the police, but I thought she might have been scared like me, but then she was mad so maybe she just wanted to get away from me."

"Try calling her."

Taylor took her phone out with a shaking hand and called

Roxy. She used her real number because it hadn't occurred to her to fake it. Thankfully, Roxy didn't answer. "If she's mad at me still, she might not answer. I don't know. What if the person who killed Albina got her? What if they think we know something and want to eliminate her—and me?"

"Don't worry about that. That poor kid wasn't murdered."

Taylor's phone pinged.

But there was literally no one around who could have given Jonah a head's up to send a snap.

"What? Are you sure?" Taylor pressed the palm of her hand over her phone. She didn't want to see it.

"Sure I am. The kid died of anaphylactic shock, or my name isn't Joseph Baker."

She was taken aback for a second. "Your name is Joseph Baker?" Baker was her mom's maiden name. Was security-guard Joe another cousin she'd forgotten about?

"Yup." He laughed. "No relation. But that poor kid wasn't murdered. Not that the cops are saying, but I saw her with my own eyes. She was laying there, swelled up, looking dead, her hands in her purse like she was trying to find an emergency rescue inhaler, or an EpiPen."

Taylor relaxed back into the chair as though his words were the good news she had been hoping for. "You must be very observant to have figured all of that out."

"The paramedics said something to the effect, but it looked pretty right to me. My brother has an EpiPen and has gotten close a couple of times. Not a pretty sight."

"What does that look like?"

"She was swole up pretty good, and her face was all red. I wouldn't wish that on an enemy. Here." He offered Taylor a hand to help her out of the chair. "Go make some calls. I'm sure you'll find Roxy. She's not one to stay mad long."

Taylor accepted his hand and followed him out of the room.

"I wish they'd make an announcement about that kid

already," Joe said. "It's no fun workin' at an event full of people who think a murderer is on the loose."

While they talked, a hoard of people pushed through the front doors. Hundreds of them. At least as many as were in the meeting room for Bruno's morning talk. It was Sunday, the day of the quilt show that was open to the public.

This was going to complicate snooping.

Then again…if Joe was right, there wasn't any need to snoop.

Taylor took a deep breath and felt her shoulders relax. She let herself get swept up in the crowd and funneled into the room with the quilts on display. Then she checked her phone.

No snap. Just a text from Hudson. Taylor thought she knew the difference in the alerts, but she was under stress. He asked if she had time to chat, so she called.

"First," she said when he answered, "You're lovely to check on me."

"Not gonna lie. I'm worried. I can cut out of this job early if things get dangerous. I've got a substitute for myself lined up."

"Don't do anything crazy. Think of the extra money."

"I'd rather think of you not getting killed, if you don't mind." Hudson's deep firm voice was a comfort, even though she wasn't worried at just this moment.

"But you don't know yet. I've had good news." She relayed what the security guard had said about it being death by allergy.

"Death by allergy…," he mused. "But could it have been murder by allergy instead?"

"I mean…anything is possible." This wasn't the first time someone had suggested this, and Taylor did not like the way it sounded, felt, and definitely seemed correct. Why couldn't it have been murder by allergy? Give Albina a strong dose of something that could kill her, then hide her medicine. "I heard it said that she hadn't had any underlying medical conditions…"

"Don't trust everything you hear," Hudson cautioned. "Even this thing about allergies. Maybe there's a poison that looks like an allergic reaction."

Taylor leaned against the wall behind her, feeling slightly defeated.

Swarms of quilt fans, the hundreds of hoped for tourists the event had been in aid of, wandered the large room, bubbling over with excitement. This was what her work and effort had been for. Not for YouTube views. Not to sell her mom's patterns. She wanted to put Comfort, Oregon on the map. To increase its esteem in the craft world so that the businesses and residents could thrive for years to come.

A woman in a sweatshirt embroidered with 'Witches get Stitches' walked past with a small group. Her voice carried as she said, "Yes, I told you this was the one where the famous author got murdered."

Taylor shivered.

How many of these guests were here for the quilts, and how many were here for the murder?

And was her goal of increasing tourism an even better motive than cash?

"I don't want you to quit this job. But if you happened to finish early, I wouldn't turn down your company." This was as close to begging for help as Taylor was comfortable with.

"Gotcha," Hudson said. "And love you. I'll call later."

"Thanks. And hey, today is a good day. Lots of people here. Albina's death didn't keep them away."

"That's good news." They ended the call.

Taylor stared ahead of her, not seeing the people or the quilts.

"Were you talking about the murdered Amish writer?" a voice whispered in Taylor's ear.

Taylor stepped away from the speaker and turned. "Yes, yeah. I was."

"Can we talk? I think I know something important." The whisperer was as close to being Taylor's doppelganger as could be, if you ignored that their faces weren't a thing alike. Otherwise, they had the same lanky build, dishwater hair, and indifferent clothes.

Taylor followed the woman to a quiet corner where the beginner quilts were displayed. Even the blue-ribbon winner in the beginner category wasn't interesting enough to draw a crowd.

"I only came today because of the murder. I'm not actually a quilter." Her eyes darted side to side. "I'm a dedicated fan of Amish fiction, and this series has been a huge controversy for quite a while."

"The theory that it was written by computer?" Taylor asked.

"Yes. That one. I know some kid online claims to have proven it, but when all four books came out at once in the spring, we superfans knew right away. It was clearly computer-generated nonsense. We've boycotted the series, and so it hasn't been the money maker it might have been otherwise."

"How do you superfans organize a boycott like that?"

"Let's not get into that now. There's something more important."

"Okay. Go on." Taylor stuffed her disappointment. As self-appointed sleuth, she wanted all information possible.

"I am afraid we caused her murder."

Taylor tilted her head and considered this woman. She seemed deeply concerned but had picked Taylor, a complete stranger, to tell a story about being an accomplice to murder.

She couldn't actually be sane.

"Why are you telling me this?" Taylor asked.

The stranger stepped back, a look of embarrassment washing over her. "I overheard you. Saw your name badge. I thought you were an official." She looked Taylor up and down. Her khaki pants and limp white button down could have been mistaken for staff. Plus, her name badge might have been taken for something more important than it really was.

"I thought you were investigating. It sounded like it. I—" She turned and tried to melt back into the crowd.

"Wait!" Taylor reached out for her.

The woman looked over her shoulder and then sped up.

DUTCH HEX

Taylor trailed her, eventually catching up to her at a bottle neck in front of Bruno's latest quilt.

"Hold on. You're kind of right. Why don't we slip out somewhere more private?"

The stranger ran her fingers over the edge of her purse nervously and looked around the room.

"We don't have to be alone, just somewhere where we can sit down and talk. The lobby by the coffee cart, maybe," Taylor suggested.

The stranger inclined her head, a scared person's nod of agreement.

Taylor led her out of the mess of people and to a bistro table in the lobby. She ordered them both coffees and coffee cake. "You say you're afraid you caused her death. Does it help to hear that some of the officials involved think she died of natural causes?" Taylor held the warm coffee in its paper cup, glad to have something to do with her hands.

"No, it doesn't. In trying to uncover who she was and what her scheme was about, one of the members of our group posted a listing of her known allergies."

Taylor froze, then exhaled sharply. "What makes you think her death was allergy related?"

The stranger lowered her eyebrows giving Taylor the look you give a child who isn't getting it. "Everyone knows. It was announced. Her death was caused by a tragic allergic reaction."

"But I only just learned this after having to hunt down a security guard. Who announced it to you all?"

"Someone in our private group. That person is here, somewhere. I kind of thought...I thought it might have been you."

"No, I don't read Amish fiction. I'm sorry."

The mystery woman hadn't touched her coffee cake and held her cup like she was afraid Taylor had tampered with it.

"I do like westerns though, and some prairie romance, when I'm in the mood."

The stranger relaxed a little. "I need to find the person who announced the cause of death to our group. Then we can have a conference. Combine our knowledge. A large crowd like this probably has a couple people trying to get to the bottom of this mess."

"You're not wrong." Taylor sighed. She wondered, briefly, if she had also seemed annoying when she was trying to solve the murder of the chaplain of Bible Creek Care Home. She hadn't felt annoying.

"Will you help me?"

"Yes, but we don't have long. What can we do in one day?"

"More than we can do with no days. I have to go. I need to discuss the problem with the online group. Get the contact to identify herself."

"Is the group anonymous?"

"No, we're not the hackers." The stranger mistook the generic term for the rogue online group. "We're the Amish Anonymous. We just want to see the literature handled with respect. It's important to us."

"Ok." Taylor scribbled her number on a napkin and passed it to the mystery woman. "Text me when you want to meet."

"I'll contact you again as soon as I can. In the meantime, keep a low profile. We don't know how dangerous it is out here."

Taylor finished her coffee and coffee cake. Then she ate the stranger's coffee cake too. She stayed half an hour snacking and catching up on Jonah's videos. He seemed to be playing a character—someone older than his real teenage self. Someone deeply concerned for his mother and his Juvies. There was a maturity about the videos that seemed false, at least to Taylor. But also, a heart to them, as though he wanted to be this wise, caring man someday.

The comments on his videos were even more interesting than the videos themselves.

One commenter, calling herself merely Am-anon, seemed likely to be the contact the stranger was looking for. Her latest comment on his newest video was particularly telling: "Vigilante justice online is dangerous. You don't know what you are doing, Jonah. This isn't just a game. People are taking you seriously. You should calm yourself down before someone else gets hurt."

The comment was only five minutes old. Jonah hadn't responded to it, but many of his Juvies had. Am-anon was called every name in the book for questioning their Jonah's motives. He, according to his Juvies, was as pure as he was handsome. Just a boy who loved his mom and cared about a dead author.

Just a boy who loved money and attention was more like it.

But that wasn't fair. Jonah wasn't bad. But murder wasn't a game.

Two much cake and coffee left Taylor sluggish and a little sick, but she went back to the quilt show. As soon as the newest detective texted her, she'd get in touch with Shara and that loud girl, Carrie Kyle. Valerie Ritz might like to be included too. A sort of dream-team of amateur detectives.

She wished she had asked for access to the Amish Anonymous forum so she could see the list of Albina's allergies. Knowing what could potentially kill Albina Tschetter would help her figure out *who* had potentially killed her.

## CHAPTER TWELVE

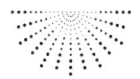

The text from the stranger who wanted to hunt down the allergy leak came right as the wait staff was serving dinner in the large conference room that evening. Taylor regretted the loss of her supper but considered it the cost of doing detective business. She texted Shara, Carrie Kyle, and Valerie Ritz, then slipped away.

They met in the café area of the lobby. Since everyone else was at dinner, they had the area to themselves.

"I like that we have good visuals from here," the woman who had called them all together said.

Taylor still didn't know this woman's name and wondered if she ever would. She'd had no idea that Amish fiction was such a cloak and dagger genre.

"The door in front of us and the full sweep of the hall behind us. It's good. Thank you all for meeting me here. I know for at least one of you it comes with a sacrifice. I'm sorry." There were two new people at the table. The mysterious stranger didn't look at them, but it was obvious she was thinking of them. One of those two was probably her Amish Anonymous contact. "We need to share our knowledge so that we can construct a picture of the actress McKenzie Forte's last moments. It's a terrible injustice that this young woman had to die. Don't you all agree?"

"Yes!" Tiny but loud Carrie Kyle was the first to speak up.

The leader of the pack put her finger to her lips. "Discretion is our best defense."

"I completely agree. I've been withholding quite a bit until now, but I think it's time to come clean, to give you all the whole story." Carri's voice hadn't quieted in the slightest. "There's a real detective here at the hotel. She's an undercover cop hiding in plain sight." Carrie Kyle stared at Taylor, pointedly. "She's playing dumb, but she has the whole thing wrapped up. I know because the chef told the maid who cleans the dorms." The more Carrie talked, the louder she got. The very discrete leader was motioning for Carrie to quiet down, but it had no effect. "The truth is, this wasn't a murder. It was a huge ruse. The paramedics were hired. The security guy is an actor. It was all fake. The death was part of the character McKenzie was hired to play. You can trust me. She's still posting things on her Facebook."

The scheduled posts. Clearly Taylor's Facebook reporting had done nothing. She didn't stop to correct Carrie, though. Her ramblings were building a picture in Taylor's mind.

"There is only one person who can profit from this—the mastermind who put it all together. The arrest," Carrie took a deep breath, "will be for fraud, not murder." Carrie's eyes were glued on Taylor.

Taylor wasn't sure if Carrie suspected her as the undercover detective or the mastermind.

"Jonah Lang got rich from it." Shara also stared at Taylor. "If he's not your mastermind, then your theory is a wash. Besides, the lady who was cleaning the bathroom in my wing of the dorms told me something entirely different, and I trust her. She's a regular at Dutch Hex." Shara fingered the cuff of her plain cotton dress.

"What was her theory?" Carrie didn't sound the least bit defensive, just more excited, if possible.

One of the new women, perhaps the Amish Anonymous contact, whispered in the ear of the leader of this motley crew.

"This maid cleaned the room after the police were done with it." Shara pursed her lips and nodded in agreement with herself. "She said that Albina didn't have a single stitch of sewing things with her."

"Yes, we all know that." Carrie's exasperated voice must have carried all the way into the dining room.

"Indeed. We all heard her talk. In light of that, ask yourself this: if she had no sewing things on her, why did she die with a thread waxer gripped in her hand?"

"Who said she did?" Taylor's heart sped up. This was potentially useful, important information. Why would Albina have had such an out of character item with her? Why was she holding it as she died? Taylor liked this tid-bit but wanted more. She wanted something better than the chef's maid's best friend said so, if possible.

"The maid. She was also in the hall when Morgan Friese found the body. She peeked in the room while he was calling the police."

"Who is this maid? Could we interview her?" Taylor asked.

"Oh no. She's very scared that it was wrong for her to look. She doesn't want to see the police because she's not sure about her papers. She doesn't want to get deported for this. There was another housecleaner there too. If you can find out who she was, she might help." Despite the very delicate nature of this news, Carrie did not get remotely quieter.

"I want the one who talked to you, not the one who might not have noticed the thread waxer. Are you sure your maid wouldn't talk to me, even?" Taylor asked.

Carrie winked at Taylor.

So, Carrie did think Taylor was the undercover cop. Maybe it was because she'd had some private conversations with Reg. Word traveled fast in the quilting set. And then again, maybe she was developing a reputation as a crime solver in the town after all.

Taylor turned her attention to the woman she suspected of being the Amish Anonymous contact. "My name is Taylor Quinn. I work with Jonah and Roxy Lang."

"Hello." The voice was quiet and low, the eyes partly hidden beneath a shag of dark hair.

"How did you hear it was allergies that had killed Albina?" Taylor asked.

"I was sitting near your table when you heard." The quiet young woman kept a very straight face. Her eyes were small and darkly lined, and she had tried to hide her freckles under thick foundation. She didn't want to be recognized after this meeting.

"So, technically, you don't know anything the three of us don't."

"I might." She pressed her lips tightly together.

"What brought you to the Expo?" Taylor turned the topic slightly. She hoped chatting would help this girl relax.

"First and foremost, I came for the Amish quilt display today. The nearest Amish community is in Montana, so we don't have access to their works like most of the rest of the country does."

"Did you get a chance to appreciate it?" Taylor tried to keep her voice conversational to draw the girl out, but it was hard.

"Yes."

"What was your other reason?"

The girl wouldn't look directly at Taylor, but she didn't hesitate either. "I wanted to have a conversation with McKenzie."

"Did you get to?"

This time the girl hesitated.

"Please tell us. Its vitally important," the woman who had gathered the group together urged.

"Yes. I did."

Taylor drew in a sharp breath.

"I came to the early bird session. She signed copies of books. She gave me three minutes. I asked her why. That was all. Just,

'Why?' And she told me to make sure not to miss the keynote address. I didn't miss it, but it was just lies. A monologue written for her to say."

"That monologue was not written by a computer." Taylor didn't say it for anyone's benefit but her own, as she was just realizing it herself. "Sue Friese runs this show. She's claimed she's a good friend of Albina's. I think it's time to talk to Sue."

"Good luck with that," the disguised Amish fan said. "I heard she left last night."

"If you will all excuse me." Taylor looked around the table. The crew were an interesting lot. From the volunteer detectives, to the obsessive fans, to that other young woman who had stayed completely silent through the whole meeting. Why had she come? Just to not be alone? Taylor squared her shoulders. She wasn't here for the company. "I'm basically staff here. I'm sure I can get someone to tell me where Sue is."

Taylor crossed the lobby, leaving the other sleuths to their deductions. But the front desk in the school office that was manned by her friend Isaiah during the school year was empty, closed down for the day. Taylor headed back to the dining hall where the dinner was still in session. An Expo employee, by the look of the name badge, stood at the door.

"I'm looking for Sue," Taylor said quietly.

"Sue's not to be bothered right now." The Expo employee's name tag said, "Trish Weaver."

"I understand. Well, maybe this is a better thing for security anyway. Can you reach them?" Taylor pulled her eyebrows together in a look of worry.

Trish looked Taylor up and down and spotted the ribbons on the name badge declaring her both a "vendor/mentor" and a "Friend of Cascadia."

She scrunched her mouth up but took out her phone and sent a quick text.

About three minutes later a security guard whose name tag said "John" was there, beckoning Taylor to the front office again.

"John, my name is Taylor Quinn. I'm one of the vendors here for the quilt Expo. I cannot, for the life of me, find Sue Friese, the woman in charge."

"What am I supposed to do about that?" John looked tired. He had big bags under his eyes and a slump to his shoulders. Taylor guessed he was her own age, but he lacked a certain energy she'd hoped to find.

"I thought you could help me find her."

He sighed deeply. "Isn't there some big keynote speech about to start? Wouldn't she just be there?"

Taylor felt stupid. Why would Sue have been anywhere else? Taylor was letting the rumors and the gossip get to her. Just because those crazy ladies said Sue was gone didn't mean it was true.

The Snapchat chime pinged. Taylor looked around but didn't see anyone watching her who might have alerted Jonah that it would be a good time to send a snap. "I'm sorry for wasting your time." Using security to find Sue had been even less effective than using it to find Roxy. She'd have to try something new next time.

John stood up with a lot of effort and a deep grunt. "Don't make a habit of it." He held the door to the little office open, then shut it and locked it behind. A very final sound.

The lobby was quiet still, so she checked her phone.

"Don't give up now. You'll get the hang of this." Taylor's mom. Smiling. Staring at the camera. Holding up a bit of yo-yo quilting. Yo-yo quilting was something Taylor had given up on in middle school. But this snap wasn't about yo-yos. It was about figuring out how Albina/McKenzie had died.

Taylor closed Snapchat and called Jonah.

He didn't answer.

She called Roxy.

Roxy didn't answer.

She cursed whoever was spying on her.

Then she went hunting.

Someone had seen Taylor sneak off with the security guard, and that person was the spy. She had to be.

Taylor headed to the dining room. She would have bet money that Trish Weaver was a closet Juvie and was the one sending Jonah tips on when to send snaps.

But Trish wasn't at her spot at the door any longer.

Taylor's chair was still empty at the table, and Bruno was still talking, so she took a seat. "How long has he been going on?" she asked the stranger next to her.

"He took a break and Sue gave a little talk, but all together, I'd say forever. This is the night of the never-ending talk about dead people." She yawned. The love light was gone from her eyes. Poor Bruno. His fans might just be getting too much of a good thing.

"In conclusion," Bruno's words, the first Taylor had paid attention to, were met with an audible sigh of relief from the crowd.

Taylor abandoned her seat again as Bruno gave his conclusion. She headed around the side of the room to the front. Sue was somewhere up there, and she wanted to find her as soon as the overhead lights came back on.

Bruno finished with a very generic prayer directed to a higher power, and the lights came on. Taylor scanned every table in the front row but did not find Sue Friese or her husband Morgan.

Bruno Stutze spotted her.

He wove his way through the crowd till he was at her side. "Let's get out of here."

There was a chair between Bruno and Taylor, but he seemed a lot closer. He had the grace not to drag her off, but he looked like he wanted to.

"I'm looking for Sue Friese. Have you seen her?"

"She went to her room after her midpoint speech. Can you believe how long she made me talk? I'm about to die. I need a drink. Are you free? Do you have time?"

"Do you know which room is Sue's?"

He looked at his watch. "I'm going to head to the bar in town. If you change your mind you can meet me there." His face was red and sweaty from being under the hot lights.

Taylor considered wandering the dorms for their guest speaker. There were a couple of apartments on campus that had been built in early days for staff but were no longer used. She figured someone like Sue would have been put up in a real apartment for the event. They were out back, towards the woods, and relatively isolated. Taylor wanted to find Sue, but she wasn't sure she wanted to check the apartments alone. "I'll walk out with you."

"Good. Thank you. I've been thinking of you. How are you holding up?" His voice was pleasantly concerned as they made their way to the main doors of the school.

"There's a lot of chaos around here, and a strange pressure on me to try and get to the root of it all."

"How do you feel about that?" Bruno sounded like a school counselor. It was kind of him.

"Tired."

He smiled. "Me too. I would very much like to take you out to dinner, like I suggested before. A real dinner, off this campus. Away from the madding crowd."

"You're kind." She didn't read too much into the invitation. She was firmly on team Bruno and Roxy, and nothing could shake the idea. Roxy deserved a nice man, and Bruno was a nice man.

When they got to the dining hall, they were greeted by more of the madding crowd, as though Taylor had conjured them.

Two officers were pulling a handcuffed woman toward the large pine doors.

Taylor ran across the polished floors. They had her mysterious stranger—the one who had reminded her of herself. "Wait!" She waved her hands and hollered.

The deputies paused.

"What's your name?" Taylor cried out.

"Beth Trager. Please help me."

"Come along." One of the deputies—not Reg or anyone else Taylor had worked with—jerked Beth's arm and took her out to their car.

Taylor ran after them, but one of the deputies stopped and barred her access to Beth and the sheriff's jeep. "Why did you arrest her? What's going on? She hasn't done anything…" Her words trailed off. She had no idea what this woman had done. Her hand went for her phone instinctively, expecting a snap from Jonah, but none came.

"Hold up there, Ma'am," the deputy said, one eye on Taylor.

"Just my phone. Sorry." Taylor held both her hands up. "Sorry!" She turned and went back into the college. She needed to find Roxy. She desperately needed to find Roxy.

## CHAPTER THIRTEEN

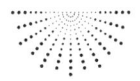

*T*aylor never did find Sue that evening, but she did find Roxy tucked in a quiet corner of the Expo work room reading on her phone.

"You look like you got hit by a truck." Roxy's face was more sympathetic than her words, which was a relief considering the tension between them.

"Could be worse, I guess." A few dedicated quilters ran their machines filling the work room with a quiet, industrial buzz. It felt safe and familiar. "I wish you had stuck around so we could talk though." Taylor pulled out a chair and sat with her old friend. The tension between them hurt, and she found herself feeling defeated over it.

"I just couldn't. The things I would have said if I had stuck around while I was still angry with Belle!" Roxy slipped her phone into her pocket. "I like you a lot, Taylor. But I love my son." Her voice broke on the last word.

Taylor had an inkling of an idea of what Roxy meant, but she still didn't see why this had to come between them. Especially if Belle and Jonah both said that Belle had nothing to do with getting the YouTube channel shut down.

"How is Jonah?"

"He's having the time of his life. He has no concept of money or the long term." Her face scrunched up in fear. "He isn't old enough to realize what he's losing."

"Then maybe it's a good thing YouTube is holding on to his cool million."

"I guess I agree with that. He thinks this is some kind of game." She rested her head in her hand. "If I hear him talk about his vulnerable mother one more time, I'm going to find him and beat him black and blue."

"He would deserve it." Taylor smiled, but didn't feel it in her heart.

"He refuses to talk to his father about the money situation. He says it's a distraction from the death which is his calling."

"His calling? But he's just a kid." Taylor tapped her toe on the polished wood floor. Even though she'd helped law enforcement a few times now, she'd hardly call crime fighting her calling.

"He's talking big and leaving the actual issue of his YouTube account alone as though it doesn't matter. Worse though, he refuses to go back to school."

"No…" Taylor gripped her hands together in frustration. Belle's set of friends had all seemed to graduate early—Belle first, then Dayton, and after bit of hard work over the summer, Cooper had been able to ditch his senior year, as well, with a real diploma to show for it.

But Jonah was different. Jonah was dropping out. Taylor's stomach fell. A million dollars earned and lost at seventeen would never make up for lacking the basics of your education. "Do you think he might actually care about the murder?" There was always a chance he could be convinced to study crime and law enforcement.

"I'm his mother, and even I can't say I believe that." Roxy raked her hand through her curls. "I just want to run away from all this. I want to go up to Seattle and grab him by the scruff of his neck and drag him home."

"I wonder…" Taylor stretched her very stiff shoulders. "I

wonder if Jonah going after YouTube for his money right now would make him or us look suspicious. Maybe he's letting that issue lie to protect us all."

Roxy gave Taylor a wan smile. "That sure would be nice of him."

The pall between them seemed to be lifting, just a little, so Taylor turned the conversation away from Jonah. "I met a strange lady today. She seemed to think she knew something important, and now she's been arrested."

"Oh?" Roxy manufactured some enthusiasm.

Taylor filled her in on the Amish Anonymous situation and Beth Trager. "I told her I'd try to help, but who knows how I could do that? I hope she calls her family from the station."

"I hope she has someone to call, too, but in case she doesn't, what do you plan to do?"

"I can only think of one thing. I need to talk to Sue Friese, who claimed to have been such good friends with our dead author."

"I think there's someone else we need to talk to." The crevice between Roxy's brows deepened. "We need to talk to my son."

Taylor took Roxy back to her house that night. They had agreed to ring Jonah's phone and flood all of his messaging systems till he finally answered. The end goal was to get him to tell them every single thing his little spies had reported back to him since Albina's death.

They camped out in the living room with mugs of tea and a box of cookies that had been hiding in the back of a cupboard, but neither of them were hungry.

They dialed and messaged and texted in silence for some time.

"I don't think he's going to respond." Taylor flopped her head back on the couch. "Not even one of those haunting snaps from my mom."

"What do you mean?" Most of Roxy's attention was on her

computer screen where a video of her son was playing with the volume down.

"He's been sending me little ten second or so snaps of Mom, from her outtakes mostly. Things I haven't seen a million times already, so they are eerie, almost real, you know?"

"They are real," Roxy said, squinting at her screen. "It's not animation or anything."

"I just mean it's almost like they're live. Like my mom is sending them. And they seem to relate to the moments I'm living. I feel like maybe he's got a spy or half a dozen of them reporting to him on what I do."

Roxy rubbed her eyes and sighed. "He's not a bad kid."

"I don't think he's bad…" But she did. She thought he was being especially cruel to her, in addition to being greedy, and at the moment, foolish.

"If some of his Juvies are reporting to him that you are in danger or distress, then he's sending the snaps to encourage you. I mean, they aren't little clips of her being mean, are they?" Roxy hadn't looked away from the Jonah video, though she had paused it.

"No…"

"So?"

"It still hurts." Taylor pulled an old quilt, one she had made herself, over her knees. She wasn't cold, but she wanted distance and protection.

"But that hurt isn't because of Jonah. It just is. It always will be." Roxy's voice had gone tender again. The encouraging, loving voice Taylor was used to.

"I just wish I knew what was going on."

"With the murder," Roxy finished Taylor's sentence.

"No, with Belle. And not just this week but the last year or more. She doesn't talk to me. Doesn't come for visits, not long ones anyway."

"Sort of like you."

Taylor didn't have to say anything. They both knew this was

true. When Taylor had left town for grad school almost ten years ago, she hadn't come back very often. She regretted it now, every day. "I have a terrible headache, Roxy. Let's talk tomorrow."

"If you hear from Belle…"

"I'll ask her everything. I'll ask her what she knows about the YouTube accounts, what she knows about Snapchat and TikTok too. I'll ask her to send Jonah home."

"Jonah swears she didn't turn him in." Roxy sounded like she was working hard to believe him.

"With so many people following him online right now, he's bound to have made some enemies. Some trolls. I swear on my mother's grave that the only thing I know for sure is that she is working on her own project. Her own content. Not for cash even, just for…the sentiment. If she turned Jonah in, she didn't tell me about it."

Roxy chewed her lip.

"My head hurts. I can't do this right now. Just…trust me, okay?"

Roxy stood and stretched, then made her way to the front door. "If you hear from Jonah again—via snaps of your mom—let me know. I'd like to know what messages he's sending.

"Sure. Goodnight, Roxy."

TAYLOR DIDN'T SLEEP long or well, so she was dressed and out of the house by six the next morning. Having a conversation with Sue Friese sounded better than waiting for a teenage boy to send a text, so she went straight to the college.

First, she went to the classroom being used as faculty lounge, but it was locked still. The coffee cart in the lobby had just opened, so she ordered a very large drip coffee to which she added a healthy amount of cream.

If she remembered correctly, Sue Friese always had one of these paper cups in her hand. If Taylor was lucky, she got her first one early and either she or her husband Morgan picked it up themselves.

The second person at the coffee cart was Kaitlyn—the girl who died her hair gray and made art quilts.

She spotted Taylor and waved shyly. Taylor wasn't sure she wanted to invite her over, but she waved in a way that implied she was open to it.

When Kaitlyn had her coffee, she sat down at the bistro table with Taylor. "I'm still here, that's something, but I don't think I met anyone who can make a difference to my future." Kaitlyn's eyes were shadowed and red, but she still had the glow that only youth can give.

"Networking was difficult after the speaker died, I suppose." Taylor sipped her coffee, one eye on the hall to the dorms. Even if Sue and Morgan were in one of the old faculty residence apartments, they'd still come in the back way, probably.

"And I don't think the experts, the ones that have real sway…I don't think they want to make room for us."

"Us?"

"The artists. The makers. We see things differently. We're ready to make our contribution, but I get the feeling that we aren't wanted." Kaitlyn's big eyes looked up and away, for all the world, like the little sad porcelain dolls her Grandma Delma used to collect.

Taylor smiled with sympathy.

Kaitlyn was facing the difference between school and the workplace for the first time.

In school you were encouraged and rewarded for showing up, for thinking different. For showing teachers something new and never done before.

In the work world, you were competition.

The men and women teaching the workshops had trained for years to get their positions, and they knew the secret.

There wasn't money in any of this.

To make a living in the arts you had to work your art, teach your art, travel for your art, produce products to sell to other artists, and then go home and work your day job.

So very few of these quilters would ever be like Bruno and do it full time.

And his dirty secret was that he paid his bills long-arm quilting other people's projects.

Kaitlyn was young, and this was the secret you only learned over time.

"What will you do next?" Taylor asked.

Her face brightened. "Some of the girls and I—Jonah's Juvies, actually—are going to collaborate! We've got a podcast planned and maybe even a zine. I think we can make a go of it."

"That sounds wonderful." Taylor remembered when zines were called blogs, and when podcasts were for experts, but look at what Jonah had done. Of course, these young artists and craftspeople—makers, she supposed—saw their future on the Internet. It was probably the only future they could imagine for themselves.

It was the only future Taylor had been able to imagine for herself, too, not that long ago. Her mom's YouTube show that was going to save the family business. "You have my card, please let me know how to find your work once it's up and running."

"I will. I can live in the basement at my parents' house and create. Like you said, I can deliver pizza or something. There's always something for people who are willing to work hard."

"And you are willing." Taylor was telling her this, confirming the thing the young woman seemed to hope was true about herself. "Hard work will make you a better artist. You'll have more to say."

Kaitlyn looked down at the lid of her cup, a soft smile on her lips. "Thank you."

Taylor could barely hear her, but it was good enough.

A line had formed for coffee while they were talking. It was almost seven now, and the early birds were after their non-fat grande worms. At the back of the line, Morgan Friese was tapping his wing-tipped foot, his eyes glued to his Apple Watch.

Taylor's coffee wasn't empty yet, but a donut sounded like a good reason to get in line behind him and maybe start up a conversation. So, she did. "How is Sue holding up?"

He didn't look up, likely assuming no one would be speaking to him.

Taylor cleared her throat and spoke a little louder. "It's been a terribly long week. How is Sue feeling?"

This time he looked up. "She's fine."

"Is there anything I can do for her?"

A look of confused impatience flickered over his face. "Thank you. I'm sure she appreciates it. She'll be giving a closing talk this morning for the quilters who aren't staying for the Master Classes." He gave Taylor a once over and seemed to decide he didn't know her. "Don't miss it. I think it will be moving."

"I wouldn't miss it for the world." They had several more minutes together in line, but he turned away, his whole attention on his watch.

Taylor hadn't locked down how to get Sue alone, but at least she knew one place and time she could find her.

❀

THERE WAS something very church like about the set up for Sue's talk. There was even a small band in the background playing what sounded like an instrumental hymn, though Taylor couldn't name the tune.

Sue Friese wore a navy-blue pants suit. The jacket had three quarter sleeves and a Peter Pan collar giving it a fifties vibe. She had a silk scarf in rose shot through with gold threads tied around her neck, to hide the age that showed up there, despite the work that had been done to her face.

Taylor could see these details because she'd taken a spot on the side of the stage, using her tablet to make herself look official to people who didn't know better, and distracted to people who did.

Sue wasn't exiting this stage without Taylor stealing a five-minute conversation with her.

It didn't surprise her when Sue opened with prayer. She spoke generically, beginning with a simple "Bless us all as we go forward" rather than addressing one higher power or other and ending with a simple ah-men. Then her sermon began.

Taylor paid close attention, hoping Sue would tell them something more about her "dear friend" Albina Tschetter, but all they got were general-well wishes for their lives as quilters. The closest she came to addressing the death of her dear friend was when she said, "And may every stitch we make be a part of our lasting legacy, speaking for us when we no longer can."

Taylor wouldn't say the applause was tepid, but it wasn't roaring either. The crowd was small but felt full, all gathered together in fewer tables, pushed close to the stage. But despite the intimacy, they were clearly worn.

Sue shifted nervously on her feet at the end, reaching for a coffee cup that didn't exist.

Where was her coffee? Not that Taylor had seen her often this week, but this was the first time she'd seen her without it.

Sue gave up her microphone for the band, who began a little folk music set with "I'll Fly Away" completing the church vibes. But the gathered quilters did not sing along.

Sue exited the opposite side of the stage. Taylor had known there was a chance, so it didn't throw her. She had her path plotted and wove her way through the front tables. She left the door Sue had exited and found her paused in the hallway, eyes closed, hands pressed together.

"Sue, I'm glad I found you."

Sue opened her eyes, but kept her fingers pressed tip to tip, at chin height.

"I need to talk to you about Albina."

"It is still too painful for me." Sue took a thin breath and held it.

"I can imagine."

Sue stood with her back to the wall, near a corner. Taylor could move to the side and give Sue a sense of freedom which might make her open up, but it also might make her walk off.

Taylor took half a step to the side. She'd rather walk fast to catch her again than have Sue's defenses go up any farther. "I can't imagine what a shock that must have been."

Sue's eyes focused on the space that had been created between them. "There are no words to describe it."

"You'd known her a long time." Taylor tried to do the innocent and sad eye thing that Kaitlyn had just been doing over coffee.

"A few years."

"We were very lucky you convinced her to join us here," Taylor soothed, speaking as though to a child.

Sue frowned. "And yet, she could have been home with her loved ones when she passed instead of here, surrounded by strangers."

"How is her husband holding up?" Taylor pushed her nerves down, hoping Sue couldn't guess how excited she was for the answer.

Sue hesitated. "They were separated, so it was…complicated."

Truth, or a cover story? "Have you been able to talk to her parents or other family?" Taylor kept her voice soft and sympathetic.

"She didn't have any family, not close family." Sue stopped, shaking her head, though her perfect hair didn't move. "I can't talk about this. I have things I need to do to close out the Expo." Sue's eyes were frantic now, scanning the hallowed halls of Taylor's alma mater, with the displays of art hanging everywhere as though even the hallway was a gallery. Behind Sue hung a charcoal portrait of a Rosy the Riveter type, but instead of strength, the face showed only the heartbreak of war.

Sue eased herself down the hall, through that gap Taylor had left for her, but Taylor swiveled so she was beside Sue, walking step in step.

"How devastating to die from an allergic reaction."

A slight flinch, not much reaction. "I don't know that they've determined her cause of death yet."

"I see. I'm sorry. You know what rumor mills events like this can be."

"Was there something you needed?" Sue's syllables were clipped and her pace increased as though she were running to the lobby now where many halls branched off with many ways to escape.

"I was hoping you'd agree to an interview for my program," Taylor said.

"Absolutely not. Under no circumstances." Sue's words popped like a cap gun.

"I think your experience could be very meaningful to my audience." Taylor paused. "I'm Flour Sax, and we are the reason you are here."

"I do not owe you for this." Sue waved her hand in the direction of the dining hall. "You think you can capitalize on my grief and profit from it. Don't think you're the first person to catch me in the hall and ask for favors. Consider this: some teenager just made a million dollars off of the death of my friend. A million dollars. Can you imagine?" The color had drained from her face, her eyes were narrow. "I put a stop to that, and I won't hesitate to stop you as well. I don't care what you think you did to bring Cascadia Expo to this campus. We are only here because I decided we would be. I owe you nothing." She said those last four words slowly. "You will not get a word from me, and I will sue you if you quote me online."

Taylor stared, blown away by the heat of Sue's reaction. "I

think you misunderstand my motives, but I won't hold your harsh words against you."

"I hope very much you will hold my words close to your heart. You are all vultures. This is the last Cascadia Quilt Expo. We will never do this again."

Sue pushed through the large, carved front doors of Comfort College of Art and Craft. Taylor let her go.

## CHAPTER FOURTEEN

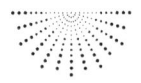

Taylor's phone immediately pinged a Snapchat alert.
Before checking it, she looked around. Trish Weaver, the lady who had gotten her a security guard the day before, was nowhere to be seen. Carrie Kyle and the other amateur sleuths weren't around either.

Valerie Ritz, the young woman for whom money was no object, was just turning the corner, but she couldn't have known Taylor had been in private conversation with Sue.

Taylor opened Snapchat to find a snap from Jonah himself this time. "I'm keeping a low profile for all of our sakes." His voice was deeper than Taylor remembered. "The Juvies are great, trust them, okay? That's all I've been trying to say with the snaps. Trust them. Trust me. Trust us. Trust Belle and trust yourself."

Taylor found herself filling with irritation. If he had time to send a stupid little Snap, surely he had time to make a call. "I trust all of them, but I trust you more. Albina's agent is there. His name is Trent Green. You have to talk to him." And with that, the snap ended.

She was sure if she tried to respond, or text, or call, she'd get no answer, but she called anyway. "Jonah, call your mother. And what do you want me to ask this Trent Green?" She left the voice message wondering if she should send a million more, because those two thoughts, her first thoughts, were just the tip of the iceberg regarding what she wanted to say.

While she waited for a reply she googled "Trent Green literary agent" and found a website with his headshot. She wasn't sure she'd recognize him in the wild, but she'd try.

She checked the lobby turned café, then the dining room, the classroom set aside as a faculty lounge, the work room, and the marketplace. She had pushed open the door to the men's room when a warm, friendly, deep voice stopped her. "Wrong door, Taylor," Bruno Stultze chuckled.

"Whoops!" Taylor laughed it off and acted like it was a mistake.

"Got a minute?" he asked.

"Sure."

They walked around the corner together. "I'm sorry I haven't been able to make good my offer of dinner. You're going to think I'm a fair-weather friend."

"Not at all. This has been a crazy week." Crazy felt right, as Taylor reflected on the emotional roller coaster the blooper reel of her mom had been putting her through.

"I was silly excited to meet Roxy—and you—I'm a big fan of your mom's show. And yours of course."

Taylor spotted Trent Green—the man himself—out of the corner of her eye. It had to be him. He was the only tall, slender man with a thousand-dollar haircut and even more expensive suit in all of Comfort. He was heading away from the general direction of the bathrooms. "Do you mind if we walk and talk?" She stared after Trent.

"Uh, sure. Yeah. So…I mean, you have my number…and Roxy does, too, right? This Expo is really slipping away from us. I have to leave early to be at the next event in time."

"Um hm."

Trent had turned toward the fiber arts wing of the school,

where most of the Expo action was being held. Taylor followed him.

Bruno did his best to keep up. "Do I remember you said you ladies aren't going to the fiber arts festival in Santa Fe?"

"Shoot! I lost him." Trent had disappeared at the turning of the hall. He must have gone into one of the classrooms, but which one? There were a dozen lining this wing of the school. "Sorry, what?"

"What's going on here?" Bruno asked.

"I'm trying to connect with Albina's agent."

"Why didn't you say so? I have a meeting with him in a few minutes."

Taylor stopped. "You're the best, you know? Everyone adores you, and they're right."

His smile started at his eyes and spread across his face. "I do my best. I'm meeting him in ten minutes at the diner in town. We're having a lunch meeting. You can come with."

🐚

Reuben's Diner was at the far end of Main Street, but this was Comfort, and it was about a mile away from the college. Taylor would have walked if it had just been her, but the day was a soaking drizzle, the kind that seeps into your bones. Bruno drove them both in his rented midsized sedan.

The diner, whose atmosphere had pressed pause somewhere in the 1970s, was quiet. Only one other table had guests. And of course, they were Taylor's Grandma and Grandpa Quinny, who were supposed to be at the beach with her Grandpa Ernie.

Taylor hung back as Bruno greeted Trent and hoped her grandparents wouldn't notice her. Not that she didn't love them, but they could be kind of a lot.

Bruno seemed like the type of man who could be trusted to make an introduction.

Trent, on the other hand, looked past Taylor like she wasn't there. She stepped forward, next to her new friend Bruno, as though she had always been invited to this meeting, but it didn't help. Trent's attention was fixed somewhere behind her.

Taylor gave him a firm smile.

"Bruno, let's go talk." Trent moved quickly toward a booth at the back of the restaurant.

"Sounds good." Bruno followed him. Taylor wanted to join them, but it was a short booth for two, with no other chairs nearby to steal. As though he had done it on purpose, she was left on the outside. Trent Green was one hundred percent smooth.

A motion from the other side of the restaurant caught her eye. "Taylor. Taylor!" And the voice that could not be ignored followed. "Come over here, we need to talk."

Taylor mutely obeyed the summons and joined her Quinn grandparents at their table.

"Sit down and eat something, you look exhausted." Grandma Quinny's style of concern could only be called martinet.

"Thank you?" Taylor smiled weakly.

"Now, don't be like that." Grandma Quinny scooted a menu over. "We've ordered big platter breakfasts. This Quilt Expo you're running is exhausting you."

"I love a good breakfast for lunch." Grandpa Quinny grinned.

"I'm not running it."

Grandma Quinny waved away the correction. "Everyone around here knows you're responsible for bringing all this business to us."

Taylor wondered if it was appreciated, and also wondered what business the Expo had brought to her retired grandparents' lives.

"Strawberries." Grandpa Quinny seemed to read her mind. "Jam. Candies. Mostly jam. Your cousins Coco and Lilly are running the booth at the marketplace."

Taylor furrowed her brow. Cousins Coco and Lilly? She tried

to place them in a family tree she had recently realized incorporated the whole town. "Jack and Hannah's girls!" She almost shouted as she remembered. Hannah was the daughter of Grandpa Quinny's baby sister. They lived somewhere on the southern Oregon Coast.

"They're visiting for a while to help. Lovely young girls."

"That's nice."

"Their parents have been calling nonstop, not to mention your aunt Jeanie." Grandma Quinny looked off toward the kitchen, but no staff were forth coming. "What with the death of your author-friend and the string of murders in this town, they are all more than a bit worried."

"I'm sure it was just natural causes." Taylor's hand went to her phone, and she glanced at Trent and Bruno.

"I'm sure you'll find out if it's otherwise." Grandma Quinny nodded in approval. "You're very good at that."

Taylor sat up. "Excuse me?"

"You're very good at getting to the bottom of things. I expect you'll resolve this whole issue quickly, if there is one to resolve. But in the meantime, please look out for your cousins."

Taylor wasn't sure she had room in her life for more cousins, but she nodded.

Bruno waived down a server and handed her a wad of cash, though they hadn't had time to eat much

"I'm sorry I can't stay to eat." Taylor also stood.

"We understand." Her grandfather reached his hand out to his wife to stop her from arguing. "Ernie is at the farm right now having a bite with Boggy and Hudson. We'll go back to the beach tomorrow. I was restless. Wanted to come home for a night. By the way, that's a nice young man you've got there.

"Thanks, Grandpa." She suspected Grandpa Ernie had been the restless one but didn't pursue it. As much as she loved these guys her mind really was on other things.

Bruno and Trent stood and went to the door.

"Sorry!" she called out as she followed the men out to Main Street.

The two men got into Bruno's rental car.

Bruno glanced back with an apologetic look as he drove off without her.

Taylor half expected a new Snapchat from her mom, but she was alone in the rain. No message from Jonah telling her what she was supposed to ask Trent Green, either.

She thought about going back in and having a meal with her grandparents, but instead, decided to think through her dilemma. After all, Grandma Quinny herself had endorsed her ability to get to the bottom of things. What would she ask Trent Green if she could?

The Flour Sax crowd were being looked at closely because of all the money they were making online. Perhaps someone else was profiting from Albina's death. Like, for example, the agent. Would he get a cut from the royalties or was his deal done with signing? She could ask that, to start, but would he answer?

Maybe she could start with questions about Albina herself. Like, was the young lady an actress who had turned author? Or maybe she could trick him into admitting she was an actress just playing an author. Her favorite TV detectives always managed to trick people into major clue reveals like that.

Taylor hustled down the block to her shop, waved at Willa who was working the register, and hopped upstairs to Clay's apartment. He was downstairs working, or at least he ought to be, and his place was a quiet shelter from the storm where she could think. And blocks closer than her own house. She pulled up Amazon on her phone. Albina Tschetter had an author page with the same photo on it that had been used in the Quilt Expo Program. The cover preview of her book showed the same picture on the back as well. Depending on Albina's contract, she might receive some sort of action on each sale.

But what about other shows she might have been trying for?

If she had been hired to play an author, would getting an acting job be too risky for the person behind the scheme?

Maybe.

But how rich were authors of Amish fiction likely to get?

Taylor Googled it.

Pages and pages of links to blogs and articles popped up. They covered everything about how indie authors were getting rich, this one had hit a million dollars, that one had a movie deal, but nothing about authors with a publisher. Perhaps because they still had discretion. Hard to say. Nobody was spilling the numbers regarding how much money authors of Amish fiction made.

Taylor did, however, find an article about a book she had heard of. A wildly popular Western series that had just been made into a mini-series on HBO. She remembered it well. It was the one that got picked up after the author had died.

Taylor sat back and stared at her screen.

The story had been simple enough.

A Shaker girl moved out West and fell in love with a Chinese doctor.

Fish out of water. Romance. Bonnets. Forbidden love.

Very Romeo and Juliet meets Tombstone.

It had been a moderately popular series of books, and then the author had died. Tragically and young.

Though the author had died over a year ago, the books were still holding tight on the best sellers' lists. Had this been the macabre marketing plan for Quilted in the County?

Taylor needed to talk to Trent Green. This death-best-seller-movie deal was motive if ever there was one, and if anyone knew who'd benefit from it all, Albina's agent did. Taylor texted Bruno. "Is Trent ready for me?"

He responded this time. "I convinced him to eat at Loggers instead of the diner. He needed to loosen up. Come on by."

Taylor ran out of Clay's place and down to her house for the car. She could walk to Loggers. She could walk anywhere, but this felt like a car emergency.

She found them at the local bar, both more than one martini into their early afternoon.

"Have one on us!" Trent was a different man a few drinks in. "We're celebrating our next best seller. Memoirs are yuge right now! Yuge! Any quilter in America will buy this. Do you know how many quilters there are in America?"

"About 3.75 million?" Taylor quipped.

He widened his eyes. "Oh, she's smart. Very smart. Watch her. Get her a drink."

Taylor shook her head. Bruno touched the side of his nose. So, this is what he had done for her. Loosened him up. Hopefully Trent wasn't too loose. Loggers, the local bar, was on the dive-side of the bar spectrum. Not the kind of place Trent looked at home, but he didn't act out of place, arm slung over the back of the booth.

"You only deal in best sellers, I bet." Taylor leaned suggestively forward.

"In my dreams." His eyes closed as a smile stretched across his face. "I dream of best sellers. All of them. All the time."

He was drunk. Flat drunk. Taylor had to jump in with both feet. "Was Albina one of your bestsellers?"

He gripped his forehead with his hand. "Poor Albina! She could have been. She really could have been. She was young, ripe, you know what I mean? Her books, not so much, but her personality? She could have sold anything to anyone, and with time, she was going to make those stupid books the best thing I ever signed."

"What about her acting dreams? Would that have ruined everything?"

He dropped his hand and looked serious. Maybe he wasn't so drunk after all. "Are you kidding me? A TV star with a series of books? That's straight up money. It was the kind of thing dreams are made of—and money. That's the kind of advertising you cannot buy. The only thing better would be if she could manage to have a love affair with a movie star, and, did you see her? It was only a matter of time."

"You must be devastated."

"Utterly. Her death is the worst. Nobody wants to see a beautiful young person die."

Taylor tried not to let her disappointment show, but this wasn't what she had expected to hear. "So, you don't know if say, her sales have had a spike since the news?"

He held his hands palm up. "Who knows. Those reports won't be ready for months. Months. Maybe? Maybe a little spike the day the news hit, but nothing we'll hear about any time soon."

"Is there anything we can do for her family? This must be a terrible shock for them."

"I don't think she had a family. No one she ever told me about, anyway."

From the corner of her eye Taylor spotted a skinny young woman she had met at the brief meeting of Amish fiction fans-turned amateur detectives. She remembered her as being somewhat threatening. The girl didn't look old enough to be in a bar. She walked slowly, her eye on Taylor.

"See that girl over there?" Taylor pointed her out to Trent. "Keep an eye on her. She's your next best seller."

He rolled his eyes. "She tell you that? Everyone thinks they are, you know, but Bruno, Bruno here is the real deal." He patted Bruno on the back.

The thin young woman stopped and stared at Taylor. She didn't know what Taylor had said. She just knew Taylor had pointed at her and gotten a strong reaction out of the man she was sitting with.

"I guess I'll let you boys get back to your celebration." Taylor got up. "Have another one on me, if you can."

Trent erupted in laughter. "Are you kidding? In the state I'm in? I'm calling it a day."

Taylor looked at her watch. Pretty early to call it a day.

"I know, I know, but I've been very stressed." He stood up and shook Bruno's hand. "It's been a real pleasure, sir."

"Same." Bruno engulfed Trent Green's hand in his own. "I can't wait to get you the manuscript."

Bruno walked Taylor out. "How about that dinner?"

"You just had lunch."

"It might be our only chance."

"Then we'd better take it." They walked out to the drizzly, gray day.

"I've read all the visitor pamphlets for the area and there's one place I'd really like to go."

Taylor had been key in getting the visitor pamphlets' ready in time for the Expo, and suspected he was going to pick Berry Noir, their fine dining winery restaurant.

"It might not sound like much, but the Flour Mill Museum has a lunch café and a tour."

She almost laughed.

Of course he didn't want to take *her* to Berry Noir. His interest was definitely in Roxy.

"Why not?" They both had cars, so they drove separately to the mill museum just three blocks down the highway, right on the edge of town.

Taylor's phone hadn't pinged in hours. She was almost sorry. She'd learned that Albina's death had been a grave disappointment to her agent and that felt like the kind of thing Jonah's Juvie's should have noticed and reported to him so he could send her a little thumbs up from her mom.

She would have loved a thumbs up from her mom right now.

There was a surprisingly large crowd at the museum. Perhaps folks who had come to town for the Expo were looking for things to do that weren't so…murderous.

Bruno bought tickets from the little booth in front of the building. "You're still worrying over Albina's death, aren't you?"

"Yeah, I am. I met a lady at the Expo who I had a nice connection with. Just a couple of hours later they hauled her down to the station. For all I know she killed that poor girl, but she reminded me of myself, so I don't want to think she did." Taylor mused on the situation with Beth Trager.

"And you want to help her," Bruno stated.

"I do."

"I get it. You're good people. You help others. But you know what? You need a break. Give yourself this hour to be entertained. Nothing bad is going to happen in an hour."

A local woman who usually bought her quilt fabric at Comfort Cozies, a newer shop down the block from Flour Sax, was leading today's tour. Her name tag said Shawna. She began with a brief history of Oregon, starting with the Yamhelas Indian Tribe, part of the Kalapooian family that lived in the Willamette Valley before the colonizers came.

She ventured through the French Catholic missionaries, the Methodists used by the United States to grab the land, the British trappers and traders, and then the Oregon trail.

And they hadn't even gotten to the milling room yet.

But Shawna's smile was big, and she was enthusiastic.

Taylor spotted the shaggy haired Amish-Anonymous member who had spoken with Mackenzie Forte to her left. The tall skinny girl who had been at the bar was with her.

"And then came the murders." Shawna the tour guide's voice dropped, and a hush spread over the small crowd.

"Our little town of Comfort, Oregon sprung up in this fertile valley like spring flowers, many years after the pioneers of the 1850s wagon trains had come through. But even though their wagon train had followed a heavily rutted path, it was still a hardship, and when they finally arrived, they knew they were at rest. They had found their Comfort.

Taylor was almost positive when they had studied town history in school the name Comfort had actually come from the last name of the wagon train captain, but she didn't correct the tour guide. After all, it could have been both.

"But the *comfort* didn't last."

The small group of visitors politely "ooooh'd" at that.

"This flour mill had been erected by the wealthy and successful Love family almost immediately on settling in this area. But the *love* quickly turned to hate."

Taylor glanced at her watch. The thought of a sandwich at the little café when this was over wasn't quite enough to make her want to stay. Not with both a solid bar burger up the road at Loggers or a nice diner burger down the road at Reuben's Diner. Shawna, the tour guide, continued with her tale, but Taylor's mind wandered.

Bruno, however, seemed mesmerized.

Bruno.

He was a nice man, and it was kind of him to have lunch with her. Since her phone was out, she sent a text to Roxy to meet them at the museum for a sandwich. It was the least she could do since he'd let her in on his meeting with Trent. Then she texted Hudson. Maybe, just maybe he was free too.

Hudson got back to her amazingly quick, but it was a disappointing sad face emoji followed by a "sorry!" He must have had to go straight back to a job after his meal with their grandfathers.

Her relationship with Hudson was a bright spot in her life right now. While he was definitely her boyfriend, they weren't rushing into anything like moving in together or getting a ring. They were just enjoying life, two grown adults in love. She felt her face warming up.

Love was a wonderful thing, and the best part was that it seemed to grow over time. She'd liked Hudson, been attracted to him early on. But as they spent more time together, his good qualities seemed to grow both in number and in goodness. The way he didn't leave messages waiting for over long. Or how he always made time for his grandpa, or dad, or her family. The way he listened without trying to jump in with a solution. He said years of counseling had taught him a few things. She appreciated it.

He was cranky in the morning, this was true, but he wasn't mean-spirited about it. And sometimes his jokes weren't all that funny, but whose were, really?

Her phone buzzed—a snap from her mom—Jonah, rather?

No, another text from Hudson. "*tomorrow. I'm yours. Any time, any place.*"

She smiled, then sent him a smiley face.

He sent a thumbs up.

They'd get to the details eventually.

The group was moving forward into the main room of the mill where the milling had occurred. Shawna the guide pointed to a rafter far above their heads. "And that was where they found him hanging."

Taylor stared.

She'd definitely missed something in the story.

Bruno let out a low whistle.

Her phone alerted her of another text. This time it was Roxy apologizing about not being able to join them for lunch.

Taylor shrugged and slipped the phone into her pocket. She thought Bruno was a catch for someone like Roxy but that didn't mean Roxy had to agree.

They moved through the milling room to a deck from where they could watch the wheel turn. Rather, they could stand and look at the wheel.

"You might be wondering what a water wheel is doing on dry ground like this, especially when surrounded by creeks and rivers the way we are. When the mill was electrified, the company rebuilt on this location. When the mill closed, as some of you might remember…" Shawna stopped to make eye contact with an elderly woman who stood a few people away from Taylor, "the historic society raised funds to move the original mill to this land and set it up as a museum."

Taylor stifled a yawn.

The group moved to an outbuilding and heard the story of a Hawaiian family who'd come to Oregon to work for the

Hudson's Bay Company in the early 1800s—by the time the mill opened the family had been in Oregon for two generations. The youngest son of the family had lived in the tiny cabin at the back of the mill, as a caretaker and security. They were keen to prevent another lynching.

Lynching! She had missed something.

She furrowed her brows and stared at Shawna. She knew her from around the town but didn't know her. Was she a historian? Paid staff? A volunteer? Who had been lynched and why hadn't she been listening?

How had there been Hawaiians in Comfort longer than English people?

And shouldn't she have known all of this?

"Thank you for taking the short tour of our little bit of history," Shawna said. "A story of love and hate, of envy and anger, but ultimately, the story of our country represented by one little flour mill."

Taylor let out a puff of breath. Who had been lynched while she was texting Roxy? Who had been angry and envious?

She wanted to go back and start over but paying attention this time.

"If you follow me, I'll take you to the The Miller's Daughter, our sandwich shop. I'm sure you all understand now how it got its name."

The crowd let out a sentimental little, "Awe."

Bruno held back.

"Not a big history fan?"

"My mind wandered. I missed something important, I think."

Bruno laughed. "I'll tell you over sandwiches."

The skinny young girl Taylor had spotted at the bar lurked near the door of the café. Her eyes seemed to bore holes straight through Taylor's skull. Taylor shivered.

## CHAPTER FIFTEEN

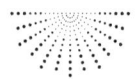

As they stepped into the newest building on the mill site, Taylor's phone pinged a Snapchat alert. "Do you see a bathroom?" she asked Bruno.

"Thataway." He pointed towards the main mill building which had a vintage tin restrooms sign secured to one wall.

Taylor headed there and locked herself in a stall.

The snap was the one she'd been hoping for all day. Her mom, smiling proudly, "We're getting the hang of this." Another voice could be heard in the background, Roxy saying, "We sure are!"

"I'm proud of us," Laura Quinn continued. "This is going to do it, you know? It's going to fix everything."

Then Roxy laughed happily.

Then the video ended.

Tears sprung to Taylor's eyes.

Sure, this was Jonah's way of saying that the two of them, or more likely, Jonah, his "Juvies", Taylor, Roxy, and whoever else wanted to get involved, were going to make a difference in the investigation. She knew that, but she didn't feel it. She felt like her mom was proud, and it hurt so good.

She stared at her phone wondering if she should play it

again, knowing that if she did, it would be the last time she could, and then her phone rang. A sound she had heard so rarely through the years it took her a moment to remember what it was. "This is Taylor."

"I've got to make this quick." The voice on the other end of the phone had grown familiar recently, what with his Internet fame.

"Jonah!" She almost shouted but remembered where she was.

"Shh," he cautioned.

"What's up?" Taylor's word choice was casual, but her heart was beating out of her chest. The myriad of things she wanted to say to him had flown away now that she had him on the line.

"Albina needs you," Jonah began, lowering his voice so that it was both deeper and quieter.

"Oh, come on…" Taylor sat on the toilet. "How can Albina need anyone right now. She's dead."

"You know what I mean. The Juvies are a good group, but you're the only one at the Expo who knows how to catch a killer."

"I'm already doing the only things I can do, you know?" Taylor chewed on her lip. "But I want to do more. You had me hunt down her agent, but I'd swear he's not a part of this. He was really cut up over her loss."

"He doesn't make more money off this?" Jonah sounded surprised.

"It didn't sound like it. You know, I think I could do more if I knew more. Are you withholding anything at all I could use? Like maybe her real name? Her family?"

"She's Allie Mackenzie. The Tschetter thing came from the Amish lady she knew. The Forte from her stage name might be made up but since Tschetter came from a real person, we're still looking for the source. No family. Raised by a single dad who died a couple of years ago. Once the Juvies got me her real name, I got the rest."

"So, is she an actor who writes or an actor paid to play a writer? Trent seemed to think she was a writer."

"You've got to find that out. You're there with her agent, so you have access. Get him alone if possible. Buy him a drink but don't let him get drunk. I've heard he lies when he drinks."

"Great. He was drunk when I talked to him," Taylor huffed.

"You've got to try again."

Taylor paused, then asked the big question. "Are you sure this isn't just because it's good ratings for you?"

"Good ratings?" He sounded honestly hurt. "I am paying out money to keep my website up. YouTube shut me down, and U of O wants to have a conversation."

She let out a sharp breath. "That can't be good."

"It's not, I promise you."

"You had a good run though…" A weight had lifted from her shoulders but it wasn't rejoicing at his failure. It was rejoicing that he wasn't a bad guy. The innocence and hurt in his voice sounded so sincere. Not that she wanted him to hurt. That was the last thing she wanted.

"You've got to talk to Trent. That's all. To help Albina."

"Sorry, Jonah." Taylor's relief faded into sorrow. Disappointment for this kid, and his mom, and all of them. Frustration that a situation so wildly out of their control had halted all their blessings.

"You're not going to help?"

"I am, I am. I'm just sorry about all of this. It's not what was supposed to happen." She closed her eyes and leaned back on the pipes that fed the public toilet. The world wasn't supposed to look anything at all like this right now. "Hey, wait. Why aren't you in school?"

He was silent.

"Don't give up on your education because of this, okay?"

He still didn't respond.

Back when Taylor had been in school, everyone had done their four years and then gone off to college. But the kids in

Belle's general age group seemed to be pushing themselves to leave early, by hook or crook, whether it was wise or not. She suspected this was Belle's influence, but who knew. Now Jonah…was just leaving? That bothered her. A million dollars in the bank didn't last very long.

"Just don't quit. I'll help you any way I can—I mean I'll help Albina anyway I can—so long as you get home and get back to school."

Jonah sighed on the other end of the phone. "Okay. But I can't yet. It's too hot down there."

"Have you been getting threats?" Taylor stood in shock and pushed the toilet stall door open.

"Not exactly, but I didn't like it. As soon as they catch whoever did this, I'll come home, and get back to school, and make up for whatever I missed. I swear."

"Okay." Taylor stared at herself in the mirror on the wall across from her. Her face had blanched, her eyes were shadowed. She had done her hair and makeup and tried to look professional today, but she still had the disheveled look of a woman in crisis. The look she'd been carrying around for two years. If ever she got herself together again, Hudson would be shocked by how healthy and nice she could look. "We got this, Jonah." She said it as much to the vision of herself in the mirror as to him. She dug deep into her newly fortified sense of self, the strength her counselor was helping her find, and tried to pass it along the phone to her young friend.

"Thanks Taylor," he said and then ended the call.

Taylor shoved her phone back into her purse and stepped forward to wash her hands.

The slender Amish fiction fan who had been haunting Taylor through the day stepped in front of the sink, glowering. "What exactly was supposed to happen?"

Taylor stood still, holding her breath. What had this girl heard, and how much of it should have been a secret?

"You will tell me where she is. You know that, right?"

"Who?" Taylor whispered.

The girl leaned in. It was a small bathroom. Taylor could smell her baby powder scented anti-perspirant. "Don't mess with me." She brought her fingertips up and shoved Taylor's shoulder.

Taylor dodged to the right, but the girl blocked her with a shoulder, knocking Taylor into the hollow metal frame of the toilet stalls.

Taylor lunged and grabbed at the girl, getting a handful of baggy flannel shirt for her effort. She pulled the girl to her. "What is your problem?" Taylor's heart raced. Strength wasn't feeding her now, fear was.

The girl twisted so expertly Taylor barely felt her move, but she was behind Taylor now, like a ghost, almost. She wrapped her skinny arms around Taylor's waist and rammed her skull into the back of Taylor's head.

"For the love! Knock it off!" Taylor elbowed the girl's side as hard as she could, but it was her funny bone to skin and bones and hurt Taylor worse than the girl.

Taylor smashed the heel of her practical shoe into the girl's foot.

The girl wavered for half a second.

Taylor took her chance and threw herself against the girl's arms, where her hands were clasped, but the girl tightened her grip around Taylor like a Chinese handcuff.

It was getting hard to catch a breath. Taylor bent over, pulling the girl off the floor, then ran forward.

This girl might be strong, but she was light.

Taylor turned, and slammed the girl bottom first into the wall behind her.

The girl's arms loosened, and she groaned.

Taylor broke free, spun around and punched the girl in the face.

The girl's head turned with the impact, and then she dropped her face into her hands.

Taylor's hand screamed in pain.

The girl lunged at Taylor, grabbed her hair in two handfuls and hit Taylor in the nose with her forehead.

Now Taylor's nose and hand were both fully aware that this girl was made of stone.

"Who are you? Are you trying to kill me too?" Taylor scuttled backward but didn't feel like running or calling the police. Something about the girl's attack spoke of fear, and something about her defense stance, head down, shoulders hunched, made her look incredibly young, like a child.

"Quit saying she's dead!" The girl was breathing heavy, and her dark mop of hair had fallen to the sides revealing a pale childlike face.

"What was supposed to happen? You told Jonah this wasn't what was supposed to happen."

"We were talking about the show, our YouTube show, the TikTok, all of that."

"I heard you talking about Albina and helping her. She's not dead. She can't be. Just tell me where my sister is." Her face crumpled. What had been anger dissolved into the tears of a child.

"Allie McKenzie doesn't have any family."

The shaggy haired girl choked back a sob. "How do you know her name?"

"Jonah's Juvie's. They know everything. Surely you know that." The crying girl was much less threatening now. She must have had a metric ton of anxiety compressed inside of her that had finally exploded.

"I know about the Juvies. I know about Jonah, and I know about you. You're all making money from this, but Jonah wouldn't have killed anyone. That's why I know she's not really dead. So where is she? She couldn't have died from her stupid allergies. Where is my sister?"

"She didn't have any family," Taylor said it again, even though it was a mean thing to do. She wanted to prompt more outpouring from the girl. When people explode like this, they spill information unconsciously. The last thing Taylor wanted was for the child to get her guard up again.

"Quit saying that! I'm her family. She was my sister. For four years, while our parents lived together, she was my sister. I saw her on a TV interview. I've been looking for her for three months now, and I finally found her here, but now they say she's dead."

"Why are you with Amish Anonymous instead of Jonah's Juvies?" Taylor asked.

"I don't care about Jonah, or quilts, or anything. But Allie wrote an Amish book, and that's how I found her here." Her eyes seemed to have emptied all their tears. Her face was flushed but uninjured, despite the punch that seemed to have broken Taylor's hand.

The skinny youth was shaking, every sinewy fiber of her scrawny frame.

"How old are you?" Taylor asked, gently.

Her mouth compressed into a line.

"Oh please, please say you aren't a child," Taylor muttered, thinking about how miserable she'd be for the rest of her life if she'd punched a child in the face.

"I'm not a child," the girl spoke through clenched teeth.

"You're eighteen, aren't you?"

The girl crossed her arms over her chest.

"And for a few years, this young woman was your glamorous older sister. Oh, honey." Taylor opened her arms for a hug, and the childlike young woman fell into them sobbing. "Did I hurt you? I will never forgive myself. Let me get you to the doctor, please."

"Just take me to my sister." Her words came through sobs, so desperate, so weak.

"Where is your mother?" Taylor murmured, stroking the girl's hair.

"She's in prison."

"Shh. Let me take care of you." Taylor patted the girl's thin shoulder and hushed her. She was at least two inches taller than Taylor and as strong as an ox, but she felt like a baby deer. Taylor held her and let her cry. A meal with Bruno was off again. She might have given this broken person a concussion. She needed to see a doctor.

When the girl had calmed down she led her out of the bathroom. "Bruno?" Taylor found him spinning a rack of post cards in the café. "Bruno, I'm so sorry, but I need to get to Urgent Care over in McMinnville."

He lifted an eyebrow but didn't question her.

Taylor ran the shaggy haired girl—Lizeth was her name—to an immediate care clinic a half an hour away. She didn't know what the girl told the doctor, but while they were there, Taylor had a doctor check out her hand. Not broken, but it was planning to hurt long enough to teach her not to punch children in the face.

THE ATMOSPHERE in Taylor's little Audi was tense and awkward as they drove back to Comfort. Taylor attempted to bridge the long empty space. "Where are you staying?"

"In a four-person dorm room at the school."

"Do you feel safe there?"

She shook her head.

"If I offer to let you stay with me, will you feel safer?" Taylor hated leaving the girl at the school with strangers and was greatly relieved when Lizeth nodded. Anyone at the Expo could have poisoned Albina, and if they were to find out Lizeth was related…

"Then let's go get your stuff." They collected Albina's small bag from a crowded dorm room and went back to Taylor's little house just up the street. "How far from home are you?"

"I go to school in Portland."

"You have a dorm room there?" Taylor asked.

"Yeah."

"Do you have transportation to get back home?"

"Yes. A bus ticket."

"Lizeth, I think your sister is dead. From what I can tell, she died of a reaction to an allergy. Can you tell me what she's allergic too?"

"Let me think." Lizeth slumped into the sofa.

Taylor's head ached as bad as her hand, and though Lizeth had no fractures or concussion, she was beginning to bruise up around the eye. She had an ice pack from the doctor, but she just held it in her hand, squeezing it gently.

"How is your eye? Do you want to put that on it?"

Lizeth lifted the ice pack to her eye. "I remember she was allergic to dogs."

"Anything else?"

"She never ate tomatoes, but I don't know if that was an allergy."

Taylor's phone pinged.

That was well-timed.

Laura Quinn's warm smile stared out across the work table. "It makes her face get red and itchy. But does that matter when a Mounds Bar is around? Nooooo…," and she laughed. At some point in the past she had been talking about Taylor's coconut allergy to Roxy when they should have been filming. Taylor looked around and shivered. Her theory that Jonah was being fed lines would have to be abandoned. She and Lizeth were alone, in Taylor's own house. He had no way of knowing they were talking about allergies at this exact second.

"Who's that?" Lizeth sat up, interested.

"Um…" Taylor stared at the phone as the snap disappeared.

"Her voice sounds like yours." Lizeth fiddled with her ice bag. "Sorry. Didn't mean to listen in, but you had it on speaker phone, I think."

"Yeah. Uh…" Taylor set her phone face down on the nicked and dinged coffee table. "Have you ever heard of contact dermatitis? Or maybe Oral Allergy Syndrome?" Taylor changed the subject from the snap itself. Even though she had to share the clips with Jonah, they still felt like they were just for her.

"No." Lizeth shook her head.

"Contact dermatitis is when you get a rash from your allergies. Sometimes people can get a rash from eating something that is similar to their hay fever triggers. That's called Oral Allergy Syndrome part. Did your sister ever get rashes that you remember?"

"One time, yeah. She bought some makeup that made her break out. She was pretty mad. That was shortly before our parents broke up."

"Do you remember anything about what brand of make-up it was?"

"Nuh uh." She laid her head on the back of the sofa, the ice pack to her eye.

Taylor's phone chimed again, this time a text from Jonah. "*News from the Juvies. Important.*"

"*Do you want to call?*"

"*no. They saw you with AA.*" She assumed he meant Amish-Anonymous.

"Lizeth," she corrected him.

"*Yeah, saw you getting her stuff and leaving. She knows stuff about Albina. That's why I sent snap about allergies. To remind you to ask. Belle said it was too vague. Ask AA about allergies.*"

"*Was just doing that,*" Taylor replied.

"*Awesome. V. Ritz, a good Juvie, sent a message.*"

"*I know her. Money no object.*"

"*Right. Her. She heard your man Bruno make a date with a gray haired girl. 9 pm tonight a Reuben's. Will get him a lot of money.*"

"*Bruno is not my man.*" She almost told him about Bruno's interest in Roxy but remembered at the last minute that Jonah might not like thinking about his mom having a romantic life. "*What does this have to do with Albina?*"

"*Don't know yet. You find out.*"

Taylor gritted her teeth. If this did have something to do with

Albina, she needed to go, but she hated leaving Lizeth. *"What about Lizeth. Don't want to leave her alone."* Taylor rolled her neck and felt a satisfying pop, but it didn't relax her.

*"Definitely don't. She could be in real danger."*

Taylor looked across the little room at Lizeth. She was injured, but that was Taylor's fault. Sort of. And sort of Lizeth's fault. Taylor had been careful-ish about only defending herself. But still. Taylor had a sinking feeling that Lizeth was in more danger now than she had been before they met.

## CHAPTER SIXTEEN

Taylor was glad her punch hadn't broken Lizeth's jaw. It was bad enough to sit across from the young lady while her eye got blacker. She couldn't have handled it if Lizeth had to drink her dinner.

"It's okay." The way Lizeth shoveled in another bite of country fried steak made Taylor wonder when she had eaten last. "I attacked you. You didn't know I didn't have a weapon or something. Plus, I'm strong. Wiry strength. You get it when you have to fight for a living."

"As nice as you are to say that, there will never be a time when I think it is okay that I hit you."

She smiled. "Thank you for dinner."

"The least I could do. I remember being your age. College kids rarely get enough to eat." Taylor picked at her meatloaf. It had sounded comforting but sat heavy on her plate.

Lizeth dabbed at her mouth with a napkin. "I have a meal plan at school. I get plenty of food."

Taylor didn't believe her. The meal plan only fed Lizeth while she was on campus, which she definitely was not at the moment.

"Besides, Mom gets out in six months."

Taylor didn't want to explain to her that a mother with a

record would have a hard time finding well-paying work, so she didn't.

They had a booth across the dining room from Bruno. Kaitlyn, the young woman with the trendy gray dye job and the idea that she was going to make some kind of huge cultural impact with her artwork sat across from him.

It was nine, and Lizeth and Taylor were both hungry.

They were too far away for Taylor to listen in, and in the far corner, so she couldn't walk past slowly on her way to the bathroom or the front door, either

Her phone pinged, so she got it out. This time it was a video of Jonah. She almost turned it off. "First, thank you all for your hard work. Second, we are almost there. Third, there is a new video. Go watch it for a summary of the work so far." It blinked off.

"How much do you know about Jonah Lang?" Taylor asked.

"Just that all the girls love him. I tried to watch one of his videos about my sister, but it kind of made me mad. I could see right through him. He just wants attention."

"You're probably right." Taylor tapped her phone screen and considered this. Jonah had wanted attention and money. Or he wouldn't have gone to all the work to become an influencer, or whatever his weird hybrid online life could be called. But he had been sincere in his fear and in his desire to help figure out what had happened to the author. She was sure of this. And even if his motives had been less than perfect, couldn't the information he'd been gathering be useful? She posed this question to Lizeth.

Lizeth scrunched up her face. "Watch his video if you want, but what does anybody here know? You were the only person who acted like you knew anything, so I really thought you were in on the fraud. But you sure don't seem to be now."

"Beth Trager from the online group Amish Anonymous acted that way too," Taylor said. Beth was still locked up, as far as Taylor knew.

Lizeth shook her head. "Nope. No way. She acted, that's true, but she didn't act like a woman who knew something. She had some kind of axe to grind but was as dumb as a rock."

"You think so?" Taylor cringed. She'd felt some kind of kinship with Beth, but maybe it had just been because they were both neither retired quilters nor Jonah's Juvies.

"Why el``se would she get herself arrested?"

"I'm sure she didn't do it on purpose." Taylor tried to smile.

"Oh yeah?" Lizeth passed her phone. "Read that. I screen capped it."

It was a tweet to the Yamhill County Sheriff's office from an account called "Am-Anon-89". "Wanna know why she died? Talk to me. I can wrap it up in a quilt for you."

Taylor sucked in a breath. "Can we be sure she posted that herself? Or that that is the reason she was arrested?"

"I know she's Am-Anon-89. The other Amish Anonymous contact told me. Beth posted this. And look at the time, it was posted right before we all met. She was arrested pretty fast after that."

Taylor's gut felt like it was full of rocks. "But it's still so vague. Yeah, attention seeking, but not necessarily a confession."

"She's an idiot," Lizeth muttered. "If she really wanted to help, she would have just called." Her shoulder's slumped, and the color faded from her face, except around the eye that Taylor had punched, which was growing darker red as they finished their dinner.

Taylor and Lizeth went back to Taylor's little house on Love Street. It was a quiet drive and things didn't get much livelier as Taylor showed her guest to Belle's room. But a couple of hours later, there was a light knock on Taylor's bedroom door.

Taylor shut her computer, somehow not wanting Lizeth to see Etsy open to a search for vintage linen.

"I can't sleep, can you?" Lizeth sounded like a child, which made sense, since she was only about eighteen.

"No. Do you want to watch Jonah's videos?"

"Yes."

Taylor grabbed her laptop and they went downstairs to the kitchen. She put the kettle on, then opened Jonah's desk chair detective website.

In a matter of days Jonah had been able to upload more than thirty videos, most of them between a minute and five minutes long. Taylor and Lizeth scrolled down to the most recent three videos. Less than fifteen minutes of material, but it looked like plenty for the moment.

In the first video, Jonah addressed the detectives in his horde of merry Juvies. The most compelling moment was when, with tears in his eyes, he declared, "If we can find justice for our friend—don't you feel like she's one of us? —then we could do it again, for another innocent victim. What do you say Juvies? When we nail down the lunatic who killed Mackenzie Forte we can help another family in crisis."

Lizeth shuddered. "I wish he wouldn't call her that. Her acting coach chose the name and she hated it."

"I'm sorry. Do you want to message Jonah and tell him how you feel about it?"

"No." She pulled the edges of the thin mauve afghan from Belle's room around her tighter. A crocheted blanket…rare in the home of obsessive quilters.

The next video was him responding to specific emails. Lots of thanks, little meat.

But the final video—the one he had asked them to watch—was much more interesting. "I've interviewed an eye-witness," he began in a hushed voice. "We'll call the witness 'Terry.' Terry was in the hallway when Albina's body was found. Terry reports that Albina's eyes opened and closed. Terry reports that the person who called for help knew Albina was still alive. That makes me question the very basics of this case. My friends, my compadres. Did Mackenzie Forte actually die?" The video stopped on the question.

Lizeth squeezed her eyes shut. "No. She didn't."

Taylor exhaled slowly, trying to find the right words before she spoke. This promise of hope was criminal. Jonah shouldn't have posted it. "The paramedics must not have made it there in time...."

Lizeth dropped her eyes to the pine tabletop. "She's not dead. I won't believe it."

Taylor reached out to pat her hand, but it didn't seem to help.

"If Jonah thinks she's alive, then so do I." Lizeth stood with painstaking slowness and made her way back upstairs as though walking through water.

❦

TAYLOR WOKE up to a text message from Bruno. "Breakfast?"

Lizeth was sound asleep still. Taylor's hand and head throbbed. They were crying out for the pain pills the doctor had sent Taylor home with, but she only took Tylenol. She didn't want her head to be in the clouds today.

Taylor listened to the quiet house. It seemed that Lizeth was still asleep. Taylor was glad—she seemed like she could use it.

She responded to Bruno with one word: *where?*

"Meet me @ front desk."

Taylor cleaned up fast and left a note for Lizeth. She wanted to make sure Lizeth either stayed put or found her again, so she didn't leave her a spare key. She was aware this was a manipulative move, but it was well meant. She just didn't want this girl running off and getting herself into more trouble. The next person she attacked in a dark corner could be armed.

Taylor found Bruno waiting patiently at the front office of Comfort College of Art and Craft, his eyes sparkling, his smile sincere. He even had a look of satisfaction to him, relaxed shoulders, calm demeanor.

"I've got the inside scoop on a good breakfast today." Bruno grinned.

"We could just eat in the dining hall. They do serve breakfast at the Expo." Taylor glanced down the hall. Now that she was back where the suspects were, she hated to leave again.

"I know this is your town, and you've probably tried every place at least five times, but all the ladies right now are talking about the new coffee shop Comfy Cuppa. Apparently they've partnered with that Tillamook Cheese Factory Outlet place and have some outstanding omelets this week only."

He looked very excited, and Taylor did want to hear about his meeting last night, so she went along with it.

The café wasn't crowded yet and they were sitting at a little table with coffee and omelets in no time. "How's your stray kid this morning?" Bruno asked after savoring a few bites of a classic Denver omelet. "And if you are up for it, tell me what the heck happened last night."

"She's doing well. Thanks for your concern. To be honest, I think what happened last night is better left in the bathroom, but I can tell you this, Lizeth is a young woman deeply concerned about the fate of Albina."

"Did we finally find a relative?" He cocked his eyebrow.

"The poor kid is alone in the world." Taylor felt bad exposing Lizeth's life. She seemed so vulnerable. "She strikes me as desperate for a connection. She is having a hard time accepting that Allie is gone. But no, she's not technically family."

"What makes her think Allie is still alive?" He used Albina's real name, and it gave Taylor a warm feeling to hear it.

"There's a rumor going around that someone saw her eyes flutter open before paramedics arrived. I suggested that just because they fluttered then doesn't mean the paramedics were in time, but honestly, what do I know?"

"That's a good question. Maybe we should make some kind of list."

"Of suspects and clues? I've got a running tab in my head, but I don't know how much is wise to share." She grinned ruefully at him, finally acknowledging to herself that this guy was on her list. He'd been a little too interested all along, and though she thought the chance to do a lot of extra talking at a quilt Expo wasn't enough motive for murder, that didn't mean he didn't have something else. After all, he was talking to Allie's literary agent. Maybe he wanted to write a book about this or use this death as a hook for his own ambitions. There was money in books, after all. Just look at Steven King.

"You want to save your friend's son, right?" Bruno tried to entice her to give up her ideas.

"Sure. And that nice lady Beth. And if possible, everyone else here from a murderer on the loose." She shivered, remembering her own showdown with a murderer. It had been an event she never wanted to repeat.

"But you don't want to let me into your confidence." He frowned.

"You must admit we hardly know each other."

"How can that be?" He smiled that friendly smile of his. "We've shared meals, we've gone sight-seeing, we've worked together, we've experienced a crisis. We're practically family."

"No." She shook her head and pushed her plate away. "You're a likeable man, Bruno, and I appreciate the way you've been keeping an eye on me. But you're a stranger, no matter how many things we've done. Anyway…" She smirked at him a little, thinking she could lighten the mood by teasing him. "I thought you had an interest in my friend Roxy, not me."

He blushed. "I sure haven't seen much of her, no matter how much I hang around with her best friend." He held his hands up in surrender. "But you're a nice lady, and I certainly don't mind spending time with someone who's not trying to use me to get a foot up in their career. God bless the people I meet at these things, but if they don't want to be my next missus, they only want me to make them famous."

"Such hard luck to be well loved and influential." She laughed honestly at his problems.

He laughed. "Okay, okay. Keep your secrets. I'm fairly sure you don't suspect me too much, or you wouldn't be here. But, you didn't want to come, and you aren't eating. So, what are you after?"

"You caught me. I have an agenda. Someone said you had a suspicious late-night meeting at the diner."

"I saw you there. Why didn't you just join us?" Bruno asked.

"You'd hardly do anything nefarious if I were at the table with you." She took a tentative bite of her spinach and feta omelet.

"Not nefarious. That young lady has a lot of ambition. She's one of the many who wants to piggy back on my name to launch her career."

"I'd heard she thought she could make you rich."

"Sure, that was her pitch. She thinks she's the first girl ever to quilt in a way that makes a statement. Thought if we collaborated it would elevate my work and launch her."

Taylor groaned. "These kids!"

He lifted his eyebrow again.

"I know, I know." She waved her hand. "I'm not old, but at thirty, I finally see how obnoxious we can be in our twenties."

"Fair enough." He smiled that big, fatherly grin that rounded the apples of his cheeks above his bearded mug. "I let her down as gently as I could."

"They all want immediate fame and fortune. They see it happen again and again online, like with Jonah, and they want their piece of it."

"The girls, those "Juvies" claim they love him, but I've noticed a ripple of resentment too. After all, he doesn't even quilt."

Taylor laughed. "How had I missed that? Of course, he doesn't and of course they'd resent it. Shoot, I do, and it's my fault he's rich and famous."

"It won't last." Bruno bent his attention to his food, clearly enjoying it.

"You and I know that, but the younger kids, the ones who are seeing things explode around them for the first time, probably don't realize how the fall from fame can be even faster than the rise was."

"Are you thinking one of the Juvies would have killed someone just to make it look like Jonah did it?" Bruno chewed on this idea and on his toast.

"That's far-fetched, but isn't it all?" She didn't reveal her thoughts on the matter to Bruno. After all, who was Jonah but a younger, cuter, and more famous Bruno? Sure, Bruno had talent at long arm quilting, but that wasn't that impressive. Maybe he'd resented the boy enough to plan an elaborate murder.

She shook her head. The idea was too far-fetched. If death of Allie McKenzie aka Albina Tschetter aka Mackenzie Forte wasn't an accident, then the motive had to be more specific than this vague idea of professional envy. After all, the means were so specific—allergic reaction, or some kind of poison that mimicked allergy. A specific, organized mind at work wasn't motivated by a vague threat. "Besides, the Juvies aren't looking to take Jonah down. They want to rise up with him. They want Internet fame. They want Netflix docuseries. At least that's what my sister wants." Taylor hadn't meant to bring Belle into this, but it happened anyway, and might be a nice distraction as she let her subconscious mind sort through the problem.

"What does your sister do?" Bruno asked.

"Right now, she's a career student, though a young and successful one. I suspect she's going to be a historian or a professor. Or maybe a documentary filmmaker. She's got a Bachelor's of Arts in…" Taylor suddenly couldn't remember. "Anyway, she's got a BA that she started and finished early. Not even twenty yet. She's just a baby."

"My daughter is about that age. I worry about her. She wants to quilt because it's what her mom and dad do-did-do-whatever, but what she doesn't seem to understand is that our boring day jobs paid for our hobby for a long time before our hobby paid for itself."

"It's a common misconception," Taylor agreed. "I don't know

where we get the idea that life can be both fun and profitable. Someone always has to do something mind numbingly dull to feed the dreamers."

"What was your mind numbingly dull work?"

"I make my living supplying materials to artists. And, if I'm being very honest, I love it. I love business more than quilting. Though, my real dream job would be advertising exec at Wyden and Kennedy, writing copy, directing commercials, and that kind of thing."

"Good dream. I sold cars. I loved it too. I worked for Ferrari." For a moment, he looked wistful, like maybe he secretly believed Ferraris were cooler than quilts. "Even though I sold cool stuff to good guys for lots of money, in the end it was just a lot of boring paperwork."

Taylor couldn't help but laugh. "Yeah, selling Ferrari. Very boring. You know, even though I've heard your story now at least twice, I don't quite get it. Why on earth did you leave Ferrari for long arm quilting?"

His eyebrows drew together, and his mouth curved down. "When Dana got sick nothing mattered but her. I couldn't spend evenings and weekends at the showroom anymore. I had to be with her. I worked less, I made less, I cared less. And when she was gone, I decided to live an entirely different life."

"And you're a good salesman. Something many of the people in the arts aren't." Taylor mused on this. Jonah was a good salesman too. And her mom. Entertaining. Charismatic. Good listeners. She could listen, but the other two things she struggled with.

"It makes a difference," Bruno nodded in agreement.

"It makes all the difference." They finished their breakfast and left again. Though her mind had gone a million different directions during their breakfast, that one thought remained: in the end, your success hung entirely on your ability to sell your work.

In what way had the actress-author failed to sell, and is that what had gotten her killed?

※

Taylor went back to her house to check on Lizeth, but she was gone and hadn't texted or left a note.

She settled into Grandpa Ernie's recliner with her phone. She wished Roxy was here to complain with about kids these days. She'd enjoyed that part of her breakfast with Bruno. But she wasn't, so Taylor checked for new content from Jonah, keeping her eye out in particular for anything related to Allie's ability to sell books.

Jonah did have a new short video on his website. Looking very sincere he stared into the camera: "Another innocent woman has been arrested. My mom and her friend are still alone and unprotected at the Expo, working to get this woman free, but so far have come up empty-handed. Juvies, I need you now more than ever. If you were at the Cascadia Quilt Expo during the first two days of the event, please message me. Write me a long email. Tell me everything you saw and heard. I am reading everything with extreme care, and you never know if you saw something that you don't realize was important. Thank you."

That much was true. Taylor shot off a text to Jonah: *Thanks for your help. Please forward me all the emails.*

She didn't look forward to combing through the ravings of Jonah's fan-girls, but someone had seen something. They had to have. They just didn't know it was important.

She let her head rest on the back of the chair. The Expo was coming to a close, and it was looking like the whole thing would be packed up and everyone gone before they could learn what had really happened.

And yet, she didn't know if anyone would really be allowed to leave. But that question was easily answered. She dialed the sheriff's office and asked for Reg. "Hey, this is Taylor," she said, when transferred to him. I haven't heard from you in a while, but the Expo will be closing soon so I thought I'd check in."

"Okay."

"So…I was wondering, will everyone be allowed to leave? Even if there's no arrest?"

Reg paused. "The guests of the Expo will be able to leave."

"Um….me and Roxy too? And Beth Trager?"

He cleared his throat, but then laughed. "Just don't leave the country, okay? And remember the sheriff isn't too happy with you after what happened at the old folks' home. Try to keep out of this."

"Yes, definitely." She crossed her fingers, just because she could. "But if you hear anything…."

"I absolutely will not tell you." His gruff tone hid a teasing lightness, she was sure.

"Now, the other day you did ask me to pass stuff to you…"

"Since you haven't yet, I'm guessing you haven't learned anything."

"You're right. I haven't heard anything new, but Jonah put out a call for people at the Expo to email him with any information. I'm having him forward them to me. I'll let you know if I find anything."

"Sounds good. And…take care of yourself."

"Thanks. Talk to you later." He hadn't told her anything new or anything about the Amish fiction fan Beth, but he had chuckled. And if she was in serious danger or if Roxy had been, he never would have laughed at her. It was a relief, she realized, to feel that Reg thought her an annoying and laughable interference rather than either a murderer or possible victim.

Taylor felt like it had been years since she'd spoke to Roxy, so she called her.

"Jonah is going to send me all the emails he's going to get from his Juvies," she said after Roxy greeted her.

"That's good." Roxy sounded distracted.

"We might find out some great info."

"Sure, good to hear."

Taylor had the feeling Roxy was in the middle of something and was hit by that childish feeling of being left out. "Am I interrupting?"

"No, sorry." The sound of a chair being pulled across hard floor echoed in the phone. "What's news? Are you on campus right now?"

"No, I'm back home. I picked up a stray yesterday and wanted to check in with her."

"You did what?" Roxy was paying close attention now.

Taylor told her the whole story of Lizeth, leaving nothing out.

"That will teach me to check out," Roxy said at the end of the story. "Sorry I've been distant. It just seems like there's so much going on. I've been at the school trying to work out Jonah's troubles."

"Sue Friese told me she reported Jonah to YouTube. Did I tell you that?" Taylor interjected. She wanted to take the heat off herself, since Jonah was off with Belle in Seattle.

A quick breath escaped Roxy. "No. You hadn't said."

"All that time I was afraid it had been Belle," Taylor admitted.

"So was I."

They spent a few moments on the phone in silence, each of them feeling something strong in light of that. Taylor broke it. "But it was Sue. She did it."

"It makes more sense than Belle. She and Jonah are great friends. Now if only we could pin the murder on Sue, as well," Roxy said.

"We don't have anything better to do."

"How about we meet at the dining hall for lunch?"

The scheduled lunch was a couple hours away still. Taylor wondered for a moment why they had to wait so long to connect but agreed.

The only question now was if she should spend her spare time trying to catch up with Lizeth or trying to find out what had become of Beth Trager after the deputies had taken her away.

The answer was neither. She really wanted to read the emails that Jonah was sure to have started forwarding. She opened her emails on her phone hoping there'd be something already.

And, in a happy twist, she had plenty to read.

※

TAYLOR MET Roxy with a new sense of what had been going on around them and the idea that Jonah was a lot wiser than he appeared. What she had taken for shameless fame grab was actually a pretty good way to crowdsource a solution to the crime.

The dining hall was far from full, and the line for the buffet lunch of sandwich fixings and pasta salad was short. "Do you want this?" Roxy handed Taylor a brown paper gift bag with the Cascadia Quilt logo printed on it as they waited for their turn to fill a plate. "It's the swag they gave us as vendors when we checked in."

"Sure." Taylor hooked the bag over her arm, glad for the little peace offering between friends. Perhaps the fear that Belle had turned Jonah in for violation of terms of service had been keeping Roxy away. If so, Taylor was very glad they had straightened things out. Right now, they both needed a friend they could rely on.

CHAPTER SEVENTEEN

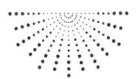

When Taylor's phone pinged after lunch, she was prepared for a new snap from Jonah, cheering her on for taking care of his "elderly" mother. Instead, it was about his website. "New vid. You need to see this one. It should direct your next actions." Taylor was distracted by the logo at the corner of his video. A pair of scissors that had a remarkable resemblance to a skull. It was creepy. She almost told him so but decided not to pick a fight over his online brand.

But she did go to his very phone-friendly website and watch the video. She used her blue tooth headphone and made herself conspicuous in a comfortable leather and wood arts and crafts era armchair in the front office. She felt a strong need to be near people.

After a quick introduction, the video went to split screen, one side Jonah, the other the girl with the cherry red hair and the white glasses. Valerie Ritz, one of the wide field of amateur detectives on the case and a strong candidate for head of Jonah's Juvies. Valerie was dressed like any young woman in her early twenties. Ripped jeans, baggy flannel top, large Doc Marten boots. But being a Ritz, of the hotel Ritz family, Taylor suspected each rip in her pants added a zero to the ticket price. And she had probably bought the plaid at auction from Francis Bean herself.

"Thank you for having me on your show." Valerie sat at a table in a dorm room—easily recognizable as Taylor had lived in the dorms when she was a student here. "I have a lot of information that I feel is necessary to get out, especially to anyone still at Cascadia Quilt Expo. Right now, the Expo is in its second week of events, the master class series, and I hope that Sue and Morgan Friese are still on site. I know this has been very hard for them, and they might need to retreat and recover, but their strong leadership is necessary at a time of crisis like this."

"I doubt they're allowed to leave yet," Jonah added. "The place is crawling with sheriff's deputies right now, correct?"

"Yes, very much so." Valerie's lips were pressed in a thin, grim line.

Taylor looked up from her phone. No deputies, as far as the eye could see.

"Let's get right down to business, Valerie. You say you have some information for us, and I say I have some for you. Why don't you go first?"

"Let's be clear from the start. I will not reveal my sources in a video, but I am not hiding my identity because I stand personally behind my facts." She fiddled with a stack of index cards, tapping them on the table to straighten their edges and then fanning them. "First, we have information on Albina Tschetter's real identity. She was an actress named Allie Forte. She has a background in adult entertainment."

Taylor's heart dropped. Not out of disdain for people in adult entertainment, but because she thought Lizeth would hate having that said about her sister.

"Forte decided to rehabilitate her image and took a stage name and an author name as well, hence the confusion between Mackenzie Forte and Albina Tschetter."

Jonah interrupted. "This is game changing news. Are you sure you aren't going to be able to share your sources?"

"Positive. I need to protect them. The publisher would not want to be identified with an adult entertainer, so they have a reason to want the actress silenced."

"Aren't you afraid that saying this online will make you a target?" Jonah's face slowly drained of color. He looked like a scared teen in over his head.

"It's a risk I have to take."

Jonah sat for a second in awkward silence, then spoke: "Her death brought this info out. I wonder. Maybe the publisher would have had more interest in keeping her alive."

"That's a valid theory," Valerie said. "In addition to changing careers, agents, even her name, Albina Tschetter was on a campaign to create a background and image for her new identity. In light of that, she joined a small church group—a cult known in Hollywood as The Sisterhood. Not much is known about this group, but they seem to be exclusively focused on financial success for the members of their church."

"Very interesting." He leaned into the camera. "Juvies, could you help me out? Could you please research this group and get back to us immediately with what you learn?"

"While we do not know what The Sisterhood believes or teaches, we do know that the woman who wrote as Albina Tschetter is dead, and this cult group was her touchstone at this time in her life. Cults, Jonah, are very dangerous."

"I'm glad you wanted to get this info out there. It's wild. I know my friends will follow up on it and help to verify what they can. In the meantime, please consider this: We have an eyewitness who says that Albina Tschetter was not dead when the paramedics were called. I have not, in fact, come across anyone who can say beyond a shadow of a doubt that she ever died."

Valerie nodded, slowly, her eyes narrowed. "It makes you wonder, doesn't it?"

"What also makes me wonder is the large deposit recently made to the business account of Mackenzie Forte. We know this is her stage name for acting and that she hadn't been in anything recently. One of the Juvies works at the bank and believes that the deceased had been paid a large sum of money, either a lottery win or maybe a payment for services rendered. You can guess which way I am leaning."

"Maybe she was paid for her silence." Valerie's vocal fray was intense.

"Maybe she was," Jonah nodded, his eyes still wide and vulnerable. "If someone out there can confirm that this girl," he held up the publicity photo of Albina Tschetter dressed as a conservative author of Amish fiction, "ever worked in the adult entertainment industry under the name Allie Forte, you would be providing an invaluable service in the name of justice. Valerie, thank you again."

"Thank you, Jonah."

The video ended.

Taylor's heart was racing, so she closed her eyes and counted slowly to twenty, first in English, then in Spanish. Then backwards. If all of this was true, and Allie had been killed to keep her identity as an adult film actor quiet, then Valerie and Jonah had just made a dangerous video. Taylor was too far away to protect Jonah from what he'd just done, but at the very least she could check on Valerie. She also wanted to check on Lizeth, who'd likely have heard this by now and would be devastated.

Taylor walked every inch of the campus but didn't manage to pin down Valerie, or anyone else she recognized. The crowds had slimmed. Registration for the second week of events had been a tiny percentage of the main show, and an ominous pall hung over the dark and quiet campus.

She gave up the hunt for the moment. She hadn't seen Lizeth either and hoped the girl might be at the house waiting to get back inside.

Taylor found Lizeth slumped against the back door of her little house on Love Street. She looked like she had seen a ghost.

"Can I come in?" She looked up at Taylor, her eyes shadowed, red, and puppy like.

"Please do."

Lizeth unfolded her long limbs and followed Taylor into the house. "How did that girl Valerie know?" Lizeth fell into one of the pine dining chairs, pulled her knees to her chest, and wrapped her arms around them.

"You saw the video?"

Lizeth pressed the heal of her hand to her eyes. "How did she know that about us?"

"You have to help me out. What did she say about you?"

"Allie wasn't an adult actress, that was my mom. And that girl got the name wrong, but close. Mom's stage name was Hallie Forte. I think that's why Allie picked Forte for her stage name. She and Mom got along really well. Anyway, Mom met Allie's dad in the club."

"The dance club where she worked?"

"Mom wasn't a dancer. She worked in adult film." Lizeth's chin jutted forward.

"Sorry. What club do you mean? The one she called The Sisterhood?"

"I don't know where that girl got that name. That's not what I remember it being called, but they could have changed it."

"What name do you remember?" Taylor moved about the kitchen fussing with things while she talked. Moving scrappy reusable grocery bags from the counter to hook on the back of the door, pulling down mugs and boxes of tea and cocoa, filling the little steel kettle and setting it on a burner.

"Mom called it the Ladies Club. Dad and some other guys were always there, but all the leaders and teachers were girls. It was a lot of self-help stuff. They got Mom out of the adult entertainment industry, and she stopped drinking back then. Who do you think told Valerie about us?"

"I can't even hazard a guess. Do you think Allie was still a part of the Ladies Club?"

"She could have been. We liked it there. They had good snacks and let us watch movies on a big screen TV."

"It sounds like a good group." Taylor couldn't see anything wrong or cult-like about a group that helped families get free from addition, out of dangerous work, financially stable and offered good snacks, too. Maybe her meter for what was good was on the low end, but the program had worked, right? Lizeth's mom had quit drinking and the adult film business. At least for a while. "Maybe it's not bad that it's known. What could it really hurt, after all?"

Lizeth rolled her eyes like she was Taylor's kid sister. "But it wasn't true—I mean about Allie. She wasn't in adult movies. They shouldn't say that about her."

"No, you're right. They shouldn't make things up about her—or if they aren't sure, they should check. There's no excuse for confusing Hallie Forte and Allie Mackenzie."

Lizeth nibbled at her fingernail. Her eyes looked like they were ready to spill.

"I want you to make yourself at home here, okay? Whatever is in the fridge, it's yours. Use the TV, computer, all of it. Take a long hot bath if you want, even. Can I make you something to eat?"

Lizeth shrugged.

Taylor sat at the table with her. "I want to head back out and see what I can dig up. But I don't like the idea of you running around out there on your own. Are you willing to stay here till I get back?"

Lizeth nodded weakly.

"There's a spare key hanging by the door in here, but if you're willing to just nestle in and wait, I'd appreciate it. It just feels dangerous right now. For you, I mean."

She sniffled as though she were about to cry. "I understand."

Having elicited promises to take care of herself, stay put, and not let anyone in, Taylor left to find Roxy.

She called and texted but got nothing. She longed to hash this all out with her old friend—someone who really knew Jonah and could help her figure out which of her fears were reasonable and which were a waste of time. She thought of calling Hudson and had the terrible realization that through this new challenge she hadn't really thought to turn to him for help. She stopped at a bench by the front door to the college and dialed his number out of guilt.

After a quick and enthusiastic greeting, they made a date for dinner at Reuben's.

But there at the campus, Roxy was nowhere to be seen.

After a few turns around the campus, Taylor found herself in a quiet corner. Tucked in the back of the ceramics and pottery wing of the school, one of the numerous arts and crafts' wood and leather chairs sat next to a steel and wire table with a small bronze and stained-glass lamp. A foggy memory of hiding in just such a corner some seven years ago as a student tugged at her. Why had she hidden here? Had it been boy trouble? Or something to do with a class she was struggling in? Either way, the corner felt like shelter, and she gladly took it. She settled into the chair and pulled out her phone. While she waited for Roxy to get in touch, she could check her emails again.

After more than an hour of carefully parsing the dozens of emails Jonah had forwarded, Taylor gave up. Apart from one Expo attendee who had seen the author in quiet conversation at a suspect booth in the marketplace, she'd gotten nothing but a little headache. Taylor checked over the lists of booths in her Expo catalogue and spotted The Ladies Club. That was the group Jonah had mislabeled The Sisterhood. They had been giving out coffee by the hundreds. But it hadn't seemed anymore questionable than the Herbalife booth or the Scientology readings.

She ran her fingers along the walnut chair arm—worn from

decades of artists seeking refuge. She felt worn down too. Tired at her heart level. Did she really have it in her to give her all to these people she didn't know? To sacrifice her own business interests for some random hunt for justice? She closed her eyes and tried that slow, careful breathing again.

Lizeth's young, pale face with its blackened eye came to mind. Parentless, unless you count a mother in jail. Without siblings. And with a hair trigger fight or flight.

Someone had to help this kid.

If Lizeth had been her baby sister, she'd want someone to help her. And then there was Jonah with his big, scared eyes, trying to seem sophisticated and smart online, but constantly putting himself at risk. And that one lady—what was her name? Beth. Yes, Beth Trager who'd been dragged down to the sheriff's office. The woman who'd reminded Taylor of herself. This list of people who needed someone, anyone, to look out for them did nothing to relieve her heart's burden, but a text came that did help.

"*I know our date is still half an hour from now, but I couldn't wait. Am drinking a coke at Reuben's and thinking of you.*"

A smile that started somewhere in her pulse spread on Taylor's tired features. God bless Hudson. "*Coming now,*" she replied.

🏵

To Taylor's great relief, her heart did a little flip when she spotted Hudson in a back booth at the diner. She had worried that not thinking of him constantly during this crisis meant she didn't love him enough. Over the last two years her mind and heart had been stretched and tested on what exactly love meant, what it should feel like, and how one should respond to it. She had loved her mom and sister desperately, so she had thought. But she hadn't had much of a relationship with them before her mother's death. But she had adored Clay, who hadn't deserved it, or maybe he had, but he had terrible cloying ways, now that she was on the other side of that relationship. All of this felt new and childish at her age, but nonetheless, it was where she was, and feeling her heart flip at the sight of Hudson felt good.

She slid into the brown vinyl seat across from him and stared at his handsome face. He wore a clean flannel and was freshly shaved, hair combed even.

"Why does it feel like a year since I've seen you?" she asked with a soft sigh.

"It's been a long few days. I didn't like it." He reached for her hand and gave it a squeeze. Neither of them looked at their menu. "I haven't seen anything about the deceased author in the news. Are they still thinking it's a murder?"

"I called Reg to ask him some questions. He implied that they had no idea what on earth was going on." Taylor stroked his rough hands with her thumb.

"Doesn't sound like Reg."

She chuckled. "He wouldn't tell me anything."

"Jonah's off the hook then?"

"I wish I knew. And I wish he'd come back home. He made me some promises about his school work, but how much can you trust a teen-millionaire?"

"Not as far as I could throw him, though…" He glanced at his thick, strong arm and winked.

"The only thing is," Taylor's smile faded slightly, "he's still playing detective online, and today he said some risky stuff." She explained the Hallie/Allie confusion and also the suggestion that the publishers had killed the author to keep her past quiet. "Between hiding her dirty past and killing her to make the book a best seller, one does look twice at the publisher."

"Unless it's a very small business with one lunatic in charge, I highly doubt it." Hudson's deep voice was reassuringly confident.

"The lunatic doesn't have to be in charge of the publisher, do they? They could just be like, on the account or something. My idea of how a publisher works all comes from that Sandra Bullock movie though."

"Mine, too." He wrinkled his nose. "I hope you don't take this the wrong way, but are you sure you should be messing around with this? I get it that you feel protective of Roxy and Jonah, but…"

She nodded. "I hear you, but things are more complicated than that now that Lizeth is staying with me."

He sucked in a breath with a quiet whistle. "I love that you care about these young people and their troubles."

"But?"

"No buts. I appreciate it. I can see why you're involved." He turned to his phone and gave it some serious consideration. "My extra work dries up tomorrow. Do you mind if I hang around?"

"Keep us girls safe?" Taylor blushed.

"Yes, and I've missed you."

"You're more than welcome. I wouldn't want just any man around the house, but I'll take you."

"Awesome. I'll go home to get my stuff and swing by your place tonight."

A shiver of anticipation ran up and down both her arms. The long nights held less panic when she wasn't alone.

They parted after dinner with a quick kiss. She had a take-out container with two turkey roll-ups for Lizeth just in case there hadn't been anything tempting at the house.

Flour Sax was an easy stop between the diner and her house, so Taylor decided to drop in and see if Roxy just happened to be there. The shop was closed at this hour, but Roxy might have gone by for any reason, like to pick up things for their booth at the Expo. The booth neither of them had set up or manned for days.

The shop was locked and dark, but Taylor let herself in anyway. She trusted Clay and Willa to run it smoothly, but that didn't mean she wasn't curious how things had been going while she was out of the office. The Comfort Quilt Guild had hoped these two weeks would bring in tons of business for their little shops, but likely the death had put a damper on shopping.

The back of Flour Sax was tidy and lightly vanilla scented, the way Taylor liked it. She ran her hand across the edge of a shelf of fabric—no dust. Fabric shops could get incredibly dusty, especially back in the work area where machines would be whizzing away during classes.

Footsteps overhead meant Clay was home. She thought she'd run upstairs real fast to check in, make sure the store had everything it needed, then get home to Lizeth.

She took the stairs two at a time, knocked, and bumped the door lightly with her shoulder. It wasn't on the latch and swung open.

Clay stood at the little stove on the kitchen wall, shirtless, laughing, his eye on the door to his bedroom.

Roxy stood in the door, also laughing, wearing nothing but an oversized man's pastel Flour Sax Quilt Shop Polo shirt.

She saw Taylor.

Her laughter stopped.

Taylor's heart hit her ribs like a bouncing basketball. She caught her breath.

Clay turned her direction and grinned.

Taylor took a step back. "Sorry!"

She tried to pull the door shut.

Clay laughed louder.

Roxy shushed him.

Taylor stepped backward and felt her foot hanging off the edge of the step. She caught the handrail.

She was being stupid.

Clay and Roxy were adults.

Just because Clay had been *her* boyfriend who *she* had lived with for four years did not mean….

Didn't it?

Words like "girl code" fluttered through her mind

Roxy.

Roxy!

Not old enough to be her mom.

But older than Clay.

But she herself was older than Hudson.

But what did age matter?

But why Clay? He was such a rotten little…

But was he?

Yes.

But *was he?*

And why Roxy?

Her mind spun: names, words, adjectives, both kind and unkind, fighting for primacy.

Clay wasn't to everyone's taste, with his insinuating ways. He was a little manipulative but not harmful, as far as her own experience had gone.

But Roxy was gold. Platinum. Exceptional. Surely, she couldn't love *Clay*.

The door opened slowly and Roxy stepped out, barefooted but wearing pants now. "Hey, Taylor, um…."

Taylor cleared her throat. "You've been hard to get a hold of."

"Sure, I know." Roxy ran her hand through her wild, curly hair.

"You've not been staying on the campus, have you?"

Roxy shook her head.

"Um, sorry for interrupting. Just, um, let's talk tomorrow, okay?"

"Sure." Roxy chewed her lip, looking very young and pretty. Because however much older she was, it wasn't like she was old-old or anything. Mid-forties? And Clay was late thirties? It was fine. Normal. Same as her and Hudson. But still….

Taylor stumbled as she turned on the stairs and left.

She was absolutely sure she did not want Clay Seldon for herself.

But that didn't mean Roxy could have him.

## CHAPTER EIGHTEEN

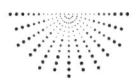

Lizeth took just one of the rolled sandwiches Taylor offered her. "Are you sure you don't want some?"

"I'm sure." Taylor put the takeout container in the fridge.

"Where have they hidden her? I'm getting scared," Lizeth murmured.

Taylor sat on the hard, wooden kitchen chair with a thump.

Lizeth slowly unrolled the tortilla and picked at the filling. She fed herself a sliver of red pepper.

"I know what Jonah said, but just because she wasn't gone yet when the paramedics called doesn't mean she's still alive."

"If she had been definitely dead when they found her, then she would be definitely dead now, but she wasn't. She was still alive then, so she might be alive now too." Lizeth didn't make eye contact. Maybe her hope sounded as far-fetched to her as it did to Taylor.

"How long has it been since you've seen Allie?" Taylor needed to turn Lizeth's mind from the hope that Albina was alive. She wasn't. Period. End of sentence.

"Years."

"So, you wouldn't know anything about that cash deposit Jonah reported she got."

"Maybe it was royalties?" Lizeth picked up another thin slice of red pepper but put it back down again.

"Could be. What about her dad, do you remember what kind of business he was in?"

"He was a builder. House builder, I think." Lizeth scrunched up her face in thought.

"Was he successful?"

"When we lived with him, we lived in a big house." Lizeth had a far-away look on her face. Like the big house they'd lived in had been a dream.

"Do you think he might have left Allie a sum of money, and maybe she just came into it?"

"Like a trust fund?"

"It's an idea."

"I don't know." Lizeth nibbled at a small bite of the cold roast turkey.

"When was the last time you heard from him?" Taylor picked up her coffee cup, but it was empty and had been sitting on the table for a very long time.

"He used to send me Christmas cards till he died. Called me his girl still."

"He sounds lovely." Taylor set the cup down. She would have loved even that much from her father—but firefighting is dangerous, and longing can't change the past.

"He was my favorite," Lizeth sighed.

"Did you hear about his will after he died?"

"No, we were living in Mexico at the time."

Taylor longed to ask the girl to check her bank account and see if she had come into any money, but she had no reason to think Lizeth's almost-step-dad from years ago had left her a trust fund. And as she was several years younger than Allie, even if he had, she probably wouldn't have gotten it at the same time.

Taylor reached out to her and laid a hand on her shoulder.

"I wish there was a way to talk to him." Lizeth shifted from Taylor's touch. "Sometimes I miss him more than I miss Mom."

This girl had Taylor's whole heart right now. When this was all over, Lizeth would still be alone, and for the rest of her life she'd have to handle a mom with addiction issues. She'd be the adult in their relationship whether she was ready for it or not.

It made Taylor want to adopt her. Pay her college fees. Bring her home for Christmas, but Lizeth wasn't a shelter dog waiting to be adopted. She was a young adult who could decide for herself where she turned for support. And that might just be with her mother, even with all of the issues that come with addiction.

Taylor's phone was silent. No calls. No pinging Snapchat alerts. No texts. No thumbs up from her mom telling her she was on the right track.

Lizeth quit picking at the food she hadn't eaten so Taylor took the wrapper, folded the food back up in it, and put it in the fridge with the rest.

"I think I'll go, um, laydown." Lizeth looked to Taylor as though asking for permission.

"Please do...but eat more sometime today, okay?"

Lizeth didn't respond. She just dragged herself out of the kitchen and upstairs.

The kitchen door popped open, and for half a second, Taylor was afraid it would be Roxy or Clay wanting to "talk about it" but it wasn't.

Hudson held a single rose in one hand and a backpack in the other. "Let me take you out."

"You just took me out to dinner." Taylor accepted his rose, and then a long, lingering hug followed by a kiss.

"Loggers is hopping tonight."

"I like a dive bar as much as the next girl..." She wrinkled her nose.

"Hopping with quilt Expo ladies. I drove past on my way here, sort of cased the town actually. I know you won't rest till you have your answers, and I wanted to see if there was any place we could go to scratch that itch."

"There aren't many options." Taylor glanced at the clock. It was early still, just nine.

"Nope. The horde of quilty ladies were easy to find. Are you up for it? If not, that's okay too." He gave her another squeeze.

"Yeah. I'm up for it."

---

A CLUSTER of master quilters had commandeered one corner of the bar. The young gray-haired fiber artist named Kaitlyn was with them. As was Shara, who thought of herself as a detective, and Valerie Ritz, who had been featured in Jonah's video. These four were surrounded by much older women with tired, but satisfied faces. Taylor and Hudson joined them.

"You're the one that got arrested first, aren't you?" a quilter in a handmade batik patch work jacket asked Taylor.

"That was my friend, Roxy."

"Did she tell you about it?" The lady in the quilted jacket had the raspy voice of a lifelong smoker. An unfortunate sound that made Taylor think her quilts must smell terrible.

"She wasn't really arrested. Just taken to the station. She said they asked her all sorts of questions but she refused to talk."

"Good girl." The woman turned to someone sitting next to her.

"Come, sit." Valerie Ritz patted the chair next to her. "We need to talk."

Taylor, fingers linked with Hudson, joined Valerie. She took a seat and Hudson stood behind her, leaning on the laminate wood back of the worn pub chair.

The waiter came by and took her order—she kept it simple and soft by ordering a Coke and lime. She wanted to keep her head straight.

"Did you see the video? I told Jonah to tell you to watch it." Valerie held a frothing purple drink in a daiquiri glass.

"I did. I was wondering about your contact."

"I thought you would." Valerie smiled knowingly. "I almost didn't open the emails, since the address was clearly fake, but I think I know who sent them."

"Are you able to tell me?"

Her cheeks were flushed, and her eyes, behind their big plastic frames shone with excitement. "There's a lady, one of Jonah's Juvies. I met her a few times. She asked a lot of questions about Albina that first day. Things like what room she was staying in and stuff. I think this email with the background info was from her."

"What makes you think that?" Hudson asked.

Taylor shivered, but in a good way. She hadn't expected him to get involved, but she kind of liked it. Like they were partners in crime fighting.

"Something about the syntax in the email reminded me of the girl's speech." Valerie sounded a bit condescending.

"What else do you know about this girl?" Taylor asked.

"She was super young, very skinny, and you've met her. In fact, I think you came in with her last night."

Lizeth.

Taylor thought back to all of their conversations but couldn't recall any unusual grammar or word choice issues. Of course, Taylor knew for a fact that Lizeth wouldn't have sent those messages. They had hurt her too badly. "When did you get the emails?"

"Yesterday evening."

"If that's the same girl I came in with, she's not the one. I spent the whole evening with her." She wasn't about to reveal anything to Valerie about Lizeth. But she was more than willing to fudge the alibi.

"Are you absolutely sure you were with her the whole evening?" Valerie lifted one thick, well drawn eyebrow.

Taylor's stomach clenched. She suspected Valerie might be able to prove her wrong and backed off a little. "Oh, maybe not the whole thing, but enough of it to feel fairly certain."

Valerie leaned forward. "I have another idea. What if Beth Trager sent them from jail?"

"I don't think you can email from jail." Hudson's deep voice resonated with authority. As much as Taylor would have loved to be her own authority, she recognized the value in being backed by a big strong man.

"You have a contact with the police. You can find out, can't you? If it wasn't the skinny girl, and I have my reasons to think it was, then it must have been Beth." Valerie sipped her drink through a stainless-steel straw.

The waitress delivered Taylor's Coke and Hudson's Lager. When she was gone, Taylor leaned forward too. "What makes you so sure?"

Valerie was a little wobbly, her drinky breath hot on Taylor's face. "Intuition."

Taylor's disappointment was visceral, but she nodded as though she found that a useful tool, then turned her attention to the other women at the various tables around them.

She attempted to eavesdrop her way to more information, but the voices she could hear were only talking about quilting. These pros were so dedicated to the craft that the unsolved murder from just days ago wasn't going to stop them from their passion.

Hudson leaned down and whispered, "Darts?"

"Sounds good." Taylor stood with her Coke. A little set back couldn't stop them. Some darts, maybe pool. Hudson might want a second drink. They could linger at the bar till closing if that's what it took to get some real information.

"We need to talk." Shara Schonley grabbed Taylor's arm as she maneuvered past. "Meet me outside."

"Both of us?" Taylor nodded at Hudson who was picking darts out of a board no one was using.

"Just you, and quick."

Taylor caught Hudson's eye and tilted her head towards the door. He nodded with a small smile. This, after all, was what they'd come for.

A mist had rolled down from the coast range mountains and the night air was still and icy with it. Shara stood under the one light in the center of the parking lot, surrounded by the modest, sensible cars of the quilters who had driven to the event.

"I don't know what that Ritz girl is thinking, talking in crowded rooms."

"I suspect she's too young to be thinking." Taylor crossed her arms as the chill seemed to soak through her cotton jacket.

"Hmm. Probably." Shara also crossed her arms. "Since we last spoke, I've come across a few very important items."

"I'm honored you want to share them with me." Taylor bit her tongue. She didn't want to put Shara on edge, but she couldn't help herself. She had such deep resentment, seeded and fertilized by her mother's frustration. When Shara had opened Dutch Hex, Taylor's mother Laura had been livid. Taylor could still remember her seething that a Dutch Hex wasn't the same thing as a Barn Quilt. That Amish people didn't paint Dutch Hex's on their barns. That the only reason Shara had used that store name was because it sounded like Flour Sax. She had been angrier than Taylor had ever seen.

Shara was around Roxy's age, and when she'd opened her quilt store, she'd been a young hip rebel. And business had flown right out Flour Sax's doors and into Shara's. It was easy to remember the tension, fear, and anger in their house at the time. Toddler Belle had been the only saving grace, as she always had been.

"I don't have time for whatever your problem is with me. You Quinn ladies…" Shara rolled her eyes. "I don't want to have to turn to you for help. But I don't think the other Guild members are capable of what I need."

"Why not just talk to the sheriff?" Taylor huffed a breath that sent a small cloud of mist into the night.

Shara snorted. "I've heard the way the sheriff treated you after the Bible Creek bombing."

"Fair enough. But what do you need me for?"

"To start with, I need you to listen." Shara's lips curled. She leaned forward slightly, aggressive even with her arms crossed. She wore another long dark dress with a high neckline, her hair pulled back in a severe knot. Whether Shara's vibes were sincere or not, she never strayed. Gothic Amish, and always on.

"Sure, why not?" Taylor shrugged.

"No one has reported on the cause of death, and they never will."

"Oh?" Taylor was tempted to yawn. How many times were they all going to circle this drain?

"Albina died of an untraceable poison. Something that would only poison her, in fact."

"Like an allergen?" Though she ought to have been at least polite to Shara, even Taylor found the sound of her own voice condescending.

"It would function similarly, but no. This was a poison tailor made for her, from a DNA sample."

Taylor glanced back at the bar, longing to be throwing darts with Hudson. "That sounds expensive." Of all the absurd things she'd heard this week, this was at the top.

"Exactly why we are looking for a very rich person." Shara nodded slowly as though Taylor were finally understanding.

"How did you come up with this idea?"

"Logic."

Shara's definition of logical and Taylor's weren't even in the same dictionary.

"I've been speaking with the maid who cleaned Albina's room. She says this is the only correct answer."

"And you're sure she knew what you were talking about? I'd heard she was a recent immigrant." Taylor fudged a little. The maid she'd heard about was afraid of deportation. But it didn't take English being your second language for this idea to sound absurd. "Maybe she was just agreeing with you but not understanding it."

"She understood me all right. This wasn't that maid who told us about the thread waxer. Plus, she was able to show me something no one else had seen."

"Please, I'm dying here. What did she see?" The sarcasm. Taylor would have paid good money to make it stop. She was literally on pins and needles to hear what this maid had seen, but her mouth refused to be polite.

Shara took a step back. "I really hoped when you took over your mom's store there'd be less of this rivalry nonsense."

Taylor was struck by Shara's tone—both tired and hurt. She uncrossed her arms and tried for a less defensive posture. "Never mind that. What did you want to tell me?"

"Sorry, but I do mind. I've worked my fingers to the bone to become a part of this community. It's not easy moving to a small town as a young adult, and your family has done everything they can to make it as hard as possible."

Embarrassment rolled over Taylor in waves of heat. She was as sure as she'd ever been that she wasn't in the wrong, but something in the weariness of both Shara's voice and eyes sounded sincere. Plus, everyone around here loved the Quinns and the Bakers, and most of them were related. It couldn't have been easy in Comfort for Shara, if she really was Laura Baker Quinn's enemy. "Forget that for now. What did the maid show you?"

"I'm taking a risk trusting you with this, but you've got experience and connections. And…." Shara shook her head. "I don't know. There's something about you that I trust. Even though I probably shouldn't." Shara took a few deep breaths, then stepped closer again, and dropped her voice. "The maid took photos of the room with her phone after the paramedics left."

The words hit Taylor like a slap. The kind that wakes you out of shock. "Did she! You don't happen to have copies, do you?"

"No. She didn't send them to me. Just showed me."

Taylor chewed her lip. "Okay, talk me through what you saw in the pics."

"Albina's handbag was lying open on the floor."

That was not news, but Taylor nodded anyway.

"And her suitcase was opened, rifled through even."

"Like maybe she had been looking for something?" Taylor asked.

"And her toothbrush was missing."

Taylor interrupted. "But how could the pictures tell you that?"

"That's what I'm trying to say. The maid, whose English is better than yours, I might add, said Albina's toothbrush wasn't on the counter where it had been earlier, and it wasn't in the suitcase, or in the purse, not that I could see."

"But if the suitcase was rifled through, how could you see?" Taylor pressed.

"I couldn't see the toothbrush anywhere in the pictures, but the housecleaner had a closer look and agreed."

"But what good would a toothbrush do anyone?"

"It was how they got her DNA to concoct the poison," Shara said.

"Ah. I see." Back to the absurd idea again. "Wouldn't a hairbrush have been easier to get DNA from?"

"It would be too obvious. Besides, saliva is a wonderful source of blood cells."

"I don't know…" Taylor exhaled, then laughed softly. "Considering Albina had likely brushed her teeth before bed and was dead in the morning, the murderer had just around eight hours to steal the brush, extract the DNA from the dried saliva in the bristles, develop a specialized poison just for Albina, then deliver the poison to her in a way so subtle that she wouldn't notice. That's pretty quick work." Taylor lifted her eyebrows, inviting Shara to recognize that this was not only insane, it was also impossible.

"Exactly. We are looking for a rich killer, a genius killer, and someone disguised as housekeeping or security." Shara held fast to her idea.

"Imagining for half a second that this is somehow more believable than someone overdosing Albina on something she was allergic to…or using a normal poison for that matter, what am I supposed to do about it?"

"I'm setting a trap for the killer. I need you to be in place, ready to call the cops." Shara shivered.

"Can't you do that?" Taylor looked up at the aluminum head of the lamp post. Was Shara delusional? She must be. This was the most unreasonable and unlikely scenario one could create. No one thinking clearly would have done it.

Shara shook her head. "I…have reasons not to get the attention of the police."

"Of course, you do."

Shara scowled. "Not all of us are squeaky clean orphans."

"That's not a thing." Taylor's small headache, from earlier in the day, was raging now.

"I'm setting the trap, but I want to be somewhere else when it catches the killer, okay? My past isn't everything it ought to be and that might prejudice a jury against my testimony."

Taylor wanted to walk into the dark night, letting the cold damp air sooth her agitated and pained head. But Hudson waited for her inside, so she didn't. And part of her had a feeling she owed Shara something. Even a delusional Shara. "Well, lay it on me, what do I have to do?"

"Spend your day in the lobby at the conference and watch."

"The whole day? I do have things to do." Like anything else at all, to be honest.

"It's a lot to ask, but not if it works. We could catch the killer tomorrow, we really could."

"But the whole day, Shara. It's too much." Taylor began to slowly back up, ready to turn back to Hudson.

"Okay." Shara paced under the light. "Be there at five. I'll be there before that. It's not likely to work immediately so the risk to me is lower in the morning. Then I'll have someone else spend the afternoon there, maybe Bruno." Her voice softened at his name. "Then you at five. Please. I think this will work."

"For how long? The whole evening?"

"Yes. If we can't catch him by the end of the day, we'll have lost our chance. See, the trap will be disrupted when the marketplace is closed out."

"Can I know what the trap is?"

"I don't know how much I should tell."

"You should tell me enough to keep me out of trouble and not so much that I can accidentally ruin the plan," Taylor said firmly.

"Yes, that makes sense. Let me think." Shara wrung her hands. "The trap is set in a place the murderer will be bound to visit. He'll feel compelled to go to it by nature of his personality. The reason you need to be in the campus lobby by the office is because the killer will rush out in a panic and you need to be able to grab security and stop him."

"What if he's a sociopath and able to leave calmly, or worse still, what if I can't tell who it is?"

"If I've profiled the killer correctly, and I think I have, then he will definitely panic, and you're bound to notice." She stared at her feet for a moment. "Even if it was a normal poison. Or something she was allergic to, my trap will work." Her words seemed to pain her.

"All I can do is try, I guess."

"Thank you." Shara stepped forward almost as for a hug but stopped.

Taylor didn't bridge the gap, so Shara turned, heading toward her little black Beetle parked near the light.

It seemed to Taylor the odds of Albina still being alive and hiding somewhere were better than Shara's crack pot idea of a genius billionaire lurking at a quilt Expo to kill a young actress.

Then again, half the people she had met this week suspected "Albina Tschetter" of being a plant in a scheme to dominate Amish fiction sales through the power of robotic intelligence.

Perhaps Shara's idea wasn't the craziest out there.

Taylor's only regret was that she hadn't thought to ask Shara what motive this billionaire killer might have had.

## CHAPTER NINETEEN

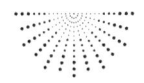

Shara was crazier than Taylor. That was just a fact, but she had Taylor's wheels spinning. What kind of trap had she set? Who would get caught in it? Would her attempt to catch a non-existent killer manage to nab the actual killer? Taylor pictured things like spilled paint in a suspicious area so the killer would leave a trail of footprints, or a hidden camera that could catch a prompted confession, but how could Shara prompt a confession? And wouldn't paint dry? And why would either of those things cause anyone to flee in panic?

Sure, if this worked, they would give the folks of the Cascadia Quilt Expo, the people of Comfort, Oregon, and anyone who didn't want a murderer running loose a great measure of relief, but it wasn't going to work. Shara wouldn't catch anyone, much less an imaginary billionaire.

And killing with a DNA-matched poison? What kind of books had Shara been reading? Definitely not Amish fiction. As Taylor rolled each of these questions around and savored them, she was left with a deep worry for Shara. Rather than wanting to babysit the campus lobby, Taylor longed to watch over Shara all day. The kind of woman who would dream up a super-villain and then try to trap him, could easily get herself hurt.

Taylor and Hudson were snuggled under the comforting folds of Taylor's Dove-in-the- Window quilt, Hudson snoring softly.

In between following social media and keeping up with the gossip, Taylor hadn't considered seeing what the police had released to traditional media, but since her mind wouldn't slow down, she hunted down the latest news on her phone. She gave a little gasp, and Hudson stirred.

She nudged him, and he rolled over, smiling.

"Yes?"

"I was just reading some news reports about the death of our author."

"Mmm." His eyes closed, but he nodded into his pillow.

"The reporter claims to know the real identity of our actress *cum* author."

"Is that supposed to be a secret?" he muttered, but she was pretty sure that's what he asked.

"I suspect so. But they've got it right: Allie Mackenzie. And they said more about her acting career. She hadn't done anything big yet but had just been signed as a regular guest star on a YouTube Premium series. She got a signing bonus."

Hudson yawned.

"The signing bonus is the money that was rumored to have been deposited in her account, I'm sure."

He rubbed his eyes. "This show was a YouTube thing, huh?"

"YouTube produced. Like a real show that YouTube pays for."

His eyebrows pulled together in thought. "That's interesting."

"That's what I thought too. Jonah has been talking about her murder all over the Internet and now his YouTube account was frozen." Taylor rubbed the back of her neck. "Maybe they shut him down when Sue complained because they didn't want the bad press."

"I wonder if Jonah knows about this." Hudson was sitting up now but didn't look like he would be awake much longer.

"Go back to sleep." Taylor patted his knee. "I'm going to make a quick call." It was late, but how late was too late to call a teenager?

She went to the hall and sent Jonah a text about the news. Within seconds her phone rang.

"Taylor, this is important." He didn't wait for her to greet him. "Be careful with this information, like about her show and her real name. I'm doing my best to only air misleading stuff."

"Hold on, what?"

"I'm doing my best. Anything I get that seems real, I pass straight to Reg. But the stuff I post is all as misleading as I can get."

"Why would you do that, Jonah?" Her head was swimming. It was late. It had been a long day.

"The more I look at this stuff, the more dangerous it seems. I know there are a lot of college girls or whatever at the Expo, but a lot of the Juvies are even younger than me. I want to keep them as far away from anything dangerous as I can."

"Why don't you just stop talking about it then?"

He didn't answer.

"The money?"

"I don't know if the Juvies would stop." Jonah's voice was worn down. Exhausted even.

"What do you mean?"

"I should send you the dms. It's nuts. Obsessive stuff. Promising to do anything for me, wanting to have my babies, weird, risk-taking kind of stuff. I thought about shutting this all down, but I was afraid someone would do something to get my attention if I disappeared. So instead I'm just trying to keep them safe."

Taylor closed her eyes and tried to remember what it had

been like to be a high schooler. How everything seemed completely intense and life or death. How everything felt like it would last forever. Even though Belle and her friends were the first ones to tell her that pop culture lasted less than five minutes, Jonah could easily feel like his fame would last longer than his show.

And maybe he was right. Not big picture fame, but in that mix of kids obsessing over him, there might be someone willing to do something dangerous for his attention.

"I understand," she said finally. "Whatever you do, then, don't come back yet."

He laughed. "I wasn't planning on it. I gotta go. If this was in the local news, I need to put out something that contradicts it, fast."

He hung up.

Taylor scrolled through the old videos on his website. She stopped at the one where he begged his fans to email him everything they had heard or seen. She suspected now that he had not been wanting to scour the emails for clues, but had instead wanted to keep the girls safe at their computers, typing lengthy emails to him instead of actively looking for a killer.

❀

First thing the next morning, before Taylor was even dressed, Jonah sent a snap.

"Find out more about the cult." He was sitting on a bed in a very generic room. She knew he'd been staying with Belle, and Belle's step-sister Ashleigh, but had no idea what kind of accommodations they had. From the look of the gray wall and no headboard, it wasn't great. "Growing up in a cult can really mess people up. Might have left Allie naïve and easy to manipulate."

She was impressed by how mature Jonah's thinking was. She wondered briefly if he was getting advice from his roomies.

"Find her agent—not the book guy. She didn't care about

books, I bet. Find the other one, the talent agent. One of the Juvies says he's called Captain. Got it from behind a paywall but it didn't have contact info." With that, he was gone.

As much as Taylor would have loved to hunt down a Hollywood agent called Captain, she didn't have the first clue where to start.

But Jonah had left her with a few thoughts. Allie had been raised, at least for a while, in a cult-like self-help group. She may have been left naïve and easy to manipulate because of it. If she had been picked for the job of fake author because of that naivety, then maybe everyone involved in this had something they wanted to cover up.

It didn't take long for Hudson and Lizeth to join Taylor in the kitchen.

"Let's get out of here." Hudson stretched, his soft white T-shirt lifting just a little to reveal a peek of tanned, firm abs.

Lizeth, draped in a thin, ragged, black sweater that reminded Taylor of Belle during her goth years, blushed.

"Breakfast on me at Reuben's," he offered.

Taylor grabbed the vintage denim jacket she'd inherited from her mom. "Perfect." She needed to think and the walk to the diner would do the trick.

Jonah wanted her to find a talent agent from Hollywood and all he had to go on was the nick name Captain. She could google the heck out of that from the safety of her own home, later. And as she walked, she realized that was probably Jonah's goal. He was trying to keep her safe too. Had he also sent her after the lit agent Trent to keep her safe? Because he couldn't possibly be involved in Allie's death?

He hadn't once said anything about Lizeth, had he? Or Beth Trager, the Amish Anonymous online lady. Were they the real keys to the crime?

She held the door open for Hudson and Lizeth. The young girl looked frail and scared, her eyes darted side to side from behind the shield of her long straight hair. She might be able to lead them to the killer, but she couldn't be the responsible party herself.

What Taylor needed was Beth and Lizeth. If she could hear from both of them and compare their knowledge the whole thing might open up for her.

---

Bruno Stultze was seated at a large booth having a hearty platter of breakfast. His brown plaid button-down had an un-ironed and traveled-in look. He waved Taylor, Hudson, and Lizeth over to join him.

The two men shook hands. Lizeth scooted in the booth and Taylor joined her. Bruno made room for Hudson.

"The Expo sure didn't turn into what we hoped for, did it?" Bruno said with a long sigh.

"No…" Taylor glanced at Lizeth.

The girl shrunk into herself.

"The death of the lovely young Albina was tragic, and I don't think anyone here can stop thinking about it." Bruno nodded at Lizeth. "I've been completely absorbed in Jonah Lang's website, but it worries me, as a father. His mom must be going crazy." Bruno's face was droopy like a hound dog. Taylor wondered if some of that was romantic disappointment as well.

"I haven't been able to really connect with her in a while…" Taylor shrugged, not wanting to tell this nice man that Roxy was hooking up with a younger man and would probably never take him up on his offer of dinner or lunch.

"What about that lady they arrested not long ago?" Bruno's brows drew together in thought. "Elizabeth, was it?"

"Beth Trager," Taylor nodded. Aviva Reuben, the niece of the diner owner, came with coffees and took their breakfast order. When she left, Taylor continued. "As they hauled her away, I promised to help, but I haven't done one thing in her favor. I feel like I've let her down."

"You know you aren't obligated to save everyone, right?" Hudson had a cup of coffee and a tired look on his face that almost mimicked Bruno's.

"Maybe she did it," Bruno offered. "The police seem like they've got their heads on their shoulders."

"Sheriff," Hudson corrected.

The thought gave Taylor pause. In her limited experience, the local sheriff had always been a couple of steps behind her own ideas, but at the same time, they had been on the right track. Except with the murder of the chaplain of the Bible Creek Care Home. But even then, they would have gotten there eventually, surely. Why did she mistrust them so much this time? Just because some Amish fiction conspiracy nut wanted her to? "They aren't idiots," Taylor agreed.

"But you've got to help," Lizeth's voice was small, almost just a whisper.

Taylor patted her hand absently. "I'm doing my best. I want to help get justice for Allie. For all we know, the officials have already done it. I just don't have enough information to act on anything yet, or so it seems."

"Speaking of information, I know you were hoping for a better conversation with Albina's literary agent, Trent Green. He's willing to meet you, but he's got limited time, and actually," Bruno glanced at his gold watch. "He suggested about half an hour from now, if that would work for you."

"Do it," Hudson nodded. "I can come with, if you want."

Taylor pressed her lips together and considered it. "Are you sure?"

"I'm yours." Hudson smiled, almost in relief.

"Great. Lizeth, do you want to come with us or go back to my place?"

"I need some air. I just....I want to take a walk."

Taylor didn't like it and nibbled her bottom lip for a moment. She had no right to ask this legal adult to stay in a safe spot, but she wanted to try. "Can you stick around the campus, maybe?"

Lizeth nodded.

"Trent said to meet him in the lobby of the school at one of those little café tables. I'll text him to let him know you're coming," Bruno said.

They sped through breakfast and headed for the school. Lizeth didn't follow them inside, though, instead she wandered toward the walking paths in the lawn.

Trent was waiting in the lobby and looked bored.

Hudson and Bruno sat at a table a bit removed from Trent and Taylor. They sat back in their chairs, sprawled out as though they were ready for a long talk.

"So, you have a stack of old self-published how-to books you're interested in selling." Trent showed absolutely no sign of recognizing Taylor from their drunken conversation in the bar.

"Actually, I was hoping we could talk about Allie Mackenzie, also known as Albina Tschetter."

He didn't look up from his phone.

"Had your client met Beth Trager before this week?"

"Who?" Trent looked up but didn't make eye contact.

"Beth Trager was recently arrested for the death of your client."

"News to me." He glanced at his phone again but seemed distracted now.

"You've never heard of Beth Trager? What about the Amish fiction online fan club Amish Anonymous?"

"Never heard of it."

"There are a lot of them here, and some of them think Allie's death may have been to spur sales."

He held his hands palms up in apology. "It will be months before sales reports are released on her books. Maybe her death got us an uptick of sales, maybe not. We might never know since this event was part of a bigger promotional package. Anyway, I just sold the books. I don't do the PR or fan stuff with her."

Taylor's phone pinged. She pulled it out hoping for some kind of encouragement or prescient tip from her mom, but the ping was just a reminder from a health app to drink more water. She ignored it and opened Amazon instead. She hunted for the best sellers list, then scrolled till she found Albina Tschetter's name.

Trent had turned his attention back to his own phone, which bought her a moment to find what she wanted. But she didn't need long.

*Quilted in the County* was the eleventh most popular book on all of Amazon. Taylor didn't have a way to find out what it had been before the murder, but she knew from her eavesdropping that it hadn't been this high.

She held the phone out for Trent. "Speaking of best seller's lists."

He looked at the phone.

He looked at Taylor. "Wow."

"Now do you want to discuss the popularity of books by recently murdered authors?"

"Are you an undercover cop?" He had a twinkle in his eye, like he was teasing.

His teasing rankled her. She wanted to be taken seriously. "No." She held the phone in front of him still, with a stiff arm.

He leaned in a little, looking at the phone more carefully. "Are you recording this conversation?"

"Absolutely not."

He stood. "I had no idea the book had taken off like that, and I had nothing to do with it. But I can't say I am disappointed." He paused to look around the lobby. "Listen, if you really want to talk about sales, you need to talk to her PR team."

"And who would that be?"

Trent had a tight grip on the back of his chair, despite the look of humor on his face. "Talk to the Frieses."

He left without a goodbye.

Taylor screen capped the Amazon rank.

She'd been hunting for Sue Friese on and off for more than a week. Pinning her down and getting her to talk were herculean feats.

Bruno and Hudson joined her at the table moments after Trent vacated. "So, that went well." Bruno frowned.

"Trent seemed honestly shocked. But was it because the book had shot up so high, or was it because he was caught?"

"Want me to follow him?" Bruno offered.

"Yes." Taylor was happy to send Bruno off. The fewer people she had to keep track of, the more comfortable she was.

Bruno left in a hurry. Trent had a small head start, but there weren't many places he could go.

But even with Bruno out of her hair, she didn't have any idea how to track down the Frieses. The idea that they knew something about Albina's PR team was tantalizing. She surveyed the lobby, looking for signs of familiar people.

The death of the keynote speaker had sent many quilters running home, and the end of the regular events had thinned it even further.

The team of faculty was now just ten professional quilters who were working with teams on specific mentoring.

Likewise, the marketplace was smaller. Anyone who wanted to stay could, but very few vendors had felt like the small crowd was worth staying for.

Roxy and Taylor had not purchased the package that included meals for this part of the Expo, living in town and all, but she thought she might find Sue and her husband Morgan in the dining room brunching with the master class students.

"Hudson, I need to talk to someone…"

"And you don't want company?"

"Maybe hover near an exit so you can jump in to save me?"

He grinned. "I'd love it if you meant that."

"Actually…" She lifted a shoulder. "I have no idea how any of this is going to go down. I suspect both of us coming up to chat might be too intimidating. But I do like the idea of knowing I can catch your eye and get rescued."

"You got it then. I'll maintain a discreet distance and watch for my cue. What will it be?"

"Hmmm…" Taylor scrunched her face. "How about if I scream help, you come running?"

"You can count on it."

Hudson followed a few feet behind as Taylor went to the dining hall. If he thought it was funny, he didn't let on.

Every quilter who had stayed behind for the master classes seemed to have shown up for the meal. Though it was a smaller group now, there was something dizzying about the circular tables, the buzz of conversation, and the wait staff bobbing around the room.

Sue and Morgan were near the front. They were easy to find because Lizeth stood at their table having a complete meltdown. Taylor could hear her from the door, as clearly as if she were standing right beside her.

"I know you had to tell the police what you saw and she's my sister, so you have to tell me too. I deserve to know and it's not a secret. If it was a secret, it's not your secret. Why would it be? It was her sickness, or death, or whatever, but she's not dead, is she? That's the secret, you have to tell me." Tears rolled down Lizeth's pale face.

Taylor hustled to the table but wasn't in time to stop Morgan Friese from intervening. She felt frozen, stuck between chairs, pushing her way to her young friend as Morgan leapt to his feet and grabbed the girl from behind.

Taylor glanced back at Hudson and shook her head no. He snarled, ready to pull the child from Morgan's grip, but held off.

Morgan pinned Lizeth's arms to the side, his fists gripped. "You aren't in your right mind. Calm down." His voice was remarkably steady for a man whose face was beet red. He stared down Taylor as she reached him. "Don't overreact. This is a specific hold for people who are panicking. She will calm down in a moment. Who is with this girl?"

"I'm with her. And let her go, whatever else you call it, that's assault."

Morgan did not let her go. "She needs a sedative and rest."

"I need the truth! Tell him Taylor. Tell him I need the truth. I deserve the truth. What happened to my sister?"

Every bit as calmly as Morgan held Lizeth in his firm grip, Sue Friese dug in her purse. "I have some melatonin. Give it to her." She opened a bottle with slow motions as smooth as her silk blouse and spilled two tablets into her hand, then held her hand out to Taylor.

Taylor did not take them. "Let her go." She reached a hand to Lizeth.

"I will let go as soon as I feel her relax, it will only be a moment."

Lizeth squirmed down till her chin was at his arm and bit him.

"Child, this is a good suit. I didn't even feel that." His voice was robotic, emotionless.

The same couldn't be said for the rest of the room. The women at the table all seemed to come out of shock at the same moment and began to holler advice. Someone told Sue to take her own damn pills, and someone else demanded Morgan free the child. Another voice said something about a spanking.

Phones came out of purses. The moment was being recorded and posted online for posterity. Taylor's first thought was worry for Lizeth's college enrollment.

In spite of the commotion Lizeth hadn't given up. She pulled one arm up, fist by her face and then slammed it back, elbowing Morgan in his groin as hard as she could.

Morgan screamed, doubled over, and fell into a chair, but he managed to keep his permanent grip on Lizeth.

It didn't matter. Lizeth was too slender for her own good, and plenty strong. From his prone position, she managed to slither out of his arms, but she didn't run to Taylor for protection. She squared her feet, bent her knees, turned one shoulder to him, fists up. "Tell me what I need to know before I call the police for your assault. I have all these witnesses."

"Someone give that girl a drink!" A master quilter with a swingy braid of salt and pepper hair tried to wave down a waiter—three waiters stood agog, enjoying the scene from a far wall.

Lizeth didn't move, didn't waver, and didn't take her eyes off Morgan. "You were there. You were the only one who saw her clearly. Not the maid, not even the paramedics. They came too late. Just tell me what you saw! What happened to my sister?"

A quivering voice rose over the hubbub, someone near, and very elderly. "Tell the poor child what she wants to know, Morgan. It won't hurt you."

He had managed a sitting position, but was bent at the waist, nursing his injury.

"Albina Tschetter didn't have any sisters."

"Say her name," Lizeth hissed.

Morgan didn't respond.

"Say her name. Say Allie Mackenzie. Say my sister's name. Tell me what happened when you saw her."

Sue stood and walked to her husband. "Why don't you just tell her what she wants to hear?"

"I only want the truth," Lizeth's voice broke.

An "awe" of sympathy passed over the diners.

"I went to Allie's room to take her and my wife down for the day. They were supposed to be having a morning meeting. When I got there, the door was ajar, and Allie was on the floor. Her eyes were open, and I thought I saw them flutter. I called her name, checked her pulse. Called 911. I did all the things you are supposed to do. I don't know what you expect me to tell you."

"She was alive. She was alive when you found her and alive when the paramedics took her away. Tell me she's still alive."

"It's just not true. She was already gone by the time the paramedics arrived."

Sue stood with one hand on his back. "You might have the

mistaken idea that this was easy for us. Please banish that from your mind. It is never easy to lose a friend, and Allie Mackenzie had become a good friend. Almost like a daughter, wouldn't you say?"

Morgan did not back up his wife's statement.

Lizeth did not move.

Behind Taylor a fork rang against a plate as someone decided to try and eat. It was the only noise.

Then her phone pinged.

And someone else's did.

Phones all around the room began to chime, ding, ping, ring, and buzz. Heads dropped to their phones.

Taylor stared at Morgan. "What about Allie's face? What did it look like? Swollen, rashy? Anything like that?"

"Yes, yes she was. Her eyes were swollen. She had a rash on her face. The paramedics said something about an allergic reaction. I don't know about her medical history, or her medicines, or anything like that, but that's what the paramedics said."

In the background Jonah's voice rose from several phones as they played his most recent snap, starting seconds after each other like he had possessed the dining hall.

Lizeth took a long, deep breath. "Where was her EpiPen?"

"I don't know. I don't know who you are, but I am sorry for your loss. I hope you can understand that we're with you in grief. This is a sad time for all of us." He looked around the room but didn't wave his hands which were gripping each other on his lap as though he were trying to control his reaction to the pain.

He was so controlled.

So emotionless.

So studied and prepared for this moment.

Sue stood next to him, a hand on his shoulder, her face a frozen mask of Botox. Or brainwashing.

"I'm sure the Ladies Club will be able to help you process

your loss." Taylor spit the words out, disgusted with the Frieses. Their talk of grief was just that. Talk.

All she received for this jab was a slight flicker of an eyelid on Sue's otherwise still face.

Lizeth turned her face slowly up to meet Sue's eyes. "That's why you're so familiar."

Sue kept her red lips shut.

"You do know me. You both do. You were the head teacher. I think that's what it was called wasn't it? You ran the meeting hall. I know you both!" Lizeth was about to lose it again.

Taylor put a hand on her back, just lightly, with what she hoped was a grounding touch.

"She sounds like she knows what she's talking about." There was just that hint of antagonism in Morgan's voice that made him sound like he wasn't happy with his wife just now.

"Yes, I was a magistrate for the Ladies Club at one time. A very good social reform organization. Were you a part of it?"

"Yes, I was. My mom and dad—Allie's dad—we were members. We were there all the time, but I was little then." A softness came over Lizeth and her shoulders relaxed.

Sue responded to it. "And this was when I was magistrate? That is so lovely to hear." She put her arm out as though to pat Lizeth from far away. A gentle motion.

Lizeth sighed. She dropped her arms. "Don't you remember me and Allie?"

"Go on, Sue. Tell her," Morgan said.

"Darling, there were so many children. Allie attended meetings when she took up acting again. That's how I met her. Her books were so charming. I knew they'd be perfect for our event here. I'm not a magistrate anymore. I just attend now and then to refresh myself."

"I haven't been since I was little."

"If you are ever back in Hollywood, I'm sure they'd love to have you visit." Though Sue's voice was calm and gentle, her face was the emotionless mask it had been the whole time. The mask of mental conditioning. Cult training. The Ladies Club was just a social organization…sure, but so was that Skull and Bones thing at Yale. That didn't make it normal.

"I think we should go." Taylor tried to lure Lizeth away from the scene.

"As should we." Morgan slowly stood.

"Morgan, you'll be fine." Sue gave her husband's shoulder a firm pat and took her seat.

Taylor led Lizeth out of the dining room as gently as she could.

Valerie Ritz sat near the back of the room, her phone up, recording their exit.

Taylor was pretty sure The Ladies Club would have a spike in Google searches tonight.

Hudson shut the door firmly behind them and stood in front of it, essentially barring it should anyone try to follow them out.

"He didn't tell me anything." Lizeth's voice broke, and she jolted, stiffening back up under Taylor's protective arm. "It was all lies."

"Lizeth, they wouldn't have arrested someone if she was alive," Taylor murmured.

"Why did they arrest that woman? What did she do? How could she make my sister have an allergic reaction?" Lizeth paced the hall outside the dining room. She needed to walk off this adrenaline rush, and maybe eat just a little more breakfast. A steady stream of calories might even out her moods.

Taylor walked with her, back and forth across the aged oak floors. "I don't know. Shall we call the sheriff and ask?"

"They'll tell us?"

"We don't know if we don't try." Taylor stopped right there and called Reg. She knew he wouldn't like her asking for more info, but she was desperate to help.

"Hey Reg, it's Taylor."

"I know that." His voice was gruff.

"I have a relative of Allie Mackenzie here, and she has some questions about the death."

"A relative?" His voice perked up.

"An ex-step-sister. Common law. You know, that kind of thing."

"Oh." Disappointment weighted the syllable.

"Can you answer some questions for her?"

"Shoot."

Taylor held the phone out.

Lizeth rejected it.

"Okay, she wants me to ask. First is simple, has Allie been released to a funeral home yet?"

"No, we haven't found a next of kin."

"Have they determined a cause of death and can it be told at this point?"

"Yes and no."

"You are confirming at least that Allie Mackenzie's body is in your morgue, and you know how she died, and that she is definitely dead?"

"Uh, yes. You're kidding though, right? Girl was dead from the second she...never mind."

"Got it. Another question: Why was Beth Trager arrested?"

He laughed, a cynical sort of bark. "We only brought her in for questioning. It was needlessly dramatic."

"But why? What prompted her?"

"Something she tweeted I think." He sounded irritated. "But it came to nothing. Off the record, it's all come to nothing so far."

"That's great!" Taylor nodded and smiled at Lizeth.

Lizeth responded with a confused frown.

"Sure, it's great. Great for Ms. Trager. Did I answer all of your questions?"

"You did. Thank you, sir." Taylor moderated her happiness. She was hugely relieved that Beth was free and that there had been nothing behind her trip to the station than questioning. And that it had merely been prompted by her iffy post online, that it was hard to remember how difficult Lizeth would take the report of Allie's death. Taylor ended the call and slipped her phone in her pocket, relieved at least that one impossible job was off her list.

"He said she was dead." Lizeth stared into the distance.

"Yes. I'm so sorry."

Lizeth stopped in the middle of the hall and just stood there. After a moment, her voice came out very small, "What am I supposed to do now?"

Taylor took her arm, like she would have done for her grandmother, and made her walk again. "You just take the next step. That's all you need to do right now. One step at a time."

## CHAPTER TWENTY

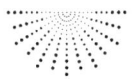

*D*arkness and chill greeted them back at the little house on Love Street. Taylor flipped every light switch to banish the gloom from the cozy front room, then gave Lizeth the other sandwich roll she'd gotten at Reuben's.

"Can I make something?" Hudson banged around in the kitchen looking for food.

"The cupboards are bare," Taylor apologized.

"Then I'll get something and cook it. I'll be back in a few." He left out the kitchen door and Taylor locked up behind him. He had a key.

Lizeth picked at it again, not eating any, as far as Taylor could see.

Instead of pressing her guest to eat more, Taylor decided to check her phone. She expected to find that the alert she'd gotten was the same Snapchat everyone else had gotten from Jonah, but it wasn't. It was from her sister Belle.

"I can't talk, but I can't just leave without telling you. Jonah and I are headed to New York. I'm going to the fashion institute and Jonah needs to get away from here, somewhere safer. I know you'll freak out that's why I'm not calling. He's got plenty of money and will put us up. We'll be cool. Don't tell Roxy." Taylor stared at her phone screen. Belle had seemed so confident and self-possessed as she spoke. Long gone was the shaggy dyed hair and overlined eyes. Her golden locks were healthy, her blue eyes wide and earnest.

Taylor absolutely one hundred percent was not going to tell Roxy that Belle and Jonah were….were what? Were they running off *together*? Like romantically?

Didn't Belle resent Jonah and his wealth? Or had he managed to win her over when he ran to Seattle to hide?

He wasn't eighteen yet, was he? Couldn't Belle get in trouble for taking him across the country? She was twenty, right? But wait, they'd had his birthday in September around the start of school. Celebrated that and his newfound fame at one shot. He was definitely eighteen. She was fairly sure.

Numbers, dates, and places all spun in her head. No, Belle wasn't twenty. Not yet. Soon, though. But Jonah was probably eighteen. But he'd promised to come home and finish school. Not quit and runaway.

And what about Belle's spot in her grad program to study… something historical. Was she just giving that up? Hadn't they paid some of that tuition already?

She called Belle but got no answer. She called Jonah, but he didn't answer either. She did not call Roxy.

"She'll be fine," Lizeth said. "She grew up sewing, right?"

Taylor exhaled slowly. Lizeth didn't know anything about her or her sister Belle, how they grew up or what they'd been through. What did she know about anything?

She'd heard the snap, sure, but that was all she knew.

Yes, yes, sure. But why fashion? She was focused on history and writing books, and…not on fashion." Taylor clenched her phone in her fist.

"People can change their minds." There was a twinge of rebellion, maybe even strength in Lizeth's voice.

Taylor didn't want to fight about her sister with a stranger, and yet, that little twinge of fight-back stirred something in

Taylor. It was good for both of them, maybe. "Sure, people change their minds, but she has to eat. What will she do in New York with no money, no job, and tuition to pay?"

"She said Jonah was paying. Isn't he a millionaire now?"

Taylor wondered. He was certainly a paper millionaire, or was that digital? But did any of that sponsorship money or those YouTube royalties actually exist in a bank account? There was no telling. "He's just a kid. He might not stick around."

"Then she'll work. Hard, probably. Anyway, why do you think she has no money?" Lizeth sat up straight on the sofa, her body tense like she was ready to defend herself. To physically fight again.

"Because…"

"She had a job, didn't she?" Lizeth pressed.

"Yes."

"Was she a wild spender?"

"No." Guilt pinched at Taylor. Belle wasn't the big spender in their family.

"Then she's got some money." Lizeth was wound tight, ready to spring. Her defense wasn't really about Belle, a girl she'd never met. It was about her. She wanted to fight for her own future. Wanted a sister who was worried about her, who would tell her she needed to be safe and take care of herself.

Taylor softened and turned the subject. "What are you studying to become?" She had her doubts that Lizeth really had a dorm room and a meal plan back in Portland, but she had no doubt that Lizeth wanted someone to push her to do well.

Lizeth jutted her jaw out. "I'm getting a business degree. Office management."

"Good for you." This was in Taylor's wheelhouse. "You can do anything you want with a business degree. What is it you want to do?"

"I want to be able to pay my rent every single month no matter who I'm dating." She got the sentence out as though it had been well-practiced. Decided, determined, and memorized.

"Good. Very good. Save up and buy your own house too."

Lizeth stared blankly. The words went over her head. It might have been one dream too many for this kiddo who had been through more in her few years than most people ever would experience. Taylor's heart twinged again. There were so many challenges ahead for this kid. This young lady. She felt older than her thirty years thinking things like "young lady" but what else was there to say?

Lizeth rubbed her hands together like they were bothering her.

Taylor seized the moment to relieve the tension in the room. "Do you need some lotion?" She opened her purse and dug around for her little bottle of Jergins but couldn't find it. The swag bag from the Expo was on the floor next to the couch so she spilled its contents onto the coffee table. Several bottles of toiletries were in the collection of stuff. She tossed a couple of small bottles of lotion to Lizeth. The other bottles were samples of shampoo, conditioner, and body wash. All were from the lady with the beekeeper booth. She had also included a lip balm.

"That bee one smells like honey. It's weird. I like this Quilter's Balm better." She tossed both bottles back. "I remember once Allie tried to use some beeswax lip balm and her whole face broke out."

"She was allergic to honey?" Taylor leaned forward and sorted all the swag. Surely the keynote speaker had gotten a significant swag bag. At least this much stuff and more.

"No...just to the beeswax, I think. She liked to eat honey, but she couldn't have too much."

"Are you sure she wasn't allergic to it?" The lotion had some kind of honey extract in it, but no beeswax. The shampoo was the same.

"No, it was the beeswax, but some honey, the unfiltered kind has like, some stuff in it, from the beeswax. I was just a kid, I don't remember."

"Beeswax. Honey." The lip balm was beeswax based. The

swag bag also included a sample piece of beeswax for waxing thread, which was probably the one found with her body, and three of the branded bandages for use as disposable thimbles. There were candies in the kit. Could Albina's candies have been tampered with? Could they have been specifically packed for her, with her allergies? "Do me a favor, Lizeth, find that list of your sister's allergies that was posted in the Amish Anonymous group."

"I'm not actually a member."

Taylor exhaled, hiding her annoyance. "I've got to see that list…it could have been a serious death threat."

"Maybe Jonah knows."

"Worth a try. He's bound to answer a question about this, especially if I don't mention their little road trip. Can you go to his website and see if he has the list posted? We can call him if not."

Lizeth dug her phone out of the deep pocket of her sweater.

Taylor organized the swag in order of things that seemed easiest to cause an allergic reaction to things that seemed least likely.

A rashy face.

A DNA specific poison.

A billionaire killer.

The missing toothbrush from the crime scene.

Albina holding the beeswax thread waxer.

Taylor tried to sort her thoughts like the items in the swag bag. She needed to piece these manic ideas together like a patchwork quilt.

Like a crazy quilt.

*Quilted in the County* was a verified Amazon best seller, whatever that meant. Probably millions of dollars.

Allie had a job with a show on YouTube Premium.

Allie was an actress and her agent was a guy who went by Captain.

Who was this Captain? How was Taylor supposed to find

him? Was that his last name or his first? Was he in town dealing with her death or somewhere in Hollywood wining and dining his next pretty starlet?

Captain….

For some reason the word felt familiar, like she'd run into it somewhere this week. In print maybe. Or she'd overheard someone say something about it.

Her phone chimed. It had been a long time since she'd gotten a message from her mom via Jonah. She longed for it right now and almost didn't check for fear of being disappointed.

And yet, she knew that her sister had just sent a message. And her sister and Jonah were together. And Jonah would send a clip to encourage her. After all, she'd just gotten bad news, and he was the self-appointed savior of women in trouble.

She grabbed the phone and swiped at it.

Her mom smiled at her.

"She will be okay, you know." The voice wasn't her mom's, but Roxy's. "Kids grow up and move away."

Her mom's bright eyes seemed to shimmer with unspilled tears.

"Even *my* kid?" Taylor's mom had that ageless look of a woman who takes care of her skin. She always had. Was this video from ten years ago when Taylor moved away or was her mom getting teary about Belle heading to college early? There were no clues.

"Yes, even your kid. But she'll be okay. Say it with me."

"She'll be okay," her mom said.

And the snap ended.

Obviously, Jonah thought Belle would be okay traveling with him to New York.

Taylor's lip curled in annoyance. That clip hadn't helped her figure out why she thought she'd heard Captain said somewhere.

"She'll be fine," Lizeth said. "Listen to your mom." Her smile was soft and sad.

Taylor gave her a matching look.

"Shoot, she probably has investments of her own, right?"

"True...." In her immediate fear over the random flight of her sister, Taylor had forgotten the healthy trust fund her sister had. Investments? Yup. Belle had investments.

Taylor had investments too.

Jonah had millions.

Everyone had what they needed.

Fleetingly Taylor thought what she really needed was a drink, but all she had in the house was a very dusty bottle of Captain Morgan spiced rum from who knows where or when.

Captain Morgan.

She froze.

Surely not.

Was Captain *Morgan* the reason she thought she'd heard Captain somewhere during the Expo?

Morgan was an uncommon name for a man. Taylor had probably heard it and filled in the blank to herself more than once, just because the words went together.

She let out a slow sigh of disappointment. She'd really hoped she'd seen the word somewhere on the Expo program or something like that instead.

Then again…what if it wasn't a coincidence? What if Morgan Friese *was* this Captain character?

Captain was just the kind of nickname you'd get in a frat or in a social club, even. Morgan and Sue knew Allie through their social club, which was probably a great way for a guy like him to pick up pretty young clients.

Maybe they had needed an actress to play the author of the book they wrote, whether with a machine or not.

It was no more far-fetched than Shara's crazy billionaire with a DNA-based poison.

Allie would have probably thought of this as just another gig, like showroom modeling.

But if Morgan was the talent agent, would he have had a reason to kill her too?

A spike in book sales seemed like such a slim motive for murder. What if they had done it and it hadn't affected sales? No. Book sales was too risky a motive. No guarantee.

Maybe they were afraid of the fraud being discovered. It was certainly the talk of the Expo. Maybe they had decided to silence the one person who could out them.

If all of those maybes were true, then why now?

Going with her theory, this event was meant to be a place to let their pretty young actress do what she did best and sell the book to the quilters, but Jonah had been on his YouTube channel telling everyone it was fake.

Had they killed her because Jonah ran their book through that stupid app?

Sue was the one who got his YouTube channel shut down.

Taylor felt like she had fallen into a mad conspiracy theory and longed for something solid. Some hard facts. She turned to Lizeth. "Any luck with the allergy list?"

"Sorry, got distracted. We're so lucky Jonah is on our side, aren't we? I mean, because of him, we will probably catch this killer."

Taylor's mouth went dry. Lizeth wouldn't be thanking Jonah if it was his work that got Allie killed. "I just thought of a call I should make." Taylor leapt to her feet and ran upstairs. As soon as she was safe behind her bedroom door, she called Reg. "I'm so sorry to bug you again," she said when she got through to him. "And this is going to sound far-fetched, but please consider it. It just…feels right."

Reg sighed. "Why not? I'm still on the clock."

Taylor laid it all out for him, as fast as she could.

"You got all of that from the idea that a man named Morgan might also be called Captain, huh?"

"I know it sounds crazy. I know. But what if it's right?"

"You're lucky I still like you," he chuckled. "I have the day off tomorrow. I'll come by and have a conversation with him."

"Really, even though the idea is ludicrous by any and every metric?"

"I think this was a murder. The sheriff agrees. I didn't say I'll be calling him right now to tell him about "Captain" Morgan Friese the killer talent agent, but it's a thread I'm willing to follow for an old friend."

"Thank you." She breathed a sigh of relief. She had her doubts about the Captain Morgan connection, but there was always a chance.

She took the stairs two at a time. Hudson was back and laying out pizza and soda in the living room.

"Seriously, you're a hero."

"It's about lunch time, I figure. Give or take, anyway."

She kissed his scruffy cheek and sat. The herbed aroma of pizza from the little family run place in Willamina, the next town over, warmed her heart. "Lizeth, you said Allie used an EpiPen, did she also take other medicines?"

"I would think so, but I don't know. Maybe I'm wrong about all of it. Maybe she had those shots and isn't allergic to anything at all anymore." Lizeth eyed the pizza but didn't take a slice.

"How do you think the Amish Anonymous group got the list of allergies?" Hudson sat on the edge of the recliner. He didn't seem interested in the food, but he asked a good question.

"Allie was so pretty, and cool, and nice, I bet she had tons of friends. Any one of them might have told." Lizeth twirled her long hair on her finger.

"Someone who is pretty and cool," Taylor used Lizeth's words because it had put a picture in her head she hadn't thought of before, "might have a lot of friends, but they also tend to have people in their lives who want to take them down a peg."

"You think some hater shared Allie's allergies with that Amish group?" Lizeth reached for the pizza but stopped herself.

"Maybe. People like to take down the successful, but they also get very annoyed by people with a lot of allergies. Don't ask me why, it's not worth explaining." Taylor wrinkled her nose.

"Jealousy," Lizeth exhaled sharply.

"Yup. Anyway, if this pretty, cool girl who was starting her career as an actress also had some books out...I could see some personality types wanting to hurt her." Taylor pushed the pizza box a little closer to Lizeth.

Lizeth's face brightened suddenly. "I messaged Jonah asking for it and he sent it to me!" She held out her own phone. "What's your email? I'll forward it." She blushed, just another kid falling for a cute boy online.

Taylor read the list of allergens twice. Hudson read it over her shoulder. It wasn't short. Beeswax was right there, in the middle. Allie McKenzie was also allergic to all nightshades, which included things like tomatoes and potatoes. She was allergic to peanuts and tree nuts, seafood, and salicylates which were found in a huge number of things like melons and berries. After reading the list through several times Taylor had no idea how Allie ate anything.

"She had to have had the shots," Lizeth offered. "How would you live, otherwise?"

"Maybe she took regular allergy medicine," Hudson suggested.

"What if someone replaced her allergy pills with Tylenol, or aspirin, or something?" Lizeth gave in and took a slim slice of pizza covered in vegetables.

"That would have been pretty bad." Not too long ago, Taylor had helped a friend whose aunt had been killed with salicylate poisoning. "If her allergy meds weren't working, she might have been taking more pills than recommended too. Whoever planned this would need access to her stuff to make the substitutions. Maybe the housecleaner at the Expo."

"What motive would a housecleaner have?" Hudson also

took a slice of pizza—an extra-large slice covered in salami, pepperoni, and sausage.

Lizeth and Hudson were a good sounding board, giving her thoughts a safety net, so to speak. Taylor would have liked to panic, what with the salicylates triggering memories of scarier times, but between the good food and not being alone with her thoughts, she was staying grounded. "There wouldn't have been time for her to have a real motive. She'd have to have been paid."

"I bet they didn't switch her pills," Lizeth threw out. "Any fool can tell if the pill they took every day was suddenly different."

A wave of appreciation rolled over Taylor. Lizeth was right. Anyone who took a daily pill would notice if it was suddenly different. "I'm glad."

"It's one less person to be involved, huh?" Lizeth offered. "Plus, less planning. If someone decided to trigger a reaction all they'd have to do is spike her soup with fish sauce and steal her EpiPen."

Taylor stared at the variety of things Allie wouldn't have been able to eat just on the two pizzas. From preservatives in the cured meat to the tomato sauce itself. No need at all to mess with a bottle of pills. All someone would have had to do was spike Allie's meals with any number of those perfectly normal foods and watch for a reaction.

## CHAPTER TWENTY-ONE

It was slightly after five when Taylor remembered she'd promised to monitor the lobby of the school for Shara. She still didn't believe in the trap, but she was curious. And antsy. And ready to see something, anything, move the needle on this case.

Lizeth was willing to nestle in at Taylor's house with a movie, but Hudson joined Taylor.

The coffee cart had long been closed, but Taylor and Hudson had brought travel cups from home and sat in the little café area. They had their phones out, ready to pose as though they were deep in thought, but also ready to record if something of real note happened.

Shara was at the office desk. Isaiah, an old friend of Taylor's, ran the front office for the college and was on duty this early evening. He had a tired look about him like he really wished Shara would let him close up and leave.

Their voices echoed through the empty hall as they discussed the timing of the Expo shut down. There were still a few days left, but everyone seemed to wish it was over.

And then Taylor heard a familiar voice coming around the corner.

She'd only heard it once before, but it was easy to recognize.

Albina Tschetter.

Mackenzie Forte.

Allie Mackenzie

Whoever she was, whatever she called herself, that was her voice in the hallway.

Taylor leapt to her feet, ready to run after that voice. Ready to find that Lizeth's hope was real. But before she made it to the corner, Roxy and Beth Trager almost barreled into her.

Roxy held a black rectangle the size of a shoe box in her hand, and Allie's voice came out of the box.

The trap?

"I'm as disgusted as you are, but I don't see how my son is responsible for this," Roxy snipped at Beth.

"Don't you? Keeping the ladies here whipped into a disgusting froth? You and I were both arrested, I'd think you would more upset with him than you are."

"You're out of your mind. He didn't make this abomination. Some sick fool did." Roxy gave Beth a significant look.

"How dare you?" Beth snarled.

Their voices carried across the lobby and caught Shara's attention. Her face lit up and she tapped on her phone as fast as Taylor had ever seen.

The sheriff.

She was calling the sheriff.

Taylor tried to suss out what the voice of Albina was saying but Roxy and Beth's fight overpowered it.

"He's a part of the problem. Just like the fool who let this child write a book. Amish. Amish! How dare she? The Amish faith and tradition is a gem in the crown of this nation. The only pure and wholesome bit left." Beth's face flushed, and her body quivered like a bow string that had been plucked.

"Don't be an idiot. The Amish are humans just like the rest of us." Roxy clutched the noisy box to her chest.

Beth thrust her jaw out. "Oh yeah?"

"*Oh yeah?* That's the best you can do to defend the Amish you say you just love, love, love?" Roxy, despite her small frame and limp, was taut, chin out, ready to fight like a bantam hen.

Beth wrenched the box from Roxy's hands, tossed it on the ground, and stomped on it. "If I ever had to hear that voice again it would be too soon!"

"And what exactly was that supposed to help?" Roxy threw her hands up. "Are we going to take this broken box that no longer plays the strange recording to the sheriff and hope they believe us?"

"I don't need the sheriff to believe me." Beth stared at the broken box. Her face wasn't as convinced as her voice.

"I do. It's my kid who's lost the most from this!" Roxy's face was red, and her thin shoulders shook.

Taylor cringed. Allie McKenzie was the one who'd lost the most. And maybe Lizeth. Not Jonah. All he'd lost was some money.

"The crime is against culture and literature." Beth's tall, thin frame towered over Roxy.

"The book was worse than the murder?" Roxy gasped.

So did Taylor.

Surely Beth hadn't meant it.

"There wouldn't have been a murder if that stupid kid hadn't interfered with what we were doing."

Roxy stared. She took a long breath and looked Beth up and down, nodding to herself. "You're jealous of Jonah."

"No! And I didn't kill that girl, either!" Beth turned to escape but froze in place. A dozen quilters, some of whom Taylor recognized, had come in behind them, rolling suitcases in hand. Bruno was at the center of the crowd laughing at something a strawberry blonde was telling him. The blonde flipped her hair and giggled.

Two deputies entered the scene from the left. Taylor hadn't

been watching the door, so she didn't notice them arrive, but they had been drawn to the fight rather than the woman waving to them from across the room.

Shara dashed across the lobby as fast as her short, Doc Marten clad legs could take her. "Sir! Sir!" she called out.

They still didn't turn her way.

"I hear one of you has evidence of a crime to report?" Maria, a deputy Taylor had worked with in the past, asked.

Roxy sighed deeply.

Bruno broke through his little crowd to join Roxy, perhaps hoping he finally had a chance to catch the pretty little woman's attention.

Taylor hung back, not sure where the best place was. She longed to be in the heart of the action, but experience had taught her that amateur detectives weren't appreciated.

"We found this." Roxy toed the broken box. "Not that it will do you any good now, but it was a box with something in it playing some audio of the dead girl. I think someone had recorded her last speech and edited it to be spooky."

"Spooky?" Maria sounded tired.

"I'm sure there's a better word." Roxy pressed her lips together.

"It was disgusting." Beth spit the word out. "The recording was of Albina Tschetter calling us all killers. I don't know how they made it."

Shara sauntered forward, beaming. "It was very simple! And it worked like a charm. Didn't I tell you it would work?" She gave Taylor a look of pride.

Hudson put a supporting arm around Taylor's waist.

"I knew it was her all along," Shara continued. "How could it have been anybody else? The death of that poor girl made her son a millionaire."

"You'd better tell me what you did." The deputy gave her full attention to Shara.

"It was simple. I knew the killer was here somewhere. She'd want to monitor the situation. No way the person who did this would leave with potential loose ends. The only real task was to figure out who did it, don't you think?" She nodded at Maria like a teacher trying to encourage a shy child.

The deputy didn't smile in return.

"I had a recording of Albina's speech and it was the work of a moment to cut and paste it to say what I wanted. It took longer to figure out how to get the box to trip so it would talk when I wanted it to, but once I had that figured out, easy as pie. God bless YouTube videos, don't you agree?" Shara did the nodding thing again.

The deputy's face was frozen in a look of disdain.

Taylor took a small step back. It was very good not to be the amateur detective in this case.

"I set it with poor Albina's books. You heard the women arguing, I think. The books were the root of it all, and the murderer, he, well, she in this case, was going to be drawn to them, with the picture of Albina on them and her own words inside. Psychologically speaking the killer had to go back one more time and probably do something awful to the books. I hid the box behind and under, you know, stacked them all around. All the killer had to do was move one of the books and the table would condemn them for who they were. It just, it worked so well I couldn't be happier." She lifted her chin, closed her eyes, and took a long, slow breath of satisfaction. When she opened them again, she beamed.

The deputy turned to Roxy and Beth. "Where did you find the box, ladies?"

"I was packing up my table in the marketplace and heard the voice from across the room," Roxy said.

"I had gone to the marketplace as well, and also heard the voice," Beth agreed.

"Who triggered it?"

Beth shrugged. "Probably one of the books slipped off. The stack wasn't particularly stable."

The deputy picked up the crushed box and the voice started up again.

"Oh! How wonderful! I'm so glad that it had only turned off. I'd be very sorry if the little device had been ruined." Shara's face fairly glowed.

Albina's smooth voice condemned them all as killers.

Shara was a talented audio editor.

She'd had to combine parts of words to make this happen.

Taylor certainly hadn't heard Albina talk about the sins of an evil genius in her speech.

Shara held her hand out for the box. "Thanks so much. You can take the killer, and I'll take the box."

The deputy showed no signs of agreeing with Shara.

Taylor couldn't take another second, though she'd fully intended on staying silent. "Shara, don't be a fool. Roxy isn't a billionaire chemist capable of creating a DNA based poison, and if she was, what would be the point of killing a person for a mere million dollars on YouTube? Your idea doesn't wash."

Shara pulled her lips together. "She had to get the poison some other way, I guess, but it's clear she did it. I successfully profiled the killer, laid a trap, and caught her."

The deputy ripped the box open, found the gadget inside, and turned it off.

The crowd of quilters fidgeted nervously. Kaitlyn, with her signature silver locks, edged off to the left, but Valerie no-price-is-too-high Ritz's slipped closer to Roxy. And coming through the crowd, pushing with his elbows, was Morgan Friese himself.

Morgan!

Taylor had one chance to test her theory, so she took it. "Cap! Hey, Captain Morgan!" she hollered and waved.

He turned instantly, looking in her direction for a familiar face.

"Captain! Why did she have to die?"

Morgan tried to push his way back out of the crowd, but Valerie and the other quilters closed the gap behind him.

"That's enough, Taylor." The deputy's words were a surprise. Though Taylor had been home for a good while now, she still wasn't used to everyone knowing her by name.

"You met her in your club. Hired her to act like an author. That's fine. Whatever, but why did she have to die?" Taylor spit it out fast before Maria, the deputy, could really make her stop.

At the back of the crowd, the perfectly coiffed head of Sue Friese bobbed up and down. "Morgan? Morgan, what's going on?"

"She was perfect for the job because she was an orphan, wasn't she?" The sick truth hit Taylor as she spoke. "Captain" Morgan Friese didn't have to kill Allie because of what Jonah had done. It had been his plan all along. Hire an orphan so when she needed to be eliminated no one would look at it too closely.

"Your name is Morgan Friese, but friends and actors call you Captain. A bad pun on your name. Who was your client? Who paid you to provide them a lamb for slaughter?" As Taylor's words became more dramatic her voice took on an embarrassing resonance, like a fire and brimstone preacher, but she couldn't stop. She was on a roll. "Someone wrote those books. Was it one of your quilter friends? Maybe even someone from that Amish Anonymous group? Did the author get mad when you hired a younger, prettier woman to pretend to be her? Was Allie's death their revenge? Then what? She comes up with another name and writes more books? What was the plan?" Taylor had lost the plot entirely. There were just so many ways it could go. Revenge. Marketing. Cover up. Only he knew what had made them murder.

The deputy was on her two-way radio but hadn't shushed Taylor again. Something about her rally held the crowd spellbound, and perhaps the deputy appreciated the free crowd control.

"Morgan, we do not have to listen to this filth, come away with me now." Sue's voice was firm and in control.

Morgan tried to get clear of the crowd without pushing anyone, but the women had developed a wonderful synergy and he just couldn't.

"If you have any idea at all what this woman is talking about, now would be a good time to tell me, dear." Morgan addressed his wife with a voice dripping in sarcasm. Throwing his wife under the bus.

Or was he?

"You're the one who wanted a younger actress to stand in for you." He didn't look his wife in the eye.

The gasp from the crowd was so perfect it felt fake.

And it hit Taylor like one of Lizeth's elbows to the stomach.

Especially as she'd spotted Lizeth, standing to the side.

"What's going on?" Lizeth's voice stood out for its fear.

Morgan held his ground now, arms crossed.

"Yes, Sue, what would you like to say about your friend Allie's books?" Taylor pressed.

"I say nothing without a lawyer, ever. Come with me Morgan." Sue's voice had tipped into panic.

"Okay, show over." The calm, tired voice of the deputy broke the television worthy moment. "Roxy, Beth, Taylor, Sue, Morgan, come with me. We need to talk." The crowd dispersed for the deputy, but they loitered in the lobby with their luggage. Like Taylor, they wanted to know how this ended.

Taylor pressed her hand to Hudson's chest, silently asking him to wait in the lobby. The deputy led the group to the small office that had been used for interviews previously. Bruno tried to stick by Roxy, but wasn't invited in.

"Sit down. All of you." Maria was firm, and her leadership skills were palpable.

Everyone sat. There weren't enough seats, so Taylor sat on the arm of Roxy's chair, and Morgan did the same with his wife.

"Sue, my dear, what's going on?" He had turned on a voice thick with false concern.

"I'm not going to say anything to anyone without a lawyer." Her face twitched as though the program that maintained her façade had a glitch.

"Me neither," Beth said. "I'm not having you lock me up again. Not one word without a lawyer."

"And as you well know, I have not and will not say anything without a lawyer." Roxy tilted her chin up, daring the cop to challenge her.

"That just leaves us, Morgan." Taylor made eye contact. "And I have nothing to hide."

"I don't have anything to hide either, but they twist your words and if anyone knows that it's me." Beth's face blanched and her eyes darted around the group. "I'm the only person in this room who did not profit even a smidge from the death of this woman. I don't know why I'm in here at all."

A vein in the deputy's temple throbbed. "You're right Ms. Trager. You're free to go."

Beth gritted her teeth, crossed her arms, and maintained her position on the plastic chair by the door.

"Since you spent so much time with Beth, you're aware of Allie Mackenzie's significant allergies." Taylor felt the strong need to direct the conversation. She'd been on the cusp of a confession from Morgan or Sue when the deputy had derailed things.

"Yes," Maria agreed.

"I wonder, do you have her things in evidence still?" Taylor asked.

"We haven't been able to find a next of kin to claim them."

"Then I suggest you test her allergy pills. I suspect it will be very easy to tell that they're actually aspirin. Maybe baby aspirin because that would be about the right size. In addition to doing nothing to prevent an allergic reaction, they would trigger a response in her."

She nodded. Taylor took it as permission to continue.

"I got a gift bag for being part of this event. It was chock full of honey and beeswax-based stuff. Allie had an allergic reaction on her face, yes? Contact dermatitis? If the contents of one set of gift products were switched with the contents of the travel bottles she had packed herself, she might have been exposed to more of her dangerous allergens."

"That's horrible." Morgan swallowed. "If you had seen her as I saw her, you wouldn't dare suggest someone did that to her on purpose."

"I'm thinking you won't find her missing EpiPen at this point," Taylor continued, "but all it would take is steady exposure to the things she was allergic to and removing her safety net. Eventually she would die in the middle of the big event, and her name would be all over the news."

"Got a motive for us?" Maria asked.

"Yeah I do. Her book is a best seller at Amazon, and with this notoriety, it will remain as such. It was their plan all along. Yes, that's what I think."

Sue Friese's face hadn't registered a word she said, but Morgan was practically convulsing. "What kind of people do you think we are? The death that child died was practically torture! And she was like another kid to us. She was a club kid! When her dad died and she came back to the club, we took her under our wings. Loved her like our own. I was her talent agent, sure. She wasn't getting the gigs we wanted for her, so when Sue came up with this…let our Allie stand in as the author, it seemed like genius, didn't it, hon?"

"I will say nothing without a lawyer present." The ice in Sue's voice put a chill down Taylor's spine.

"She was an orphan," Taylor said to Maria. "A person Sue saw as disposable. To kill her with her allergies took significant preplanning. It was almost like…like a poison designed just for her DNA." Taylor blushed as she said it. Shara's crazy idea. But somehow true.

"Sue, just tell them you didn't do this."

"I will say nothing without a lawyer present, and Morgan, I highly recommend you take the same tack."

"That's it. You two, you can come down to the station with me and call your lawyers. The rest of you," the deputy looked from Roxy, to Beth, to Taylor, "I hope I don't hear from any of you ever again."

## CHAPTER TWENTY-TWO

The story of the arrest hit the Internet news before the radio or TV, but Taylor heard it via a snap—one more outtake of her mom. "Can you believe how bad the pollen is this year?" Laura's eyes were wide and red. She rubbed at the bottoms of them both with her knuckles, trying to deal with the itchiness without messing up her mascara. "My allergies are enough to kill a person."

Taylor laughed out loud. Maybe it was the alcohol talking— she was on her second glass of local *Pino Gris*. Or maybe she laughed because it was the first sunny day in ages. A cool breeze from across the low-slung valley hills brushed against her cheeks as she and Hudson enjoyed dinner on the patio at one of the many tiny little vineyards near Comfort.

Hudson smiled. "What's so funny?"

"Jonah. My mom. Nothing. Honestly, nothing is funny about death. But Jonah sent me this snap." She held out the frozen screen. She had taken a quick screen cap of it but refused to play it again. She hadn't repeated any of them. Not yet. She knew she could have a copy of all of the footage Jonah had saved, but the snaps were different. The quick little moments devoid of their context would always feel different. New. Real. Alive. And so long as she had that second view waiting for her, that magical one-last-chance granted by the Snapchat gods....

She sighed.

She couldn't watch them again, because then she wouldn't have them anymore. And someday she might need them more than she needed them right now. "Jonah sent a snap about allergies which is obviously a comment on the arrest of Sue and Morgan."

"So, there's news?" Hudson had a pint of the darkest beer available at the little vineyard restaurant. He took a long drink.

"There must be." She texted Jonah. Then Belle. Then Roxy.

Hudson just smiled at her. When she looked up with a sheepish grin, he chuckled. "Maybe check the actual news?"

Taylor opened Oregonlive.com, but her phone rang before she could search the headlines.

She laughed again and held it up for Hudson to see. "It's Belle!"

"Then answer it?" Hudson just shook his head.

"Belle?" Taylor bit her lip.

"Hey, um, just wanted to let you know what happened."

"With you or with the murder thing?" Taylor stroked the smooth cold surface of her wine glass.

"Maybe with everything...."

Taylor didn't like the sound of worry in Belle's voice. "Okay, start with the easy part."

"The easy part. Okay. So, um, some of those Amish fiction people, the Amish Anonymous, they leaked the police report. Sue Friese hasn't admitted anything and never will, but officially Allie McKenzie died of anaphylactic shock. Her EpiPen was nowhere to be found in her things or in the hotel room. It wasn't found in Sue's stuff, either. They can't prove that anyone tampered with her food, but her purse had some snack wrappers in it. They were labeled nut free, but on examination, peanut residue was found. Plus, all of her travel bottles did contain the honey-based products."

"That sounds an awful lot like murder." Taylor swallowed. Her throat had gone itchy in sympathy. She had promised to call Lizeth if she had any news. She would, but she didn't look forward to it.

"Especially because Sue's prints were on the snack packages. It's all rather circumstantial, and we know how these trials can drag on."

The trial for their mother's murder had taken ages and had been at least partially responsible for Taylor's lingering anxiety. More recently, the man responsible for the death of Taylor's friend Sissy's aunt had only just been sentenced. "It will be a long time before Lizeth gets any justice."

"I guess we're just lucky Lizeth exists at all. Poor Allie, without her almost-sister, no one would have cared about any of this. Not really cared at least."

Belle and Taylor were only "almost sisters." At twelve years apart in age, they hadn't grown up together or even lived together for much of their lives. And though Laura Quinn had been Belle's legal guardian, she hadn't been adopted. The heart ties of the tenuous bond of almost-sisterhood were something Taylor understood deeply. She'd likely worry about Lizeth for the rest of her life. "So, this is all…if not actually good news, at least it's a conclusion for all of our efforts, right?"

"Right," Belle agreed.

"Have they said anything about the motive?" Taylor sipped her wine, glad for something to do with her hands while she waited. Why murder? That was always the question. Envy, money, sex. These were the common reasons, and when the victim was a beautiful young woman with a bright future, any of those could have been at the root of it.

"There hasn't been a confession, but the Amish Anonymous group claims to know the prosecution's case. It was a money job, like you suspected. It's easy to write books with a machine. They thought they could get rich quick doing it, and that a pretty face on the back cover would seal the deal. When the first four failed to make their dreams come true, they, or at least Sue, went for the dead-artist method of fame. I bet it's revealed she was going to launch the 'unpublished works of Albina Tschetter' as soon as she was offered a big enough deal."

"Is it just me, or does that sound unreasonably risky?" Taylor asked.

"Oh, it does. But they were so deep in fraud…if Sue had some underlying personality disorder that made her not see people as real people, you know what I mean. It's just a jump from fraud to murder with the right disorder." Belle exhaled slowly. The world was a rough place, and she was young. Taylor felt for her.

"It sounds like you have something else worrying you. What's going on? Have you made it to New York yet?" Taylor choked on the words. She did not like this plan. It was only a week old, and she still hoped Belle and Jonah would change their minds.

"No. Um. We're in Beaverton actually. Nike needed to talk to Jonah more."

Taylor said a silent prayer of thanks for Nike, but out loud only said, "I'm sorry."

"Yeah, so…"

"What else?" Taylor's heart was in her throat. What possible thing could Belle say after all of this?

"Um, so, yeah…We got married."

Taylor stared at Hudson.

He hadn't heard what she had just heard and smiled at her warmly, glad for her company, glad for the sunshine, glad for the end to their troubles.

"Who did what now?" Taylor said, her voice high and squeaky.

"Um, we did. While we were in Seattle. We were going to go to New York. The school thing was a really good idea, but we also, um, thought it would be wisest to be far away till everyone was cool with this. But then Nike called with a really good offer and we had to come back down here for a little while. Then actually, Nike is going to fly us to New York, but not for long. Just um, a couple of weeks."

Taylor couldn't hear the words, or see the man across from her, or smell the food, or the fresh air, or feel the sun on her arms. She fought for balance on her seat.

Hudson reached out and placed his strong, rough hand on her forearm. "You okay?" His touch and his voice brought her back to the table, to the Willamette Valley, to the phone call.

But she couldn't breathe right. Not right enough to speak.

"Taylor, it's going to be okay. I swear. Nike has a thing planned for him, for school. He's got to take a couple of tests, then he gets his diploma. It's something student actors can do."

Taylor still couldn't reply.

"This was perfectly legal you know," her voice got defensive. "He's eighteen and I'm almost twenty and between us, well… we're pretty rich. His dad has been putting pressure on YouTube to get us his money, so surviving's not really a problem."

Taylor took a deep breath, held it. Forgot to exhale. She wavered. Then she exhaled. "Congratulations?" her voice was raspy and forced.

Belle laughed, almost in relief. "You'll mean it someday. You love Jonah. Everyone loves Jonah. But, um, don't say anything to Roxy, okay? We had a deal. I tell you and he tells his mom."

"Best of luck to him."

"Love you sis." Belle ended the call warmly but didn't give Taylor time to respond.

The list of things she couldn't talk to Roxy about had grown over the last two weeks. They hadn't talked about Roxy's assumption that Belle had tried to ruin Jonah's career—not in depth at any rate. They hadn't discussed her military lawyer ex, Jonah's dad. Or the other ex Taylor had remembered from years before, the short cute one. Those things just weren't Taylor's business. They hadn't discussed their future filming schedule either. They had a sort of silent agreement that the break they took for the Expo would continue indefinitely. And they hadn't discussed Clay. In fact, Roxy and Clay were both away, taking a week off, Taylor could only assume as a couple. Their plan all along had included Roxy and Clay taking a week off after the Expo, and then Taylor getting a week off while Willa, their part time employee went back into retirement. They wouldn't see each other, much less discuss Belle and Jonah eloping for another two weeks.

"Taylor, what's wrong?" Hudson set his pint down and leaned forward, real concern etched on his young, but wise face.

Taylor only had one word for it, but it seemed to sum up all of her problems at once. "Teenagers."

He cocked an eyebrow, ready to listen, which was good, because it was going to be a long story.

### Emperor's New Quilt

A MYSTERIOUS ABANDONED QUILT. A sinister string of murders. Can this amateur sleuth follow the pattern to catch the killer?

After much hard work, Taylor Quinn is finally finding relief from the trauma of losing her mom. Invited to help solve the mystery of an abandoned quilt, she agrees to take on the pleasant distraction. But her innocent investigation leads her straight to a dead body with a pair of sewing shears stuck in its back.

When two journalists reporting on the stabbing are taken out the same way, Taylor faces her worst fear: A monster is targeting everyone she's talked to about the quilt. Desperate to prevent more deaths, she starts building a patchwork of clues. But piecing them together might land her in an early grave.

· · ·

Can Taylor uncover the villain before her life is cut short?

Buy Emperor's New Quilt today to sew up a chilling case!

# FLOUR SAX BLOCK

## Spin a Tale

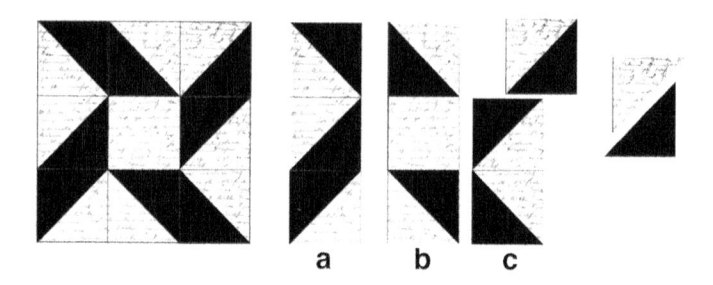

a  b  c

*A pinwheel block based on the classic Friendship Star.*
Build this with contrasting text print fabrics to create the feeling of a story spinning out of control.

**Brief Instructions**

Cut five 3.5 inch squares of text fabric.
Cut four 3.5 inch squares of contrasting text fabric.
Cut 8 squares into half square triangles.
Use 1/4 inch seam allowance and combine contrasting triangles into squares.
Build rows a, b, and c as illustrated.
Combine to form block.

ABOUT THE AUTHOR

Tess Rothery is an avid quilter, knitter, painter, writer and publishing teacher. She lives with her cozy little family in Washington State where the rainy days are best spent with a dog by her side, a mug of hot coffee in her hand and something mysterious to read.

Printed in Great Britain
by Amazon